DROPPING TRUTH BOMBS ON THE HIDDEN MINE FIELD OF LIES AND CORRUPTION!
LARRY WALLACE

DROPPING TRUTH BOMBS ON THE HIDDEN MINE FIELD OF LIES AND CORRUPTION

A Picture is Worth a Thousand Words

Larry Wallace

TABLE OF CONTENTS

INTRODUCTION

The bible states: Woe unto them that call evil good and good evil; that put darkness for light and light darkness. Perfect description of the times we live in. It is enough to make a crazy man go insane! This book is for those who still have their sanity.

"Yea, Let God be true and every man a liar," (Romans 3:4)

What was the very beginning of the downfall of all mankind? Wars, the Atomic bomb, nuclear bombs, evil dictators, selfishness, ego, accumulation of wealth, hate, religion, atheism, or the desire of men to want to control every man on earth, such as took place when Nimrod built the tower of Babel to consolidate all mankind in one place for his control, etc., etc. The subject matter is endless! But think about it, it was simply <u>words</u> of a <u>lie</u> spoken in the garden of Eden that brought the fall of man! The power of spoken words, not mighty weapons of warfare, but words! But fortunately for mankind it was the WORD that brought back mankind to his rightful place and standing with God. The name of that word is Jesus, John 1:1,2,14. Has it not been said that the pen is mightier than the sword? Weapons of warfare would not even be used if it was not for the power of words to entice men to their use. In a roundabout way this is the reason for writing this book. I believe truth needs no defense. Lies on the other hand, always needs a defense, it also needs 24/7 vigilance. Think of the little Dutch boy trying to keep the dyke from breaking by using his fingers to plug every leaking hole that springs up! But eventually he runs out of fingers and the holes just keep leaking until the dam breaks! That is the destiny of all lies. All the holes of lies eventually have to be covered or the damn will break exposing their darkness. The truth comes along and all the diligence in the world to hide the truth with lies runs out! Biblically speaking, lies (the darkness) cannot escape the truth (light). No man can hide his sins because the truth and the light (Jesus) John 14:6, John 8:12, will expose them!

I am writing this book because you have heard the saying: A picture is worth a thousand words. This book is about exposing many lies with just a single picture or screen shot. I am hoping because MSM (Main Stream Media) has become the tool for spreading lies across our nation, due to its ownership and the finance of a few families that literally control the media, these little pictures will expose the truth that have been hidden from the people! We are finding out that we have been lied to in our history books, in science, medicine, politics, government, religion, you name it, all have been lies covering hidden agendas, thus the subjects of the screen shots and pictures presented in this book.

Fear them not therefore: for there is nothing covered, that shall not be revealed; and hid, that shall not be known!" Matthew 10:26.

CHAPTER 1 CLIMATE

Put on your jacket, I mean your tank top!

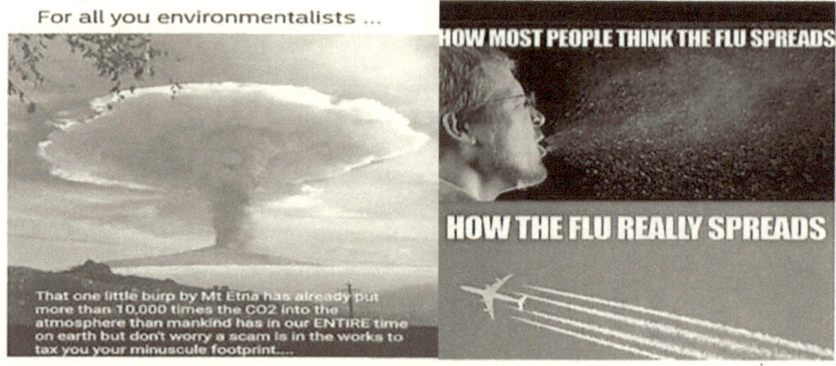

No worries, just vapor trails from commercial airliners!

Florida fires, caused by DEWs (Direct Energy weapons), I mean, a lightening strike. Paradise CA. Houses desentagrated, trees standing.

Massive Eugenics program going on all over the world, promoted by Bill Gates, Klaus Schwab, WEF, Monsanto, and the vaccine industry. They have found chem trails to be a toxic brew that includes heavy metals barium, chromium, cadmium and nickel, and other pollutants like mold spores, mycotoxins, polymer fibers, and ethylene dibromide. These toxins are absorbed through the skin, inhaled and ingested from contaminated water and foods. These toxins are linked to an increase in respiratory illnesses and heart disease. These toxins in chemtrails are called geoengineering. Geoengineering is the deliberate intervention in the Earth's weather system. Direct Energy Weapons are being used to start fires all over the nation: Paradise Ca., Florida, Colorado, and Maui, Hawaii to name a few. The population is deliberately being poisoned by chemicals in the air, Fluoride in the water, GMOs in our food, 5G radiation from cell towers, and now murder from the vaccine industry! Not counting the death of our future generation, abortions!

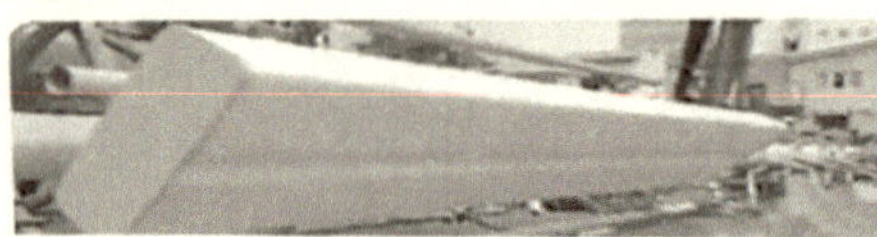

Professor Richard A. Werner
@ProfessorWerner
Residents of Miraflores in Peru, who suffered from unusual pneumonia and disseminated intravascular coagulation, forced the municipality authorities to remove a 5G tower disguised as a tree.
And with that, Covid miraculously disappeared in the area

TAKE ACTION
SAY NO TO
GEOENGINEERING!

CHAPTER 2 E CARS

Chaching Station fire

Because of low cutomers rentals

Electric car batteries catching on fire

CHAPTER 3 COVID/VACCINES

So if you still need a booster after been fully vaccinated, and testing after been fully vaccinated, and hospitalisation after been fully vaccinated, and masks, social distancing & lockdowns all after been fully vaccinated?

Then it's time to admit that you've been FULLY conned.

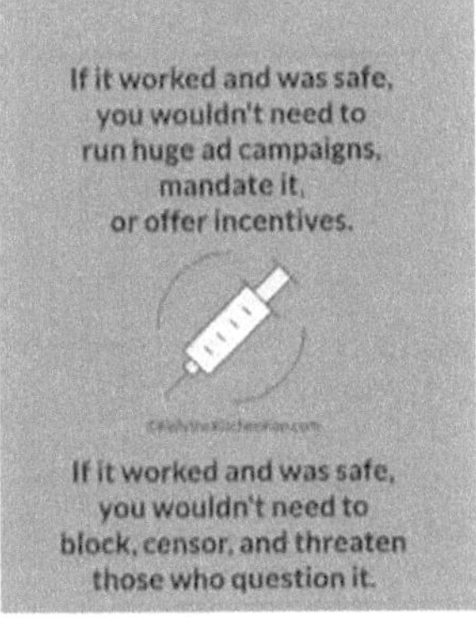

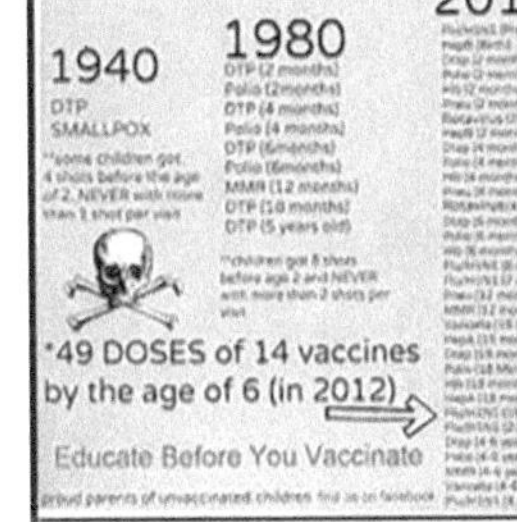

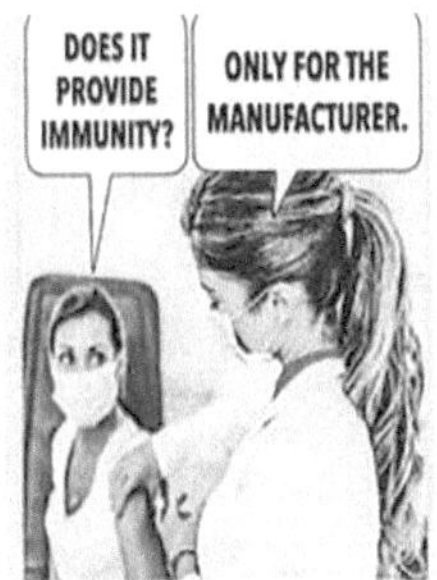

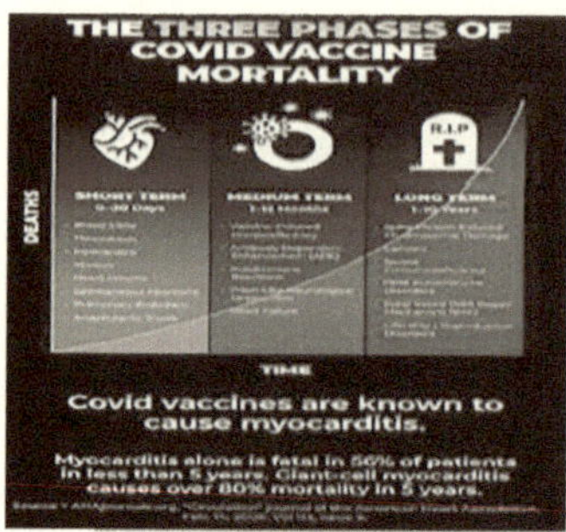

They also cause Mask phobia!

Parents send their child's mask to a lab for testing....look what they find on it

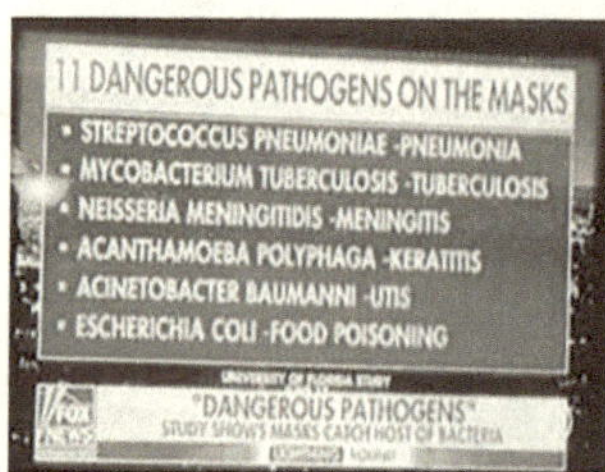

BRASSCHECK'S COVID VACCINE INJURY REPORT

The FDA and CDC's own VAERS data as of September 22, 2023

Deaths	36,286
Hospitalizations	210,138
Adverse Events	1,595,001

Source: OpenVAERS.com

This will sell like hotcakes here in the U.S.

I don't care, just give me the booster!

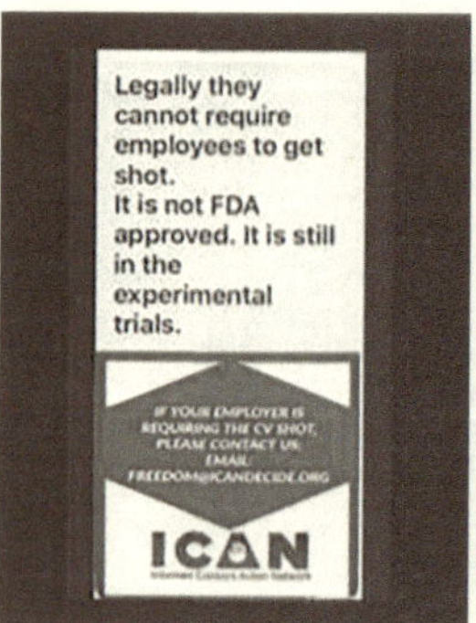

No surprise here!

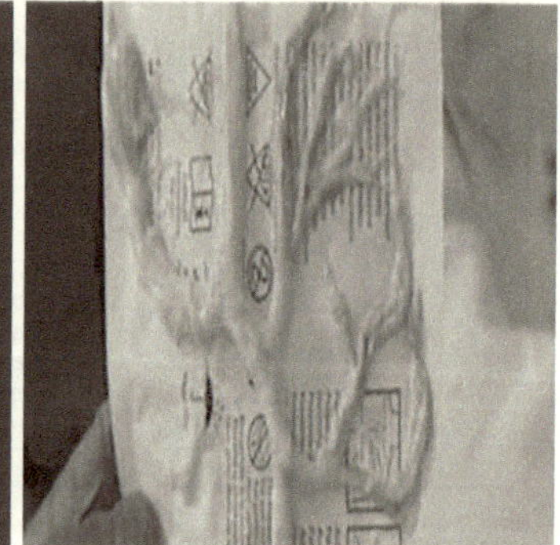

Fiberous clot found in blood after vaccine!

I will not wear it on my face
I will not wear it any place.
I will not wear it to get in.
I will not wear it on my chin.
I will not wear it on my ear.
I will not wear it out of fear.
I will not wear your stupid mask
I will not wear it.
DO NOT ASK.

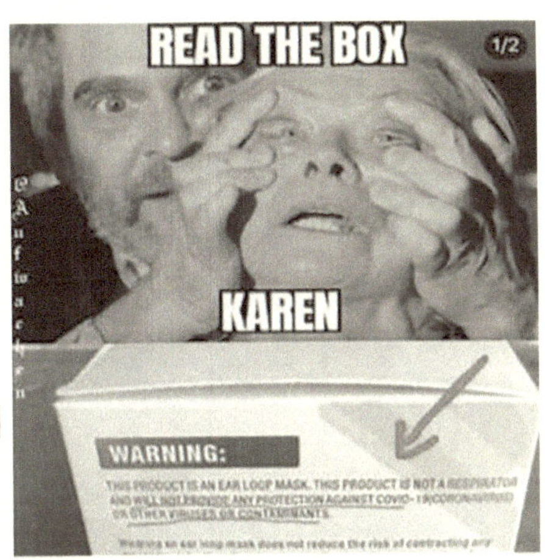

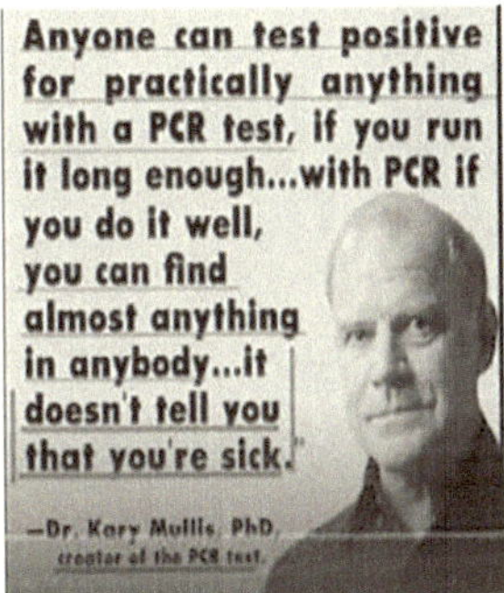

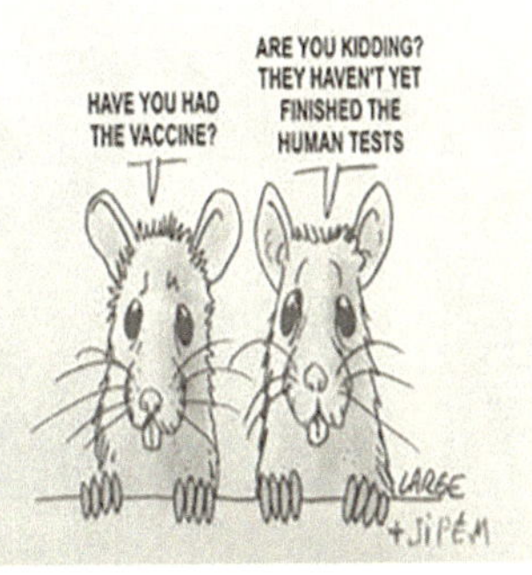

No surprise here!

Oh no, they wouldn't lie to us would they!

Don't come in without a mask!

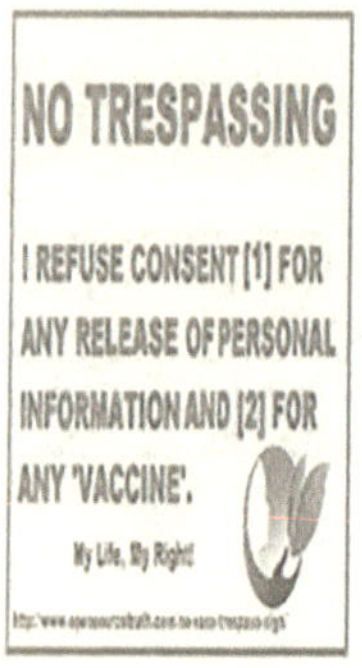

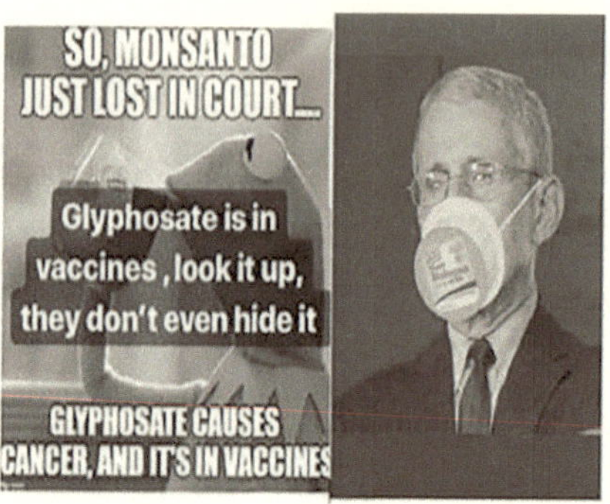

This is why your doctor gets aggressive.

Blue Cross Blue Shield pays your doctor a $40,000 bonus for fully vaccinating 100 patients under the age of 2. If your doctor manages to fully vaccinate 200 patients, that bonus jumps to $80,000.

But here's the catch: Under Blue Cross Blue Shield's rules, pediatricians **lose the whole bonus** unless at least 63% of patients are fully vaccinated, and that includes the flu vaccine. So it's not just $400 on your child's head–it could be the whole bonus. To your doctor, your decision to vaccinate your child might be worth $40,000, or much more, depending on the size of his or her practice.

Gee, they really care about my health!

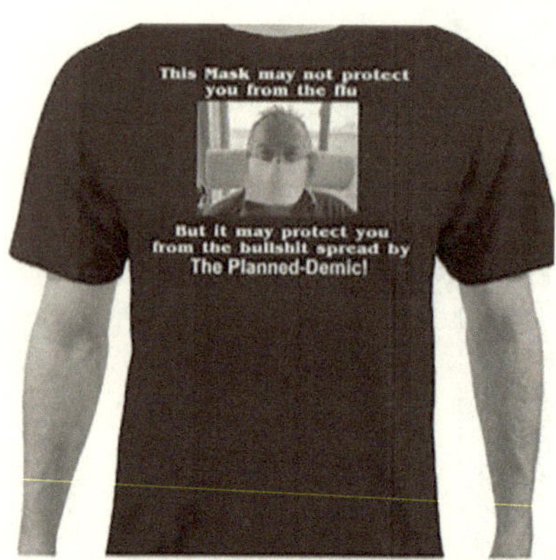

Yeah, but they are the chosen people!

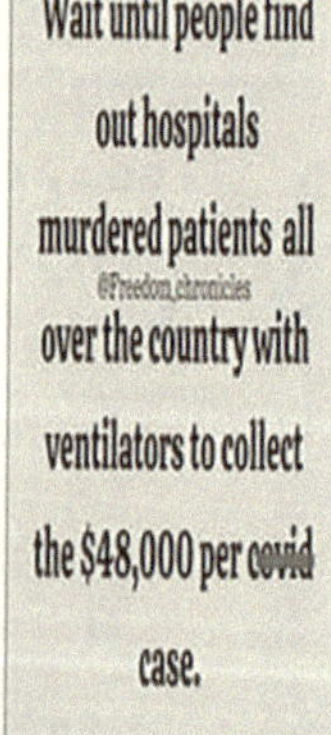

United States
Patent Application Publication
Rothschild
Pub. No.: US 2020/0279585 A1
Pub. Date: Sep. 3, 2020

(54) SYSTEM AND METHOD FOR TESTING FOR COVID-19

(71) Applicant: Richard A. Rothschild, London (GB)

(72) Inventor: Richard A. Rothschild, London (GB)

(21) Appl. No.: 16/876,814

(22) Filed: May 17, 2020

ABSTRACT

A method is provided for acquiring and transmitting biometric data (e.g., vital signs) of a user, where the data is analyzed to determine whether the user is suffering from a viral infection, such as COVID-19. The method includes using a pulse oximeter to acquire at least pulse and blood oxygen saturation percentage, which is transmitted wirelessly to a smartphone. To ensure that the data is accurate, an accelerometer within the smartphone is used to measure movement of the smartphone and/or the user. Once accurate data is acquired, it is uploaded to the cloud (or host), where the data is used (alone or together with other vital signs) to

Rothschild Patents

Unless you are promoting Genocide!

And the hospitals will get their checks in the mail!

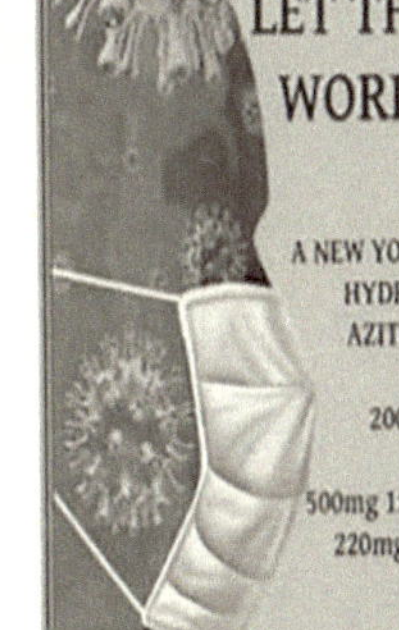

Employer's Mandating Vaccinations as a condition for employment?

1. Sidney Powell Post
When you hear that EEOC guidance says "your employer can require you to get a vaccine," this is false/ mistaken: EUAs have to have the Option to Refuse and the right to Informed Consent for EUAs. The EEOC's guidance updated on May 28, 2021, only states that "federal EEO laws do not prevent an employer from requiring all employees physically entering the workplace to be vaccinated..."[1] It does not address 21 USCS § 360bbb-3, which relates to EUAs and the option to refuse.

This is called a word game or word salad.

There is Potential Liability on Employers or Universities that Mandate Vaccines if an Employee or Student suffers any Side Effects or Death from a mandatory EUA vaccine.

See DefendingtheRepublic.org/covid

Source TG Post
https://t.me/SidneyPowell/906

CHAPTER 4 HEALTH

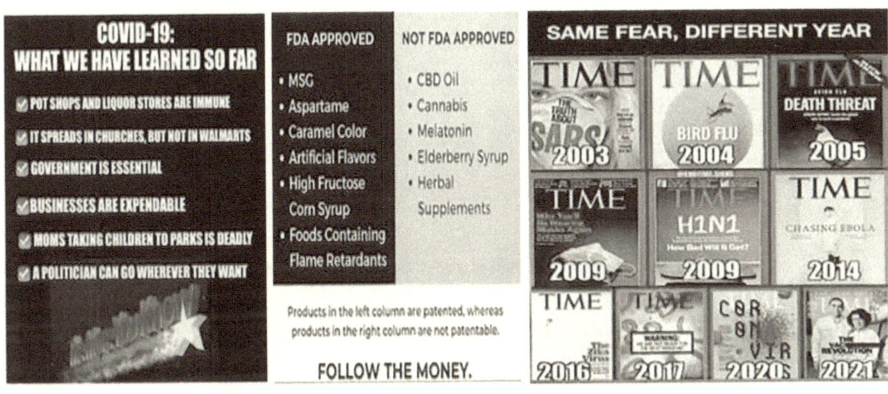

FDA (Federal Death Administration)

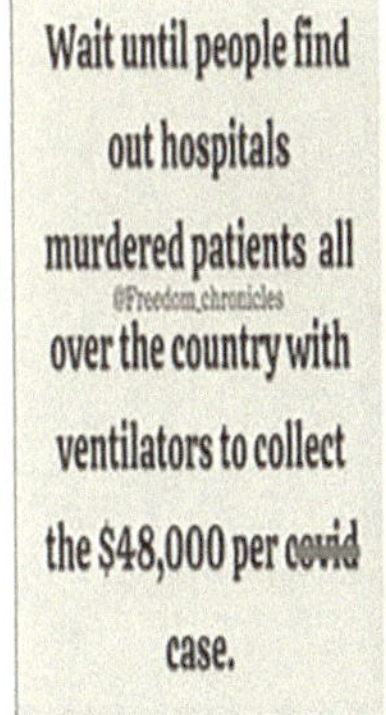

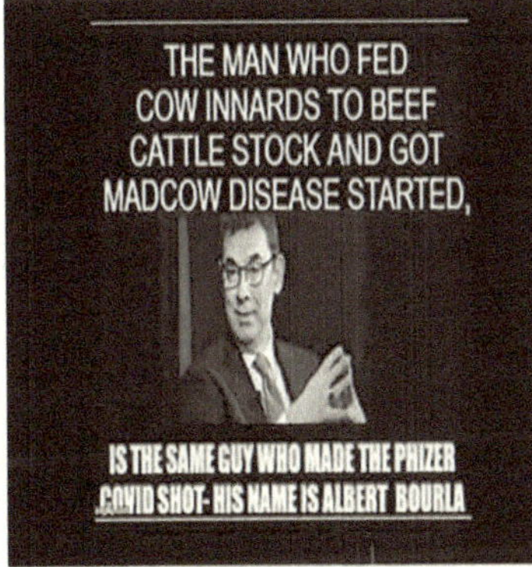

FACE MASK EXEMPT CARD

I am exempt from any ordinance requiring face mask usage in public. Wearing a face mask poses mental and/or physical risk to me.

DEPARTMENT OF JUSTICE ADA VIOLATION REPORTING NUMBER: 800-514-0301

Under the ADA I am not required to disclose any medical condition to you

If found in violation of the ADA you could be fined up to **$92,383** for your first ADA violation and **$184,767** for any subsequent violations.

Elias Trumen

1. CDC Director, Rochelle P. Walensky, is a jew.
2. CDC Deputy Director, Anne Schuchat, is a jew.
3. CDC Chief of Staff, Sherri A. Berger, is a jew.
4. CDC Chief Medical Officer, Mitchell Wolfe, is a jew.
5. CDC Director, Washington Office, Jeff Reczek, is a jew.
6. COVID Czar, Jeff Zients, is a jew.
7. COVID Senior Advior, Andy Slavitt, is a jew.
8. HHS Secretary, Xavier Becerra, is a jew.
9. HHS Ass. Secretary, Rachel Levine, is a dude and a jew.
10. Pfizer's CEO is a jew.
11. Moderna's vaccine created by a jew.
12. Johnson & Johnson's CEO is a jew.
13. Teva is an Israel pharmaceutical company with a jewish CEO.
14. Regeneron Pharma CEO is a jew
15. AstraZeneca's CEO was to take over as CEO of Israel's Teva Pharmaceuticals which means he's a jew.
But go ahead and take that vaccine you stupid goy....

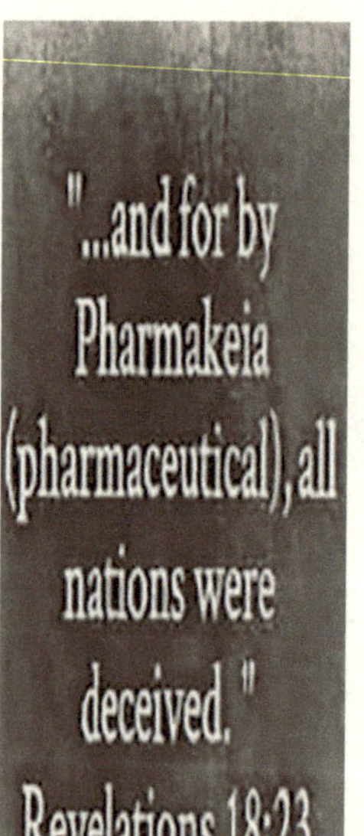

Wuhan Demic

Here is a list of what the vaccine contains:

- 2-fenoxietanol (antifreeze)
- aluminium (neurotoxin - [causes MS, ALS, Alzheimers])
- fetalt bovint serum (aborted cow blood)
- formaldehyd (causes cancer)
- gelatin (from animal)
- humant albumin (human blood)
- mononatrium L-glutamat (causes obesity and diabetes)
- MRC-5-celler (dead tissue from aborted fetuses)
- neomycin (antibiotikum)
- polymyxin B (antibiotikum)
- polysorbat 80 (causes cancer, emulsifier that opens up the blood brain barrier so the aluminum nano particles can get in)
- kaliumklorid (used in deadly injections)
- kaliumfosfat (liquid fertilizer)
- natriumborat (Borax, used to control cockroaches)
- natriumcitrat (food aditive)
- natriumhydroxid (Risk! corrosive)
- natriumfosfat (poisonous for cells)
- natriumfosfat monobasiskt monohydrat (poisonous for cells)
- sorbitol
- streptomycin (antibiotikum)
- yeast protein (fungus)
- urea (metabolic waste product from human urine)
- and other chemicals

the R N A- Va c c i n e contains nano technology.
R N A works as a genetic scissor that modifies your DNA in deep. It is your responsibility to inform yourself and to make a decision. The FDA warns of 22+ side effects including death. https://assets.publishing.service.gov.uk/government/uploads/system/uploads/attachment_data/file/940566/Information_for_UK_recipients_on_Pfizer_BioNTech_COVID-19_vaccine.pdf

⚠ 50 MILLION DIED FROM BACTERIAL PNEUMONIA CAUSED BY "MASKS" ‼ (1918 Spanish flu) ◇ What fact checkers & the media don't want you to know, FAUCI KNEW

EVERY policy government creates has unintended consequences.

Of course, SB21-142 is intended to fund abortions in Colorado. But this statement in Paragraph (e) of the Legislative Declaration has no qualifiers. https://leg.colorado.gov/sites/default/files/2021a_142_signed.pdf

Don't waste any time reacting to the intent of this policy. Lean into the opportunity.

Stay strong.

When asked whether you have taken the COVID-19 Vaccination, you might respond with:

"Every person has a right to privacy with respect to personal health decisions, free from coercion or interference from the government."

This is a direct quote from Colorado Senate Bill 21-142 which was sponsored by 16 of the 20 Democrat Senators and 31 of the 41 Democrat Representatives. Every Democrat present in both chambers voted in favor of the bill and Governor Jared Polis signed it into law on May 21 of this year.

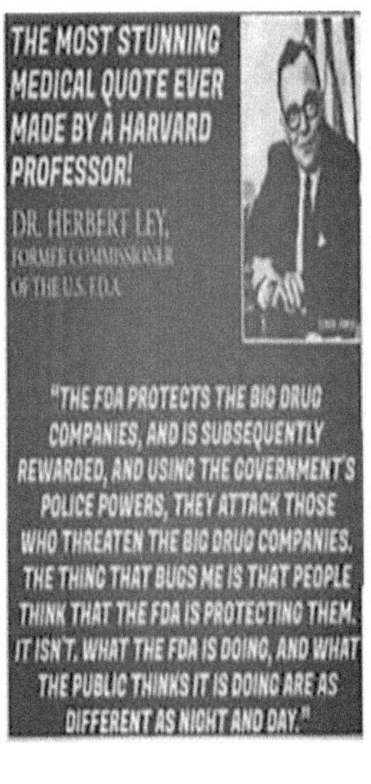

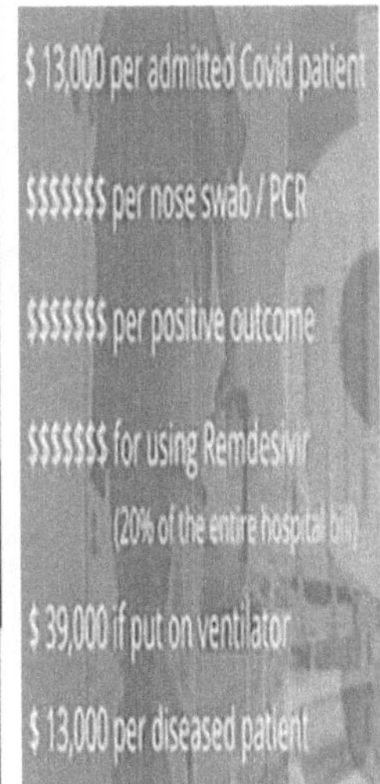

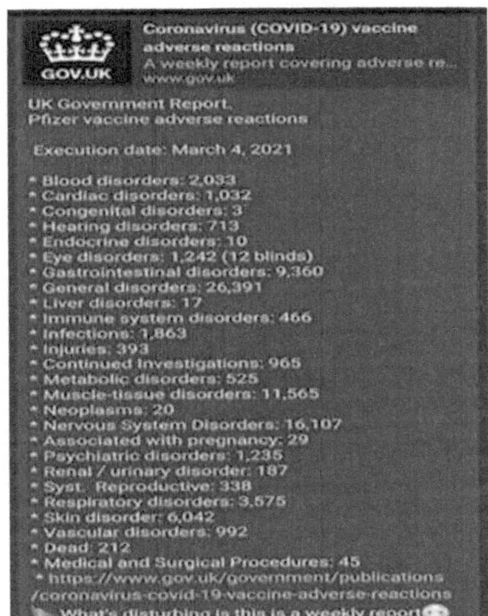

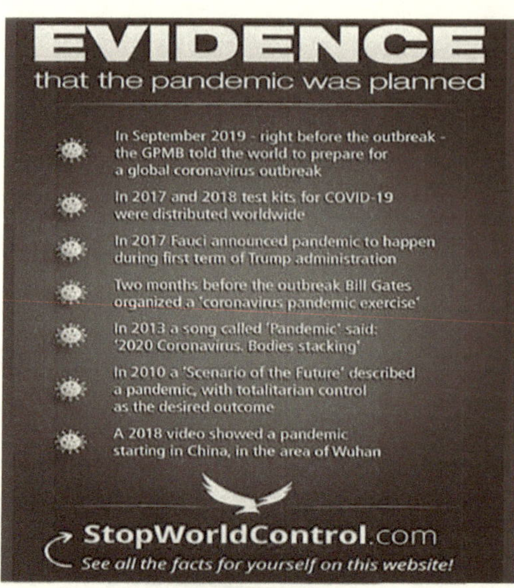

Are They trying to kill me? No worries, give me my 50th booster!

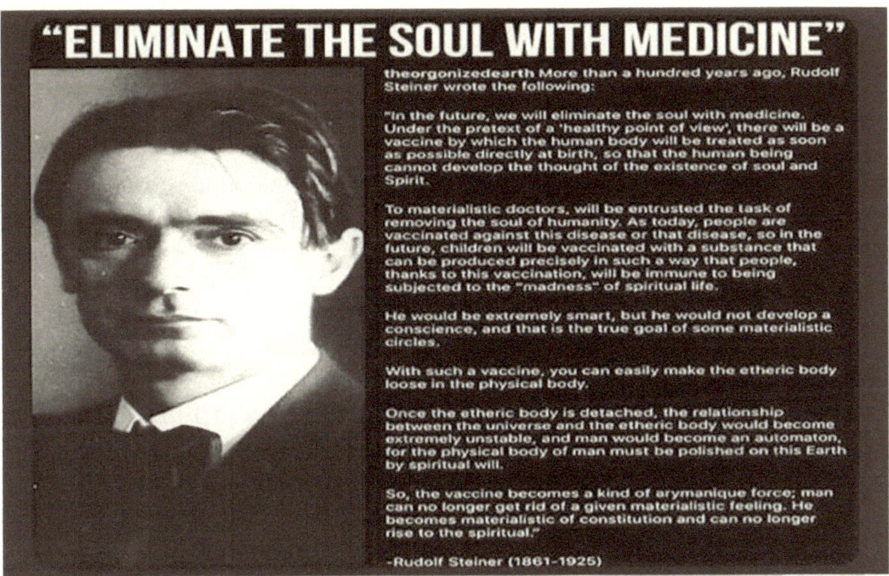

Such a nice man! You think vaccines are for your benefit?

America's Frontline Doctors exposing the medical field and the corrupt FDA

On the heels of Legacy Media *finally* acknowledging "Long Vax" side effects, we have yet another breakthrough for medical freedom and truth. ***<u>And this one is a game-changer.</u>***

The U.S. Food and Drug Administration (FDA) has agreed to remove misleading statements about ivermectin, one of the early treatment medications proven effective against COVID-19.

In a recent settlement, the FDA conceded to remove social media posts and webpages discouraging the use of ivermectin for COVID-19 treatment. They have already taken down one page that falsely advised against its use, and within 21 days, they will remove another titled "why you should not use ivermectin to treat or prevent COVID-19."

This landmark decision comes as a result of dedicated efforts by doctors who took legal action against the FDA's dissemination of disinformation. AFLDS played a crucial role in this fight, filing two amicus briefs in support of the suit. These actions compelled the FDA to retract statements that undermined the use of ivermectin, *a treatment that could have saved countless lives.*

From the beginning of the "plan-demic," we at AFLDS have known that ivermectin works well for both the prevention and treatment of COVID-19. Why? Because we followed the science. Study after study early in the "plan-demic" proved that ivermectin, with known anti-viral and anti-inflammatory properties, is a highly potent treatment against COVID-19. ***And when we began to see the Medical Industrial Complex lie to the world about its efficacy, we made sure millions had access to it.***

This epitomizes the Medical Industrial Complex›s insidious agenda—driven solely by profit and dominance. *They are not allies of our well-being. Ever.*

While President Trump was trying to promote Ivermectin for a covid cure, along with America's Frontline Doctors, the FDA along with the Medical Industrial Complex ignored them. No one was going to be allowed to introduce a cure saving thousands of lives that would interrupt the profits from their death jabs! How can the thousands of lives lost from their vaccines and boosters, not in just America but possibly millions worldwide go unpunished?

Has anyone questioned our governments involvement paying hospitals unbelievable vast amounts of money to ensure patients got the medicals deadly Covid Protocol, ensuring the jab and gave patients Remdesivir that caused nearly a 50% death rate, not counting the patients that were forced to take the ventilator which killed many more including a personnel friend of mine! Why were family and friends not allowed to visit their loved ones at such a critical time when these visits were needed the most for their well-being?

Do you think all the nurses were satisfied with the treatment they were forced to give the patients? No, many refused to continue, knowing they were witnessing legal murder. Don't believe me? Try purchasing **Brasscheck's most important book:** What the Nurses Saw: Medical Murder and COVID on Amazon. Link below

There is much more going on than just the Medial Industrial Complex lining their pockets with their deadly profits. You would have to be blind not to see the ongoing eugenics program depopulating the world by such influential Billionaires such as Bill Gates and the NWO along with all those involved in poisoning our **food** with GMOs, radiating us with 5G **cell towers**, contaminating the **water supply** with deadly Fluoride, destroying our future civilization by murdering our **unborn** through **abortions** and the continual poisoning of the **air** with the deadly Chemical trails worldwide 24/7.This brings the question, who has the unbelievable amount of capital to keep these commercial aircraft in fuel, and chemicals, paying the pilots hundreds of thousands of dollars a year, saturating the skies in the entire world? It would have to take trillions and trillions of dollars to carry out this murder mission! It could only be done by those that have trillions and trillions of dollars whether it be individual families or governments. My guess, since the banking United States Federal Reserve, which is not federal and have no reserves, but can print money out of thin air might be a good place to look into. If you or I printed money we would be arrested for counterfeiting! This is just one Truth bomb dropping onto the hidden mine field exposing lies and corruption!

When Governments have been
supressing cancer cures for decades,
then suddenly start pretending to care
about everyones health.

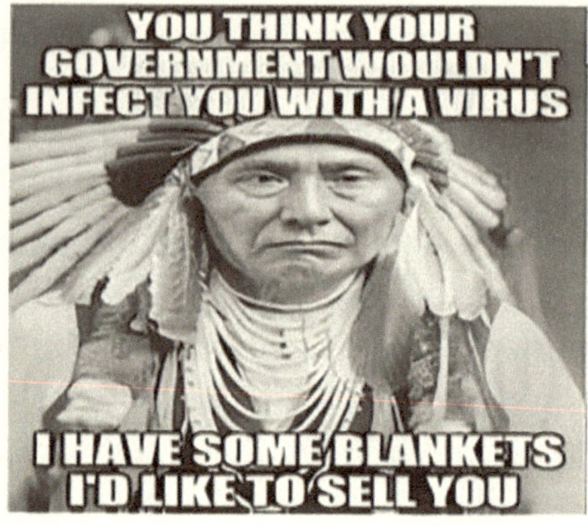
YOU THINK YOUR
GOVERNMENT WOULDN'T
INFECT YOU WITH A VIRUS
I HAVE SOME BLANKETS
I'D LIKE TO SELL YOU

CHAPTER 5 GOVERNMENT

When somebody asks me why I don't trust government:

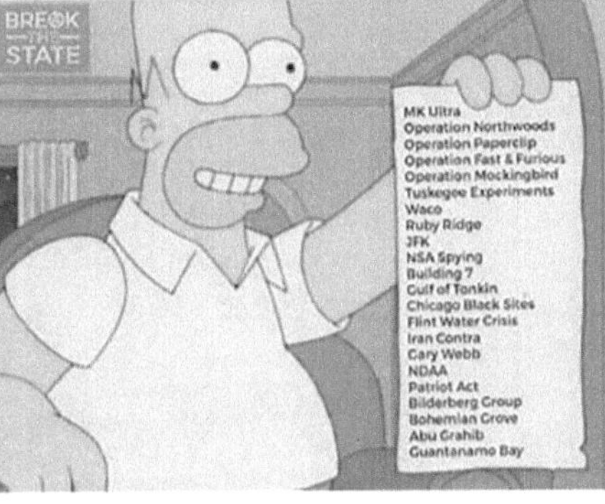

Pick up magnifying glasses in cart area!

Michelle, can I have some of your pie?

The curse of governments, 1 Samuel 8: 4-18: Israel desired to have Kings reign over them, like the nations around them, instead of God. God gave them their wish with a warning of the following consequences: He will cause your sons to fight the king's wars (the draft). He will take your fields and your vineyards and olive yards, even the best of them and give to his servants (tax money for fellow politicians). He will take your daughters and make them bakers and cooks (Women's Lib, mothers working). He will take ten percent of your seed and vineyards and give to his officers and his servants (Nearly 50% taxes today). He will take your men and maid servants and the best of your sons and your asses and put them to work, so they can cover their taxes! This was prophecy, it is today's reality!

In the event of a Civil War, I'm not afraid of the 81 million Biden voters. Half are dead and don't exist. And the rest don't even know what gender they are.

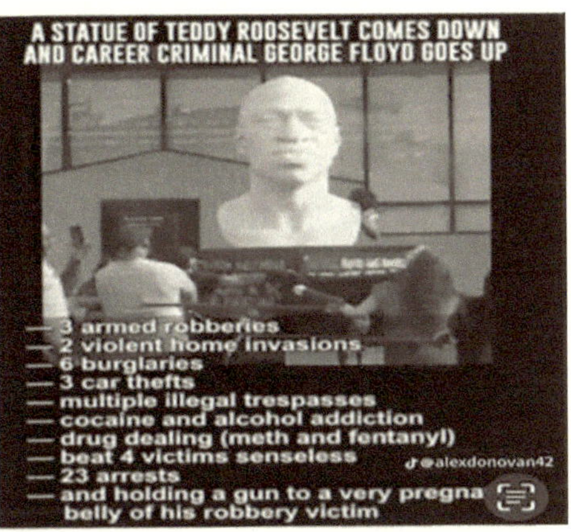

Can't be charged as a criminal, a Traitor, yes!

Proof America is under Communism, criminals immortalized

CHAPTER 6 GUN CONTROL

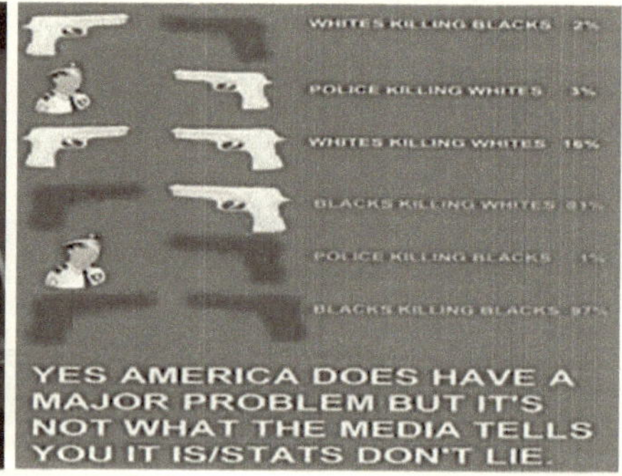

Here's my answer to your communist gun grabs: NO, and Hell No!!

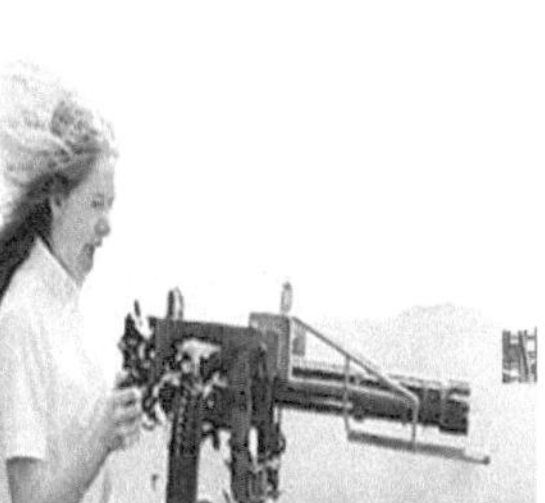

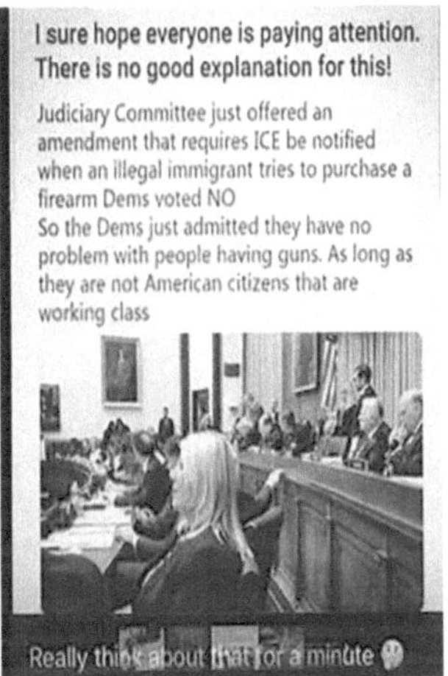

Definitely, a lot of Gun Control Dems are receiving
gifts under the table by their RED Friend!

Today is a good day to remind that you that, last year, Texas Republicans proudly changed the law to *allow* any Texans to carry a handgun *without* a permit, **background check, or training** that the state previously required.

97% of all guns are in the red territory

97% of all gun violence is in blue

Amish people after they listen to rap music for the first time

Ted Nugent posted this picture this morning
and I dont know who the artist is but it fits
how I am feeling exactly'.

CHAPTER 7 WHO DAT?

I didn't know Michelle had a twin brother?

Obama & George Clooney on some R&R

We live in a world where your kid cannot pretend to be an Indian. But a grown man can pretend to be a woman

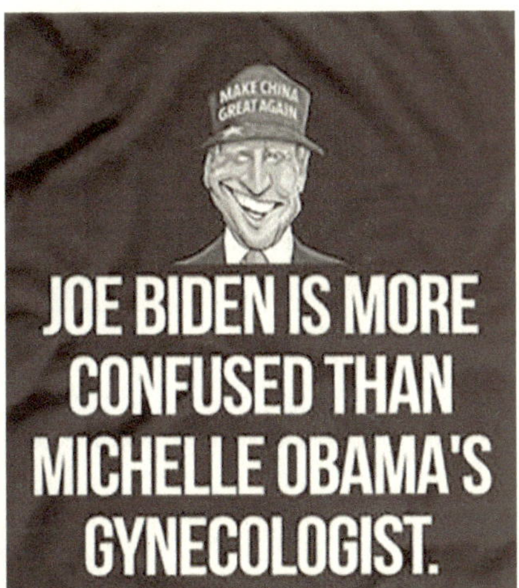

All part of the corruption of the nation and families. God destroyed Sodom and Gomorrah for just these acts against humanity and against his creation. This WOKE nonsense is not by accident. It is to destroy the moral fiber of our nation. Why? It is easier to destroy a nation that has no morals than those with morals who will stand up for God, country and family. Not hard to discern those wanting to destroy our nation, it's called Godless Zionist communism!

CHAPTER 8 MILITARY

Murdered by Jewish President LBJ Paradise CA.
DEWs, houses dustified, tree standing!

Indeed, one of the central goals of the feminist movement is to establish a fully sexually integrated military, trained, fit, and ready to engage in combat. To the advocates of this cause, it is an outrage that the United States is not moving at a rapid enough pace in their direction. But the truth is that it has moved very swiftly indeed. The United States today is the only serious military power in history to contemplate thorough sexual integration of its armed forces. And thanks to an adamant feminist lobby, a conspiracy of silence in the officer corps, and the anodyne state of debate over the issue, the brave new world of female infantry, bomber pilots, submariners, and drill sergeants may lie just around the corner.

Fox commentator Tucker Carlson, upset after seeing a photo of a new <u>pregnancy</u> flight suit, he <u>fumed</u>, "So we've got new hairstyles and maternity flight suits. Pregnant women are going to fight our wars. It's a mockery of the U.S. military. While China's military becomes more masculine as it's assembled the world's largest navy, our military needs to become, as Joe Biden says, "more feminine." Next uniform, our hairy legged soldiers wearing miniskirts!

OK, so women can fly a jet, drive a tank and shoot a rifle as well as the men. But I have heard nothing about hand-to-hand combat in time of war. As we see today transgender men are wiping the floor and beating women in every female sport. Do they think they will do better facing men in open hand to hand combat in war! The records show otherwise!

July 14, 2022

Joe Biden's transgender Assistant Health Secretary Dr. Rachel (Richard) Levine and newly hired DOE employee Sam Brinton represented the U.S. at the Bastille Day celebration at the French Ambassador's residence.

Sleeper cell

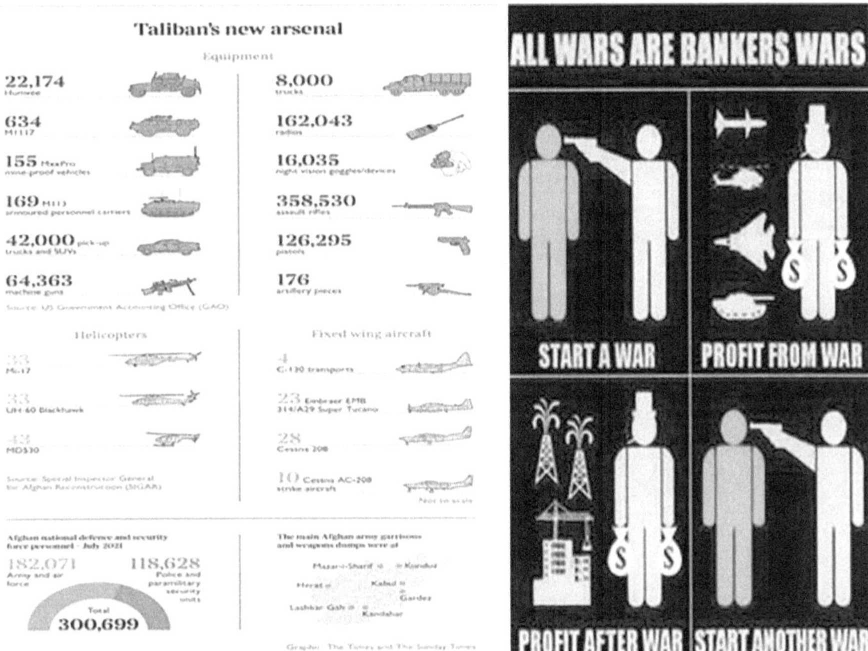

Thanks traitor Joe!

CHAPTER 9 CHILD TRAFFICKING

Crime Prevention and Justice Assistance Division | MI...
ag.hawaii.gov

OMG! Look at these Covid cases:

Australia - 20,000
Canada - 45,288
Germany - 100,000
India - 96,000
Russia - 45,000
Spain - 20,000
United Kingdom - 112,853
United States - 460,000

Oh whoops, I meant children that have gone missing so far this year without a peep from the media.

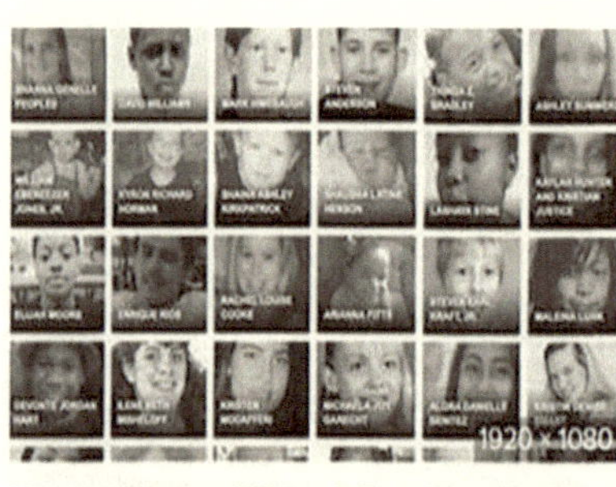

National Missing Children's Day: Help the FBI ...
kvue.com

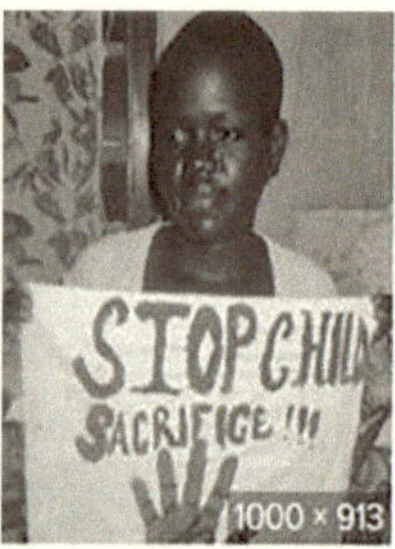

» Gideon Foundation ...
advocacynet.org

The lack of a common definition of "missing child," and a common response to the issue, results in few reliable statistics on the scope of the problem around the world.

Even with this challenge, we know that:

In **Australia**, an estimated **20,000** children are reported missing every year.
Australian Federal Police, National Coordination Centre.

In **Canada**, an estimated **45,288** children are reported missing each year.
Government of Canada, Canada's Missing – 2015 Fast Fact Sheet.

In **Germany**, an estimated **100,000** children are reported missing each year.
Initiative Vermisste Kinder.

In **India**, an estimated **96,000** children go missing each year.
Bachpan Bachao Andolan, Missing Children of India.

In **Jamaica**, an estimated **1,984** children were reporting missing in 2015.
Jamaica's Office of Children's Registry

In **Russia**, an estimated **45,000** children were reported missing in 2015.
Interview with Pavel Astakhov MIA "Russia Today", Apr. 4, 2016.

In **Spain**, an estimated **20,000** children are reported missing every year.
Spain Joins EU Hotline for Missing Children, Sep. 22, 2010.

In the **United Kingdom**, an estimated **112,853** children are reported missing every year.
National Crime Agency, UK Missing Persons Bureau.

In the **United States**, an estimated **460,000** children are reported missing every year.
Federal Bureau of Investigation, NCIC.

This, however, is only a snapshot of the problem. In many countries, statistics on missing children are not even available; and, unfortunately, even available statistics may be inaccurate due to: under-reporting/under-recognition; inflation; incorrect database entry of case information; and deletion of records once a case is closed.

One Missing Child Is ONE TOO Many

We are committed to improving the global understanding of and response to missing and abducted children.

Learn More

These Last Days News - January 24, 2018
URGENT: Forward a link to this web page to your clergy, family, friends and relatives.

Mel Gibson Exposes Hollywood as the Hub of Satanic Child Sacrifice...

"Are you so blind that you do not recognize the acceleration of sin among you? Murders abound, thievery, all manner of carnage, destruction of young souls, abortion, homosexuality, condemned from the beginning of time by the Eternal Father. Yet sin has become a way of life. Sin is condoned now, even unto the highest judge of your land and your lands throughout the world. As you have sown so shall you reap. Sin is death, not only of the spirit, but of the body. Wars are a punishment for man's sin, his greed, his avarice." - *Our Lady of the Roses, August 14, 1981*

The History Of Moloch, The Pagan God Of Child Sacrifice
allthatsinteresting.com

Don't forget, Elizabeth II & her Husband visited the Residential school in Kamloops, BC and left with 10 First Nations children who were never seen again.

NEVER SEEN OR HEARD FROM.

LET THAT SINK IN.

!!!!SHARE!!!! if you agree!

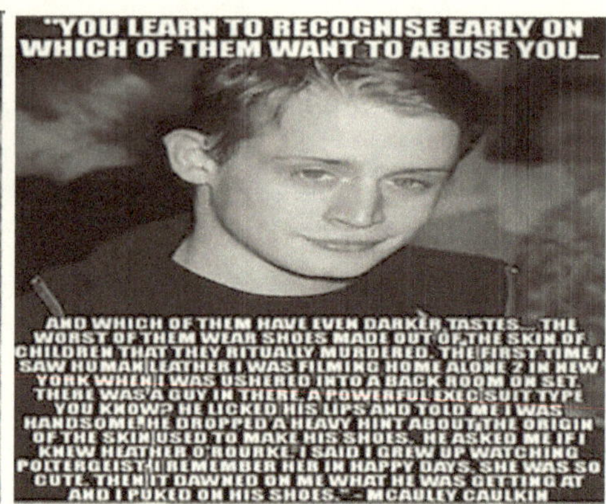

Child sacifice to molech, still happening today!

Abortion and Child Sacrifice | Answers In Genesis

10 Children Missing In Illinois Since De...
967theeagle.net

CHAPTER 10 FOOD POISONING

GMO's the way you like um! Killing more than Serial killers!

Fox News: Fentanyl traffickers caught in Connecticut with over 15K fentanyl pills disguised as Nerds and Skittles just ahead of Halloween

Former DEA Agent warns parents cartels are also targeting children. "It's deadly fentanyl, and it's flooding our streets like we've never seen... We're losing a future generation -- 300 [Americans] a day."

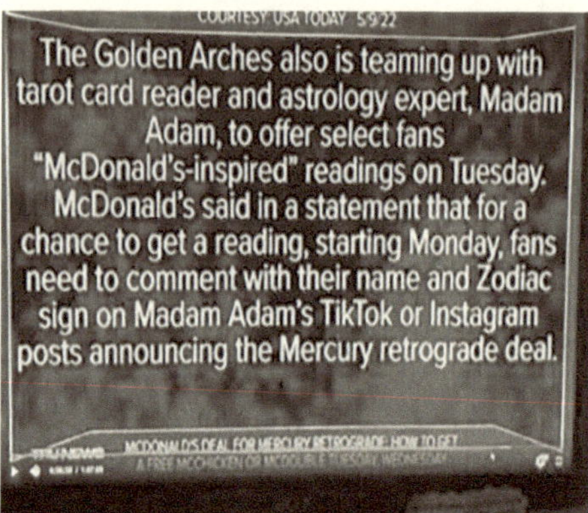

Punishment for traffickers: forced to eat a case of NERDS!

Did you know that one of the first coins in the world had a bee symbol on them? Did you know that there are live enzymes in honey? Did you know that in contact with metal spoon these enzymes die? The best way to eat honey is with wooden spoon, if you can't find one, use plastic. Did you know that honey contains a substance that helps your brain work better? Did you know that honey is one of the rare foods on earth that alone can sustain human life? Did you know that bees saved people in Africa from starvation? One spoon of honey is enough to sustain human life for 24 hours?

Did you know that propolis that bees produce is one of the most powerful natural ANTIBIOTICS? Did you know that honey has no expiration date? Did you know that the bodies of the great emperors of the world were buried in golden coffins and then covered with honey to prevent putrefaction? Did you know that the term "HONEY MOON" comes from the fact that newlyweds consumed honey for fertility after the wedding? Did you know that a bee lives less than 40 days, visits at least 1000 flowers and produces less than a teaspoon of honey, but for her it is a lifetime. Thank you, BEES! Make sure to share this post guys, I am sure many people will love to know this information Much love, Niko If you like our work and want to support us here's the link (which allows you to view some of the posts that are only for members). Thanks. https://www.patreon.com/awakenedspecies

No farmers, no cattle, no worries we will feed you! Bee colonies are being destroyed by Chem trails

115 US Food Processing plants destroyed, by whom?   No worries, eat bugs!

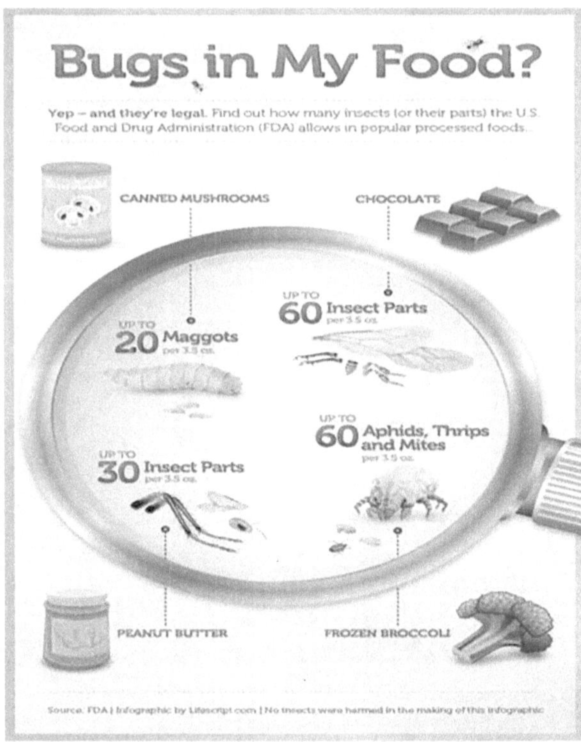

Tyson closing pork plants to building insect plants. I'll pass!
Next they will figure a way for us to eat ground glass, trust the FDA!

CHAPTER 11 FREE MASONS

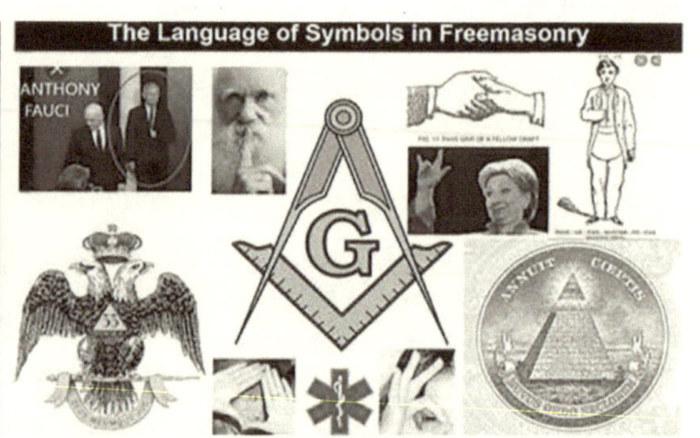

Global Elite Occultism
Since 1873, the Global Elite meets in secret in the Redwood Forest of Northern California where they practice the Cremation of Care ceremony, which is an occult ritual, an appeal to luciferic tendencies. (egotism/selfishness)

A marriage made in Hell!

CHAPTER 12 TRUTH NEEDS NO DEFENSE

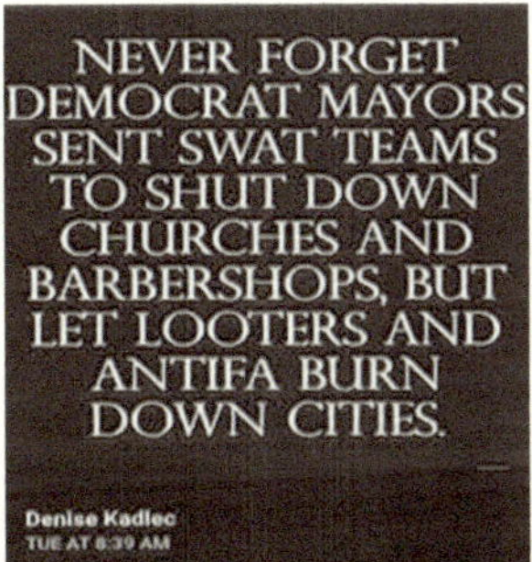

Zionism communism again!

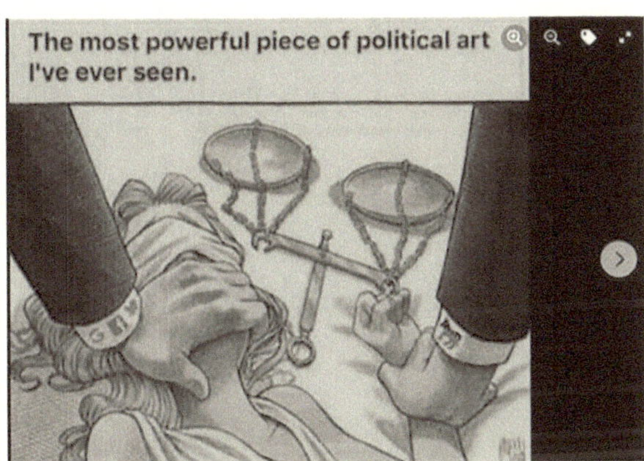

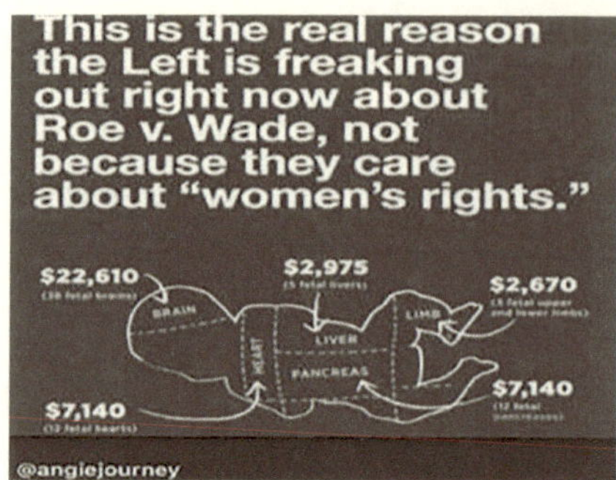

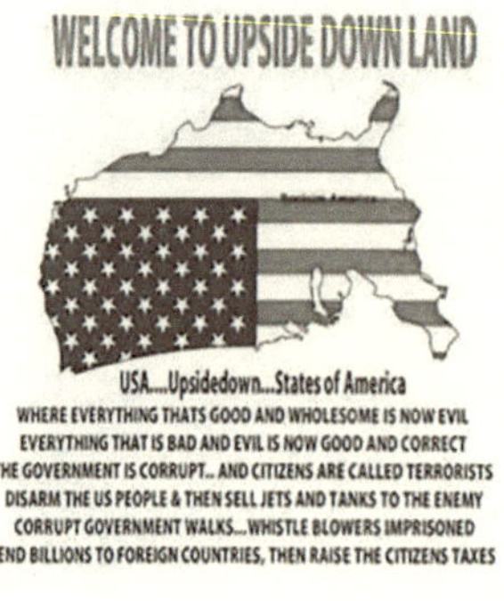

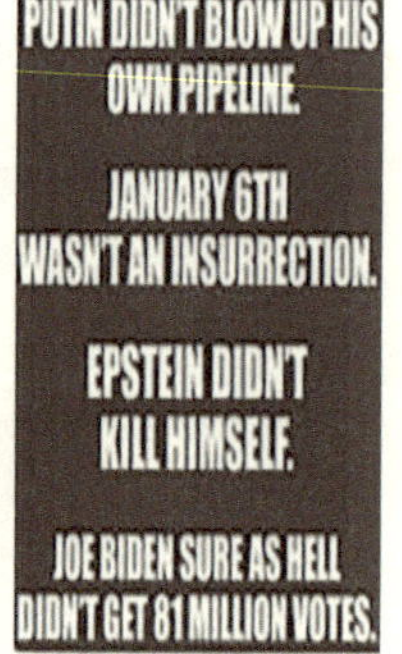

They shall call evil good and good evil, Isaiah 5:20

That is some crazy suntan oil!

Or possibly cows farting, bring out the Cow Depends!

Don't think gender matters? Go buy a rooster for eggs and a bull for milk. You will soon learn that God knew what He was doing.

Family Worth: Try 100 Trillion Dollars!

MAKE CHINA
GREAT AGAIN
JOE BIDEN IS MORE
CONFUSED THAN
MICHELLE OBAMA'S
GYNECOLOGIST.

HELL IS EMPTY AND ALL
THE DEVILS ARE HERE.

White Face
@Count58Chocula
Our Jewish director of Homeland
Security says our border is secure &
our Jewish Attorney General agrees.
Albert Bishai @ @annunakikkk · 18 Oct
Our Jewish Secretary Of State says we can
fight 2 Wars & our Jewish Secretary of the
Treasury says we can afford them

CHAPTER 13 EUGENICS

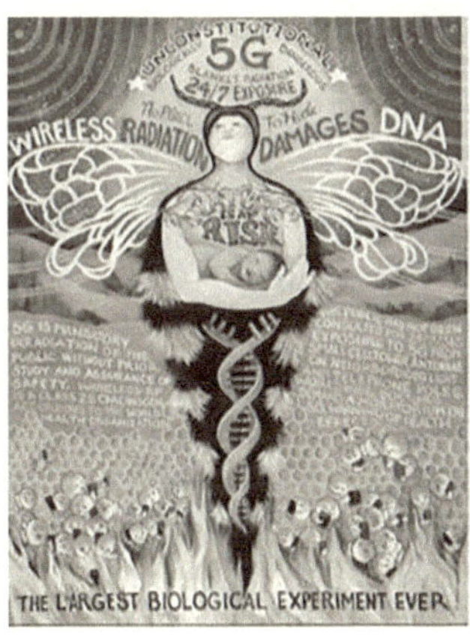

Re: Another Day Another Freek Show

Subject: Another Day Another Freek Show

Interesting – isn't it? Janet Lee

Sonlight @BillyBoysDaddy · 5m
Every election year has a disease

SARS ———2004
AVIAN———2008
SWINE———2010
MERS———2012
EBOLA———2014
ZIKA———2016
EBOLA———2018
CORONA———2020

Coincidences?

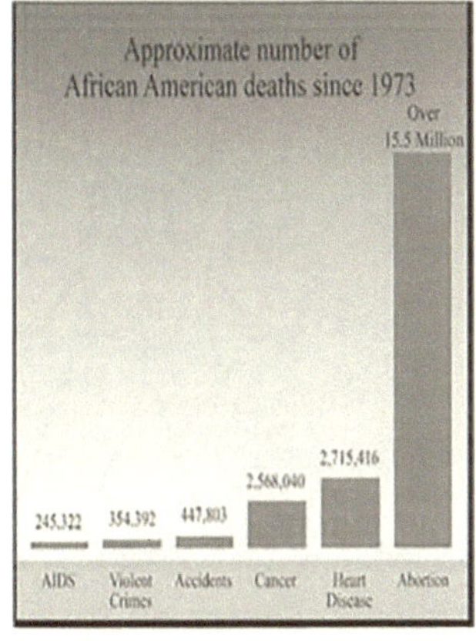

1970-2020

1312 athletes suffered from cardiac arrest and died.

2021-2022

1598 athletes suffered from cardiac arrest and died

It's always "look at the numbers" until the numbers no longer fit their narrative

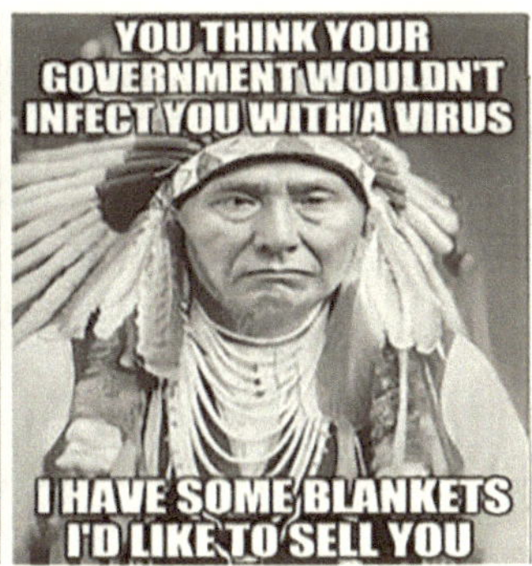

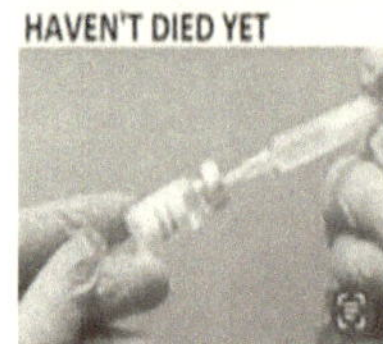

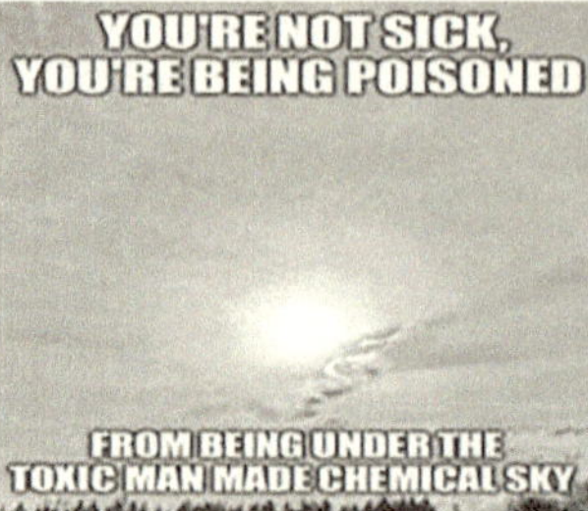

Chemical Trails

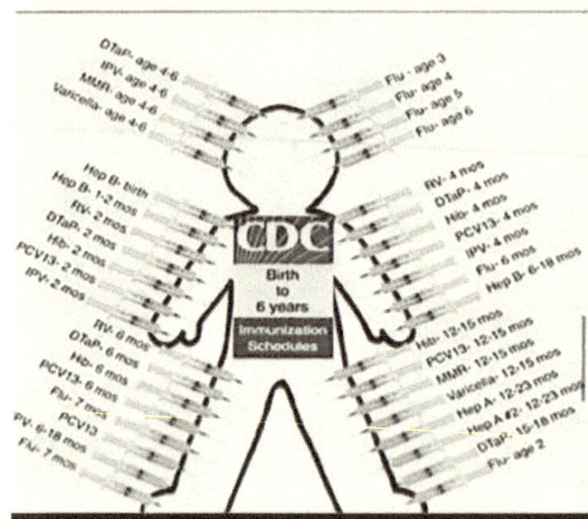

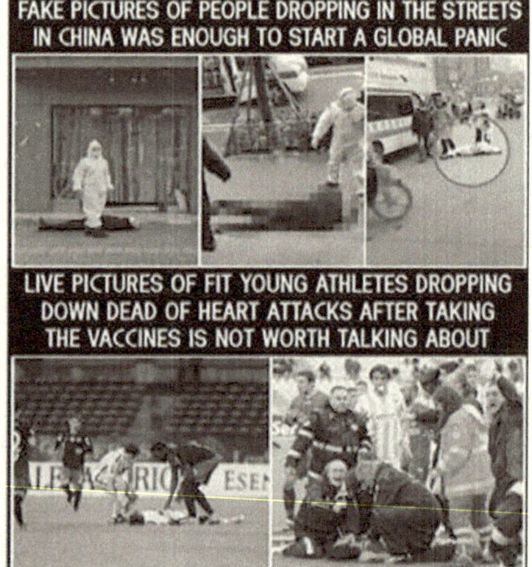

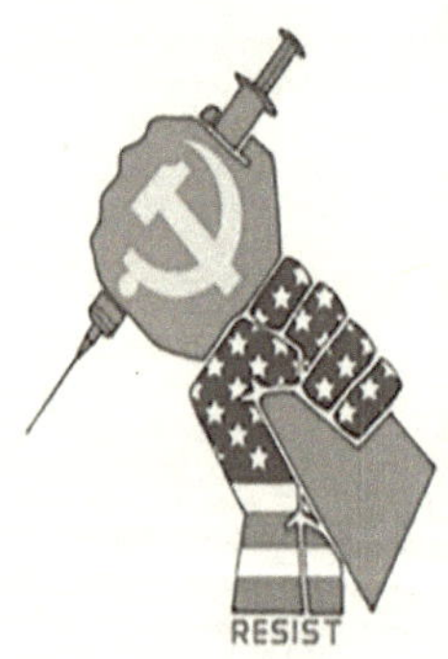

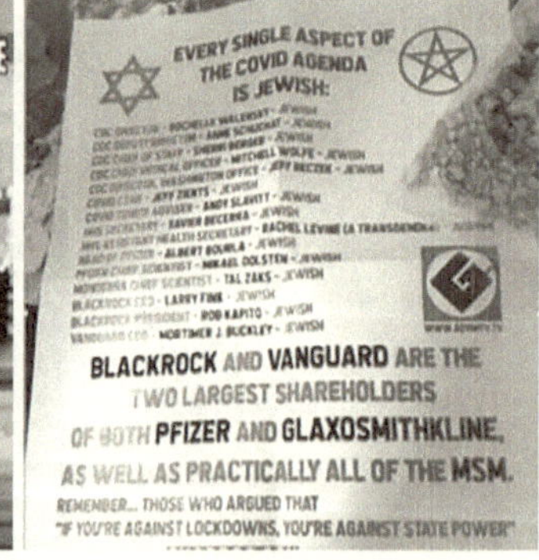

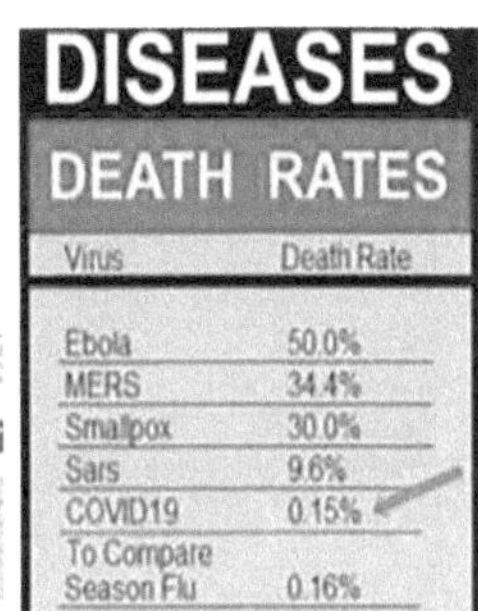
DISEASES
DEATH RATES
Virus | Death Rate
Ebola | 50.0%
MERS | 34.4%
Smallpox | 30.0%
Sars | 9.6%
COVID19 | 0.15%
To Compare
Season Flu | 0.16%

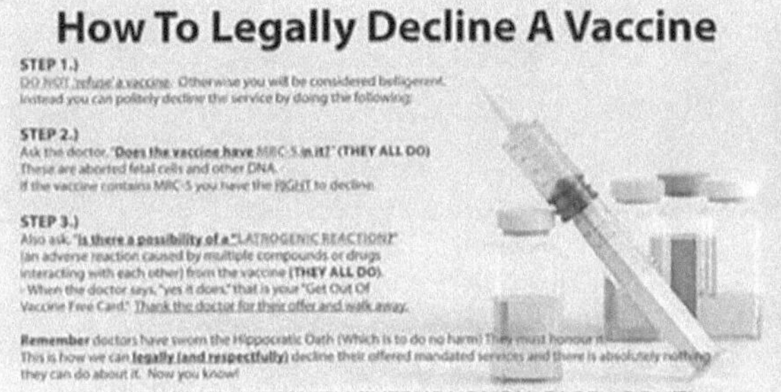
How To Legally Decline A Vaccine

STEP 1.)
DO NOT 'refuse' a vaccine. Otherwise you will be considered belligerent.
Instead you can politely decline the service by doing the following:

STEP 2.)
Ask the doctor, "Does the vaccine have MRC-5 in it?" (THEY ALL DO)
These are aborted fetal cells and other DNA.
If the vaccine contains MRC-5 you have the RIGHT to decline.

STEP 3.)
Also ask, "Is there a possibility of a "IATROGENIC REACTION?"
(an adverse reaction caused by multiple compounds or drugs
interacting with each other) from the vaccine (THEY ALL DO).
- When the doctor says, "yes it does," that is your "Get Out Of
Vaccine Free Card." Thank the doctor for their offer and walk away.

Remember doctors have sworn the Hippocratic Oath (Which is to do no harm) They must honour it.
This is how we can legally (and respectfully) decline their offered mandated services and there is absolutely nothing
they can do about it. Now you know!

PLEASE SHARE WITH EVERYONE YOU CARE ABOUT!
www.facebook.com/Holistology

Vaccination for ... Depopulation?

"The world today has 6.8 billion people.
That's heading up to about nine billion.
Now if we do a really great job on new
vaccines, health care & reproductive
health services, we could lower that
by perhaps 10 or 15 percent."

— Bill Gates
on Ted Talks, February 2010

They'll keep setting fires until
you submit to their climate
change agenda

WORLD ECONOMIC FORUM
WORLD ECONOMIC
WOR ECON FOR
WOR ON

They'll keep faking pandemics
until you submit to medical
slavery

« In the future it will be a question of finding a way to reduce the
population. We will start with the old ... then the weak and then
the useless ... and especially the stupid ones.

We will get rid of them by making them believe it is for their own
good. We will find something or cause it, a pandemic that targets
certain people ... a virus that will affect the old or the fat, it doesn't
matter; the weak will succumb to it, the fearful and the stupid will
believe it and ask to be treated.

We will have taken care to have planned the treatment, a
treatment that will be the solution. The selection of idiots will thus
be done ... they will go to the slaughterhouse on their own. »

- Jacques Attali, French-Jewish 'shadow Président of France',
interviewed in 1981 by Michael Salomon, 'Les Visages de l'avenir'
French original text at www.profession-gendarme.com

Written in 1921 explaining the deaths by vaccines!

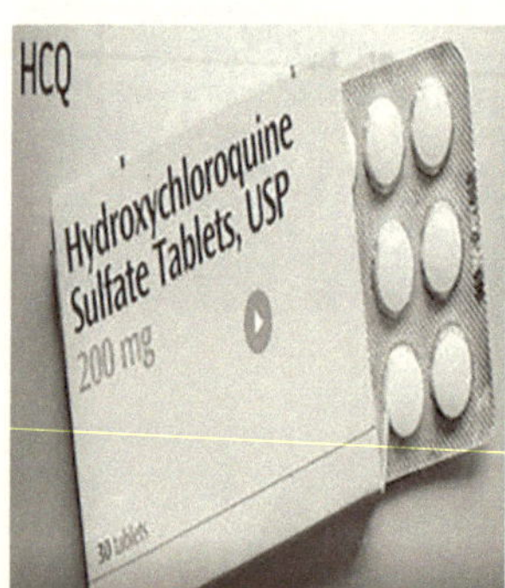

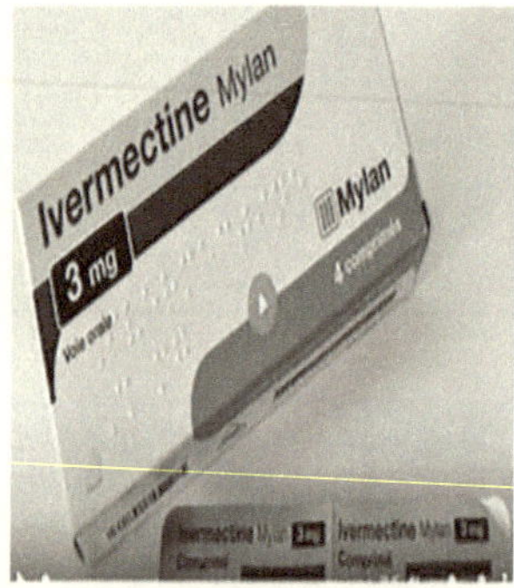

Covid cure outlawed   GMO's granted by the FDA   Covid Cure outlawed

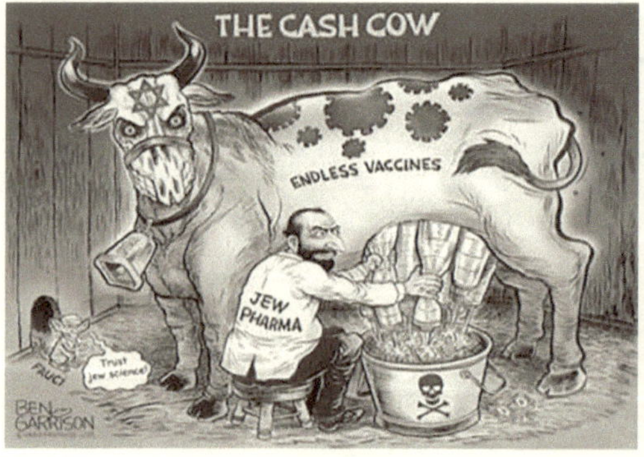

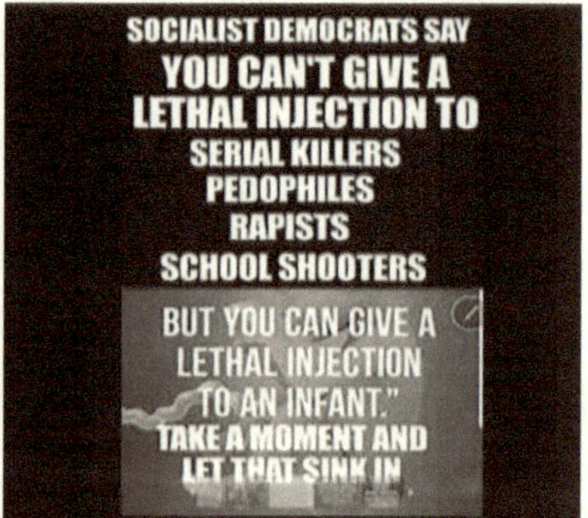

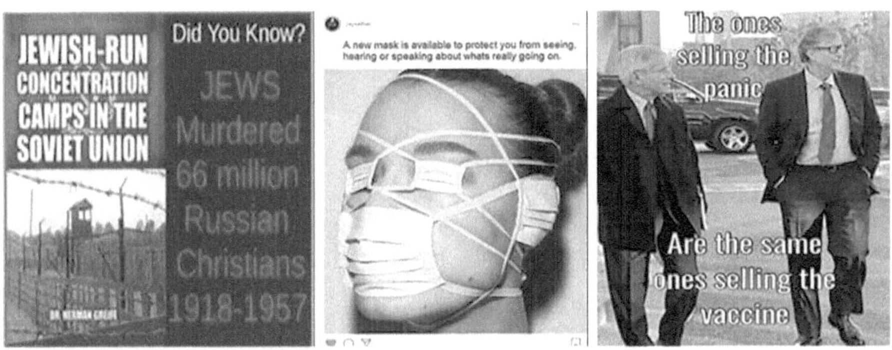

Alexandr Solzhenitsyn survivor

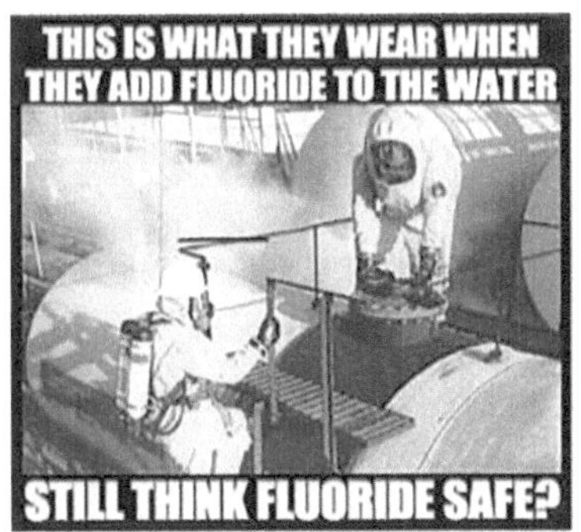

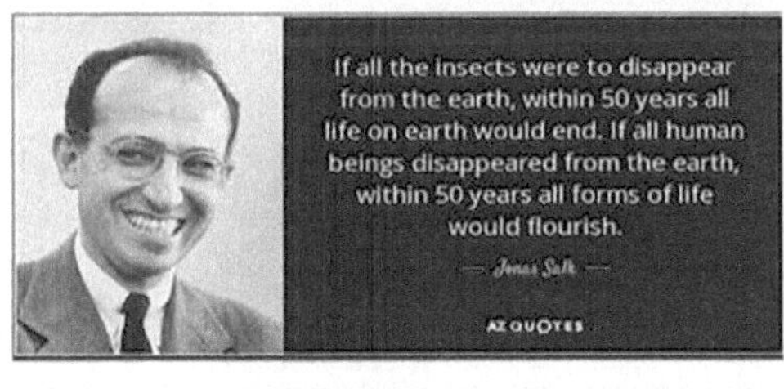

Jonas Salk, developer of the first "safe and effective" polio vaccine was a member of a Luciferian cult that aims to destroy humanity by mass depopulation and genetic modification.

Father of Mass Vaccination Wants Mass Depopulation

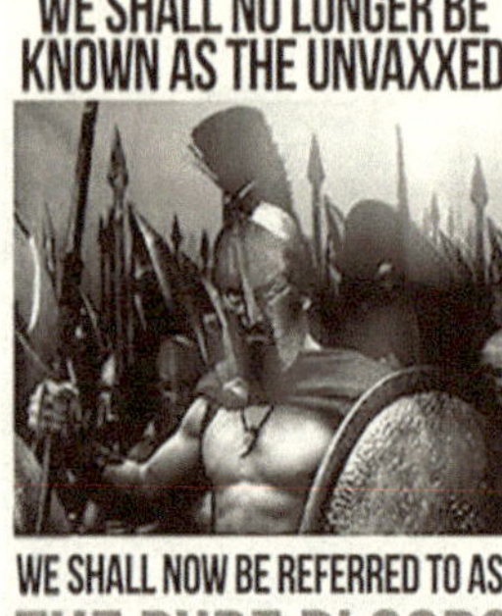

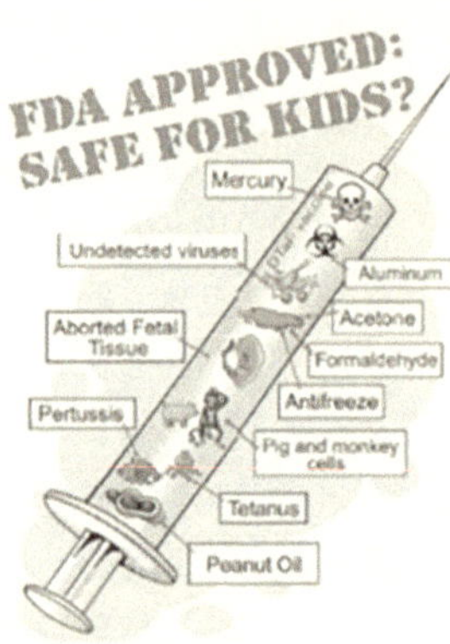

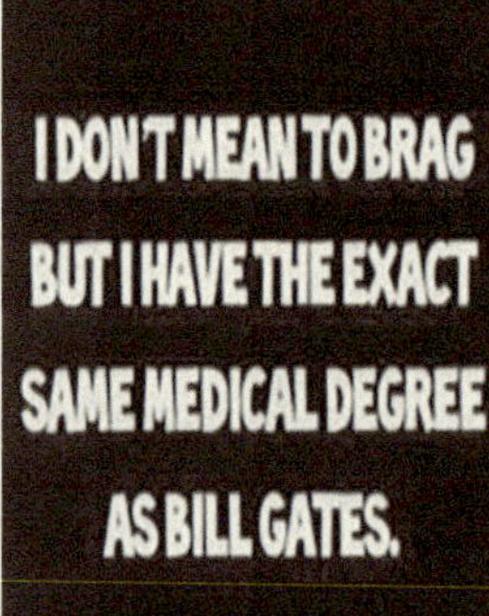

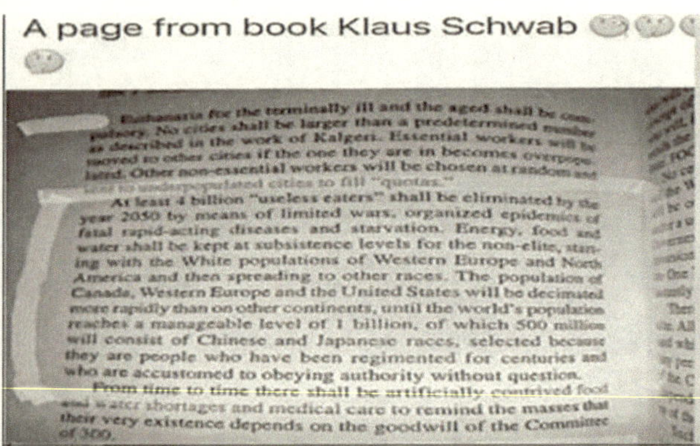

Euthanasia for the terminally ill and the aged shall be compulsory. No cities shall be larger than a predetermined number as described in the work of Kalgeri. Essential workers will be moved to other cities if the one they are in becomes overpopulated. Other non-essential workers will be chosen at random and sent to underpopulated cities to fill "quotas."

At least 4 billion "useless eaters" shall be eliminated by the year 2050 by means of limited wars, organized epidemics of fatal rapid-acting diseases and starvation. Energy, food and water shall be kept at subsistence levels for the non-elite, starting with the White populations of Western Europe and North America and then spreading to other races. The population of Canada, Western Europe and the United States will be decimated more rapidly than on other continents, until the world's population reaches a manageable level of 1 billion, of which 500 million will consist of Chinese and Japanese races, selected because they are people who have been regimented for centuries and who are accustomed to obeying authority without question.

From time to time there shall be artificially contrived food and water shortages and medical care to remind the masses that their very existence depends on the goodwill of the Committee of 300.

How much food (and drinks) does Ohio produce? Like Budweiser, Coca Cola, and Nestle for starters? This is why they poisoned Ohio-
They targeted Ohio because we feed everyone!

We have over 1,000 food manufacturing companies.

A small sample:
Conagra:

Conagra's iconic brands, such as Birds Eye®, Duncan Hines®, Healthy Choice®, Marie Callender's®, Reddi-wip®, and Slim Jim®, as well as emerging brands, including Angie's® BOOMCHICKAPOP®, Duke's®, Earth Balance®, Gardein™, and Frontera

Anheuser-Busch InBev

General Mills

Kellogg

Kraft-Hines

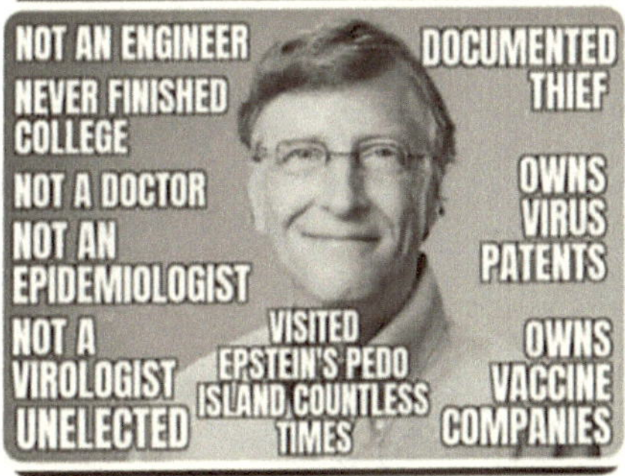

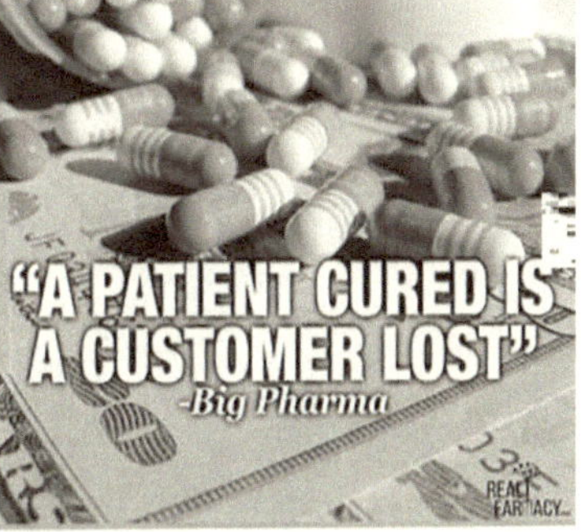

Did hospitals kill over 100,000 patients during the Covid Planned Demic?

CHAPTER 14 CORRUPTION

On this day in history, Andrew Jackson ended the Second Bank of the United States:

"I have had men watching you for a long time and I am convinced that you have used the funds of the bank to speculate in the breadstuffs of the country. When you won, you divided the profits amongst you, and when you lost, you charged it to the Bank. You are a den of vipers and thieves."

~ President Andrew Jackson, 1834, on closing the Second Bank of the United States

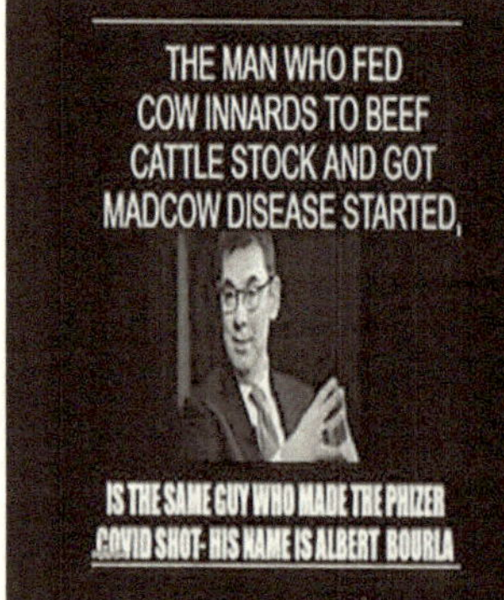

For 23 years these 3 guys invaded 9 countries and their victims exceeded 11 million souls!! What I do not understand is that noone calls them terrorists, murderers or dictators.

In Case You've Missed This...

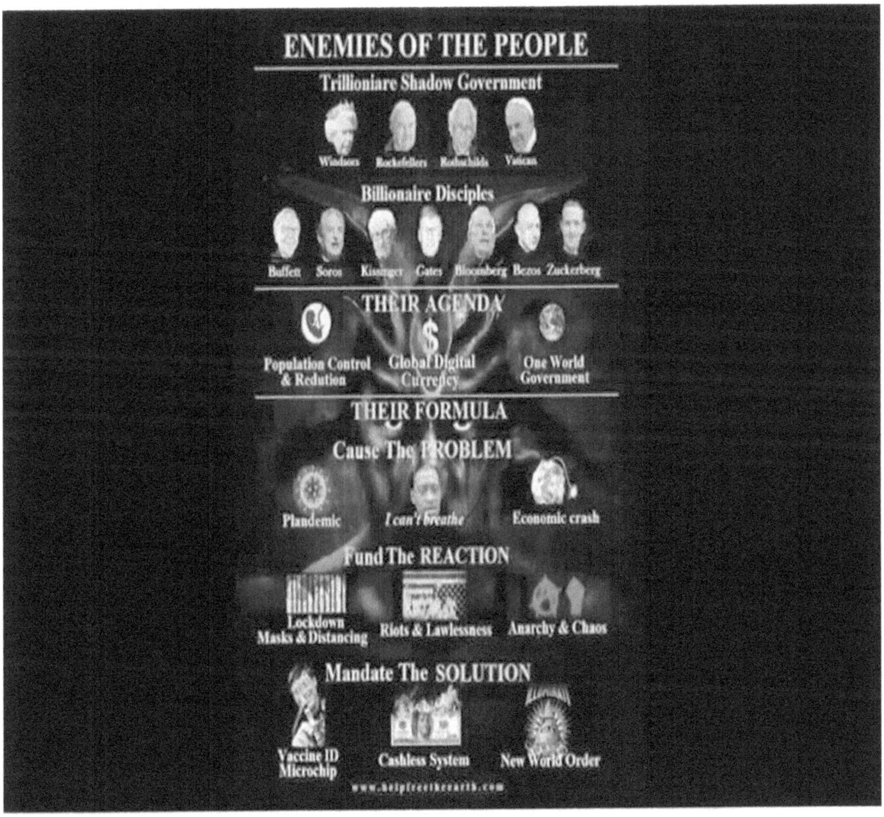
ENEMIES OF THE PEOPLE
Trillioniare Shadow Government
Windsors
Rockefellers
Rothschilds
Vatican
Billionaire Disciples
Buffett
Soros
Kissinger
Gates
Bloomberg
Bezos
Zuckerberg
THEIR AGENDA
Population Control & Redution
Global Digital Currency
One World Government
THEIR FORMULA
Cause The PROBLEM
Plandemic
I can't breathe
Economic crash
Fund The REACTION
Lockdown Masks & Distancing
Riots & Lawlessness
Anarchy & Chaos
Mandate The SOLUTION
Vaccine ID Microchip
Cashless System
New World Order

Ever wonder why Joe Biden wants to fine businesses $14,000 per unvaccinated employee but wants to give illegal immigrants $450,000?

VISIT PATRIOTPOST.US FOR THE BEST HUMOR AND MEMES

DEMOCRATS KILL A BILL FOR TUITION ASSISTANCE FOR CHILDREN OF VETERANS KILLED IN BATTLE.....

THEN APPROVE GIVING ILLEGAL ALIENS FREE TUITION...

LET THAT SINK IN AND THEN PASS THIS ON!!

Dr. Simon Goddek @goddek... · 16h
I'm tired of hearing conspiracies about how Big Mike is actually a woman.

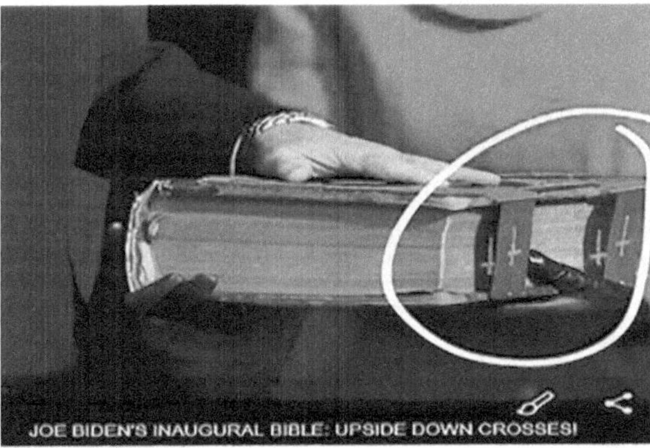

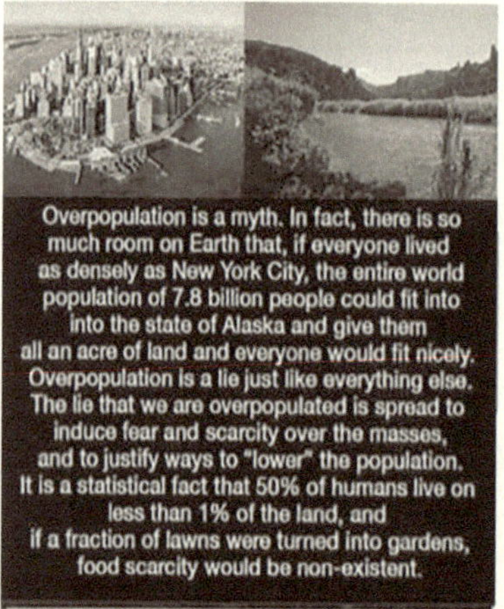

Overpopulation is a myth. In fact, there is so
much room on Earth that, if everyone lived
as densely as New York City, the entire world
population of 7.8 billion people could fit into
into the state of Alaska and give them
all an acre of land and everyone would fit nicely.
Overpopulation is a lie just like everything else.
The lie that we are overpopulated is spread to
induce fear and scarcity over the masses,
and to justify ways to "lower" the population.
It is a statistical fact that 50% of humans live on
less than 1% of the land, and
if a fraction of lawns were turned into gardens,
food scarcity would be non-existent.

"I do not believe in Communism any more than you do, but there is nothing wrong with the Communists in this country. Several of the best friends I have are Communists. I do not regard the Communists as any present or future threat to our country; in fact, I look upon Russia as our strongest ally in the years to come. As I told you when you began your investigation, you should confine yourself to Nazis and Fascists. While I do not believe in Communism, Russia is far better off and the world is safer under Communism than under the Czars."

...Franklin Delano Roosevelt
(Responding to Congressman Martin Dies, Democrat of Texas and chairman of the House Committee on Un-American Activities)

"You must understand. The leading Bolsheviks who took over Russia were not Russians. They hated Russians. They hated Christians. Driven by ethnic hatred they tortured and slaughtered millions of Russians without a shred of human remorse.

The October Revolution was not what you call in America the 'Russian Revolution.'

It was an invasion and conquest over the Russian people.

More of my countrymen suffered horrific crimes at their bloodstained hands than any people or nation ever suffered in the entirety of human history.

It cannot be overstated. Bolshevism committed the greatest human slaughter of all time.

The fact that most of the world is ignorant and uncaring about this enormous crime is proof that the global media is in the hands of the perpetrators."[1]

– Aleksandr Solzhenitsyn

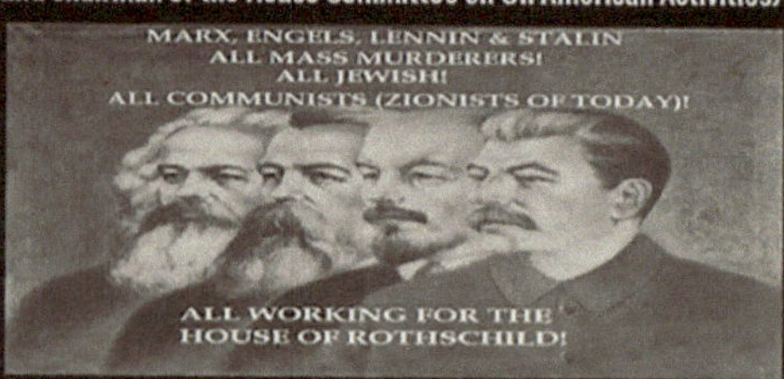

COVID19 FACTS:

The virus can travel 6', it can not travel 6'1 or greater, it can live on all surfaces except anything that comes in the mail from Amazon, it does not live in Target, Walmart, Home Depot, Lowe's or any grocery store. It's harmless in protests, riots and looting. It is only deadly in bars, restaurants, small businesses, hair salons and it can not live on your food as long as you get it to go.

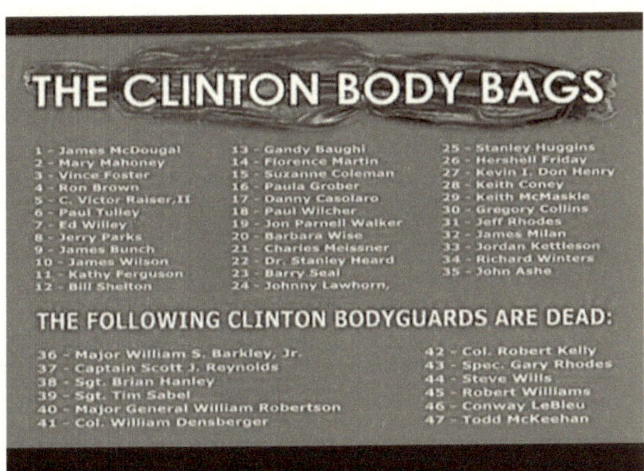

On the left is a current member of the Board of Directors of Pfizer.

On the right is the former FDA Commissioner in charge of regulating Pfizer.

Pfizer got tired of paying billions in fines for illegal marketing practices, bribing physicians, and suppressing adverse trial results so they bought the FDA Commissioner.

Why not, right ?

"Ready for the rabbit hole that connects all rabbit holes?
CHECK THIS OUT:
As many of you heard Moderna is in the 3rd and final stage of their vaccine development. Here's something many of you don't know, guess who the first CEO of Moderna was? A Cornell graduate by the name of Anthony Fauci, who was a roommate with none other than Bill Gates. Are you paying attention? It was at Cornell that Bill Gates designed the RFID (Radio-frequency identification) and patened it under US2006257852. Are you awake yet? Now let's really go down the rabbit hole. Moderna was a pharmaceutical company that started in Germany under the name IG Farben. IG Farben is infamous for it's mass production of Zyklon-B, the primary gas used to kill millions during the Holocaust. After Germany fell, IG Farben was dissolved and its assets sold off by a Nazi turned American by the name of, you guessed it, George Soros. Soros rebranded the company as Moderna. And who was the primary
stockholder of Moderna until his death? Jeffrey Epstein. His role in Moderna is where he made his fortune and established his connections. Let that sink in.
Wake up people! You are being conditioned and controlled. Now it's up to you to... share

Error: Not so. Zyklon-B was used to kill lice in Prisoners clothes, which in turn stopped the spread of Typhoid!

You do not want your prisoners dying when so many were badly needed for the Nazi war effort. Holocaust prisoners were given numerical tattoos. If they were to be immediately gassed to death, why waste time and cost by tattooing them!

Health Care and Politics

Fauci: 'No doubt' Trump will face surprise infectious disease outbreak

January 11, 2017

ADD TOPIC TO EMAIL ALERTS

Anthony S. Fauci, MD, director of the National Institute of Allergy and Infectious Diseases, said there is "no doubt" Donald J. Trump will be confronted with a surprise infectious disease outbreak during his presidency.

Fauci has led the NIAID for more than 3 decades, advising the past five United States presidents on global health threats from the early days of the AIDS epidemic in the 1980s through to the current Zika virus outbreak.

During a forum on pandemic preparedness at Georgetown University, Fauci said the Trump administration will not only be challenged by ongoing global health threats such as influenza and HIV, but also a surprise disease outbreak.

Anthony S. Fauci

WANTED
For Crimes Against Humanity

Name:	Bill (William Henry) Gates
DOB	October 28, 1955
Height:	6'8"
Weight:	164 pounds
Hair:	Grey
Education:	College Dropout
Net Worth:	$100 Billion US
Address 1:	1835 73rd Ave NE and 7400 Northeast 15th St. Medina, Washington
Address 2:	2808 Ocean Front Del Mar, California

CASE INFORMATION

Bill Gates must be stopped. His medical reign of terror and crimes against humanity are listed here:

1. Funding and planning the Covid-19 pandemic at Event 201
On Oct. 18, 2019, Bill Gates funded a simulation of todays plandemic six weeks in advance.

2. Funding the development of the Covid-19 virus
Bill Gates is a major funder of the Piveright Institute (UK) that owns the patent to the virus. Bill Gates provided Dr. Anthony Fauci with a $100 million grant, who in turn, funded the coronavirus bat research that included scientists at the virology lab in Wuhan, China.

3. Bribery and buying control over health agencies and officials
Bill Gates has used his philanthropic billions in donations to buy control over WHO, UNICEF, GAVI, PATH, NIAID and the CDC.

4. Genocidal killing, paralyzing and crippling of 1000's of infants and children
Bill Gates funded the GSK's experimental malaria vaccine that killed 151 African infants and caused paralysis, seizures and convulsions in 1000's more. In 2002, his meningitis vaccine forced on African children caused paralysis in over 50 children. In India, Bill Gates experimental polio vaccine paralyzed 490,000 children.

5. Sterilizing millions of unwilling women and young girls in India and Africa
In 2014, Bill Gates funded the experimental HPV vaccine on 23,000 unwilling girls in India. Seven died and 1200 suffered side effects. His $10 billion funding of WHO allowed them to chemically sterilize millions of unwilling Kenyan women with a tetanus sterility formula vaccine.

6. Using humans instead of animals as experimental guinea pigs
Bill Gates funded Johns Hopkins University experiments that infected 100's of Guatemalans with sexually transmitted diseases for drug and vaccine testing.

7. Genetically engineering our food with GMO's
Bill Gates invests in Monsanto and GMO Foods. Health risks include infertility, accelerated ageing and weakened immune system. Bill Gates has funded the destruction of rural farming worldwide. In the past 20 years, 35,000 farmers have committed suicide.

8. Human rights abuses including the use of citizen surveillance technology
Bill Gates crimes disguised as charity are the single greatest threat to the world economy, world health, world peace and human rights. His agenda is one world government, one world currency and a culled microchipped population of vaccinated robots.

WE MUST END HIS REIGN OF TERROR! NOW!

Innocent victims of 911 murdered by the
NWO, our governments partners!

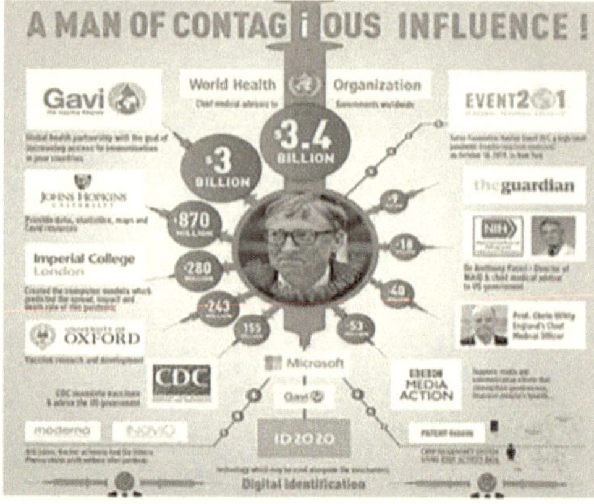

Bill, "Why such an interest in the medical field?"

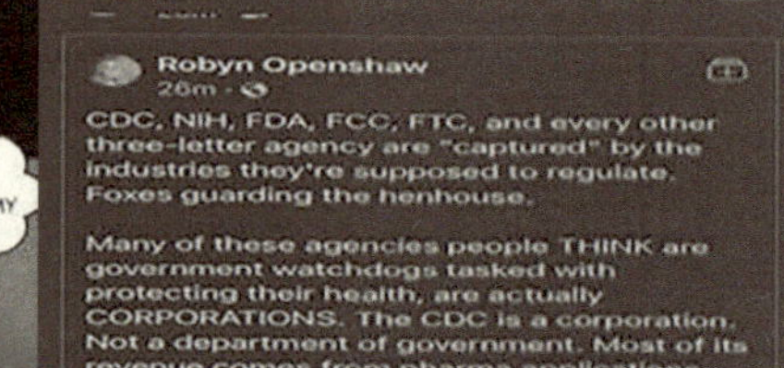

On the left is the former Vice President of Monsanto, a company that poisons everything you consume. On the right is the current Deputy Commissioner of the FDA, an agency that protects you from companies like Monsanto. This is legal.

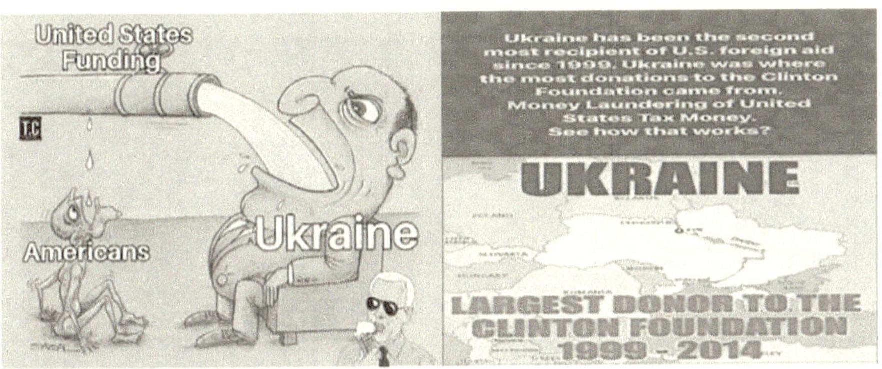

More treason that will one day be rectified!

Jacob Rothschild, recently deceased, standing before a painting called: "Satan Sommoning His Legions". Very appropiate! The Rothschilds created the state of Israel for economical purposes to protect their oil interests. The family since its beginning in the 18th century have started every major war in our history. They make fortunes providing loans to both sides of those in conflict. Even supplying Hitler with money in WWII with the design to remove all Jews to Palestine to fulfill their Jewish state of Israel. What's a few human casualties against a high gain in profits! Their Jewish trump card, anti-Semitism was created in 1848. Their net worth, 100 trillion!

CHAPTER 15 SCIENCE

FLAT EARTH CURVE BALL!

"Common sense is what tells us the earth flat." ---- *Albert Einstein*

According to <u>Pythagorean Geometry</u>, the formula for the earth's curvature is 8 inches multiplied by every mile squared. For example, one mile would see 8 inches of curvature. 8 x 1 mile squared equals 8. Two miles (8 x 2 squared equals 32 inches of curvature). Three miles (8 x 3 squared, you would see 72 inches of curvature). Four miles (8 X 4 squared, 128 inches of curvature, etc.

The math should be easily testable; however, no such curve can be demonstrated.

If the earth is curved by 24 feet over six miles, as the formula says it should, then surveyors, engineers, architects, and other professions which rely on precise measurements must factor-in the curve.

Bridges, tunnels, canals, and railroads, which stretch over vast stretches of land and sea, would have to account for curvatures . . . **But they don't!**

Covering roughly seventy -five percent of the earth's surface, **water always seeks its own level.**

Quote:

There are rivers that flow hundreds of miles towards the level of the sea without falling more than a few feet – notably, the Nile, which, in a thousand miles, falls but a foot. A level expanse of this extent is quite incompatible with the idea of the earth's convexity. It is, therefore, a reasonable proof that the earth is not a globe."

Samuel Rowbotham: "A hundred proofs the earth is not a globe" 1885

You believe Science, right? Pythagorean Geometry is science and proof the earth is not a globe! Case closed! No computer Image software needed.

Question: If the earth spins at 1000 mph and travels through space at 66,600 mph, how does a meteor that travels at a speed of 20,000 mph strike the earth and make a perfect circular crater on the earth's surface. It can't except on a perfectly flat surface that does not move!

Earths space images contrived by CGI! (Computer Generated Images).

Sun and Moon; I rely on God's word concerning His creation. Not the slippery serpents tongue as displayed on the NASA Logo. The word globe is not mentioned in the Bible. The word Planet is mentioned once, used as in a constellation, not the earth.

The earth does not move, 1 Chronicles 16:30, Psalms 93:1. The sun moves not the earth, Ecclesiastes 1:5 Isaiah 60:20, Joshua 10:12, Psalms 104: 19.

Isaiah 66:1 says: The Lord saith, I make heaven my throne and the earth my footstool. I don't know about you but I have never seen a footstool in the shape of a basketball and certainly not spinning.

The earth and sun are the same size: Enoch 78: 1-3: And the names of the sun are the following: the first Orjârês, and the second Tômâs. 2. And the moon has four names: the first name is Asônjâ, the second Eblâ, the third Benâsê, and the fourth Erâe. 3. These are the two great luminaries: their circumference is like the circumference of the heaven, and the size of the circumference of both is alike.

Sun and moon approximately equal distance from the earth: And the waning of the moon which takes place in the sixth portal: for in this sixth portal her light is accomplished, and after that there is the beginning of the waning: 4. And the waning which takes place in the first portal in its season, till one hundred and seventy-seven days are accomplished: reckoned according to weeks, twenty-five (weeks) and two days. 5. **She** (the moon) falls behind the sun and the order of the stars exactly five days in the course of one period, and when this place which thou see has been traversed. **Moon behind the sun?**

NASA space program: smoke and mirrors and fish eyed camera lenses!

God & the Scientist...

God is sitting in Heaven when a scientist says to Him, 'Lord, we don't need you anymore. Science has finally figured out a way to create life out of nothing.

In other words, we can now do what you did in the 'beginning'.'

'Oh, is that so? Tell me...' replies God.

'Well', says the scientist, 'we can take dirt and form it into the likeness of you and breathe life into it, thus creating man.'

'Well, that's interesting. Show Me. '

So the scientist bends down to the earth and starts to mold the soil.

'Oh no, no, no...' interrupts God,

'Get your own dirt.'

God is the scientist!

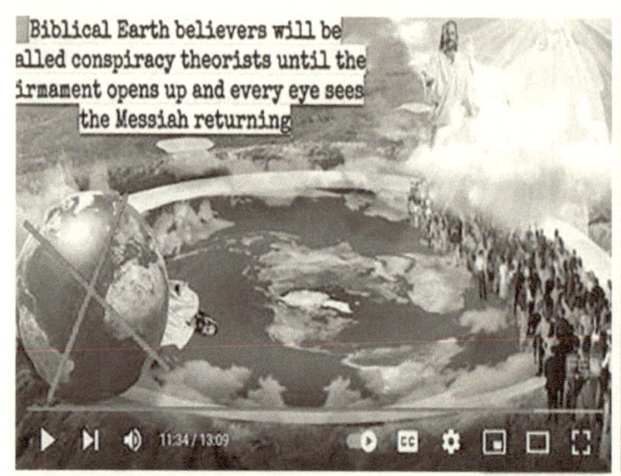

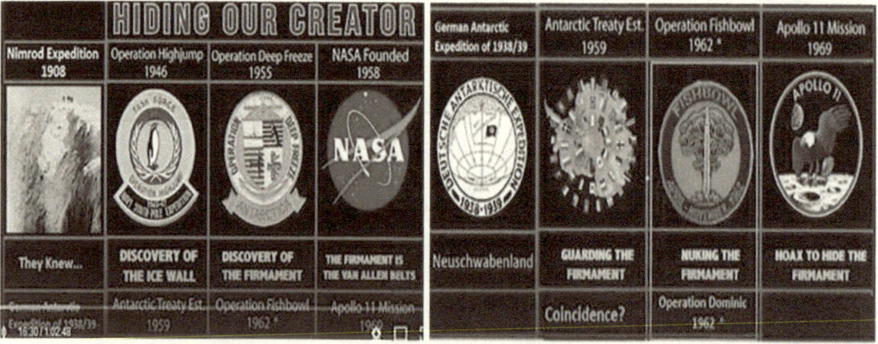

Try finding these Antactica military expedition patches!

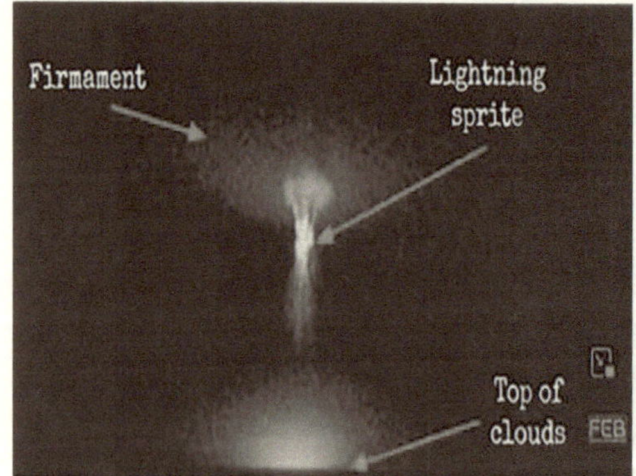

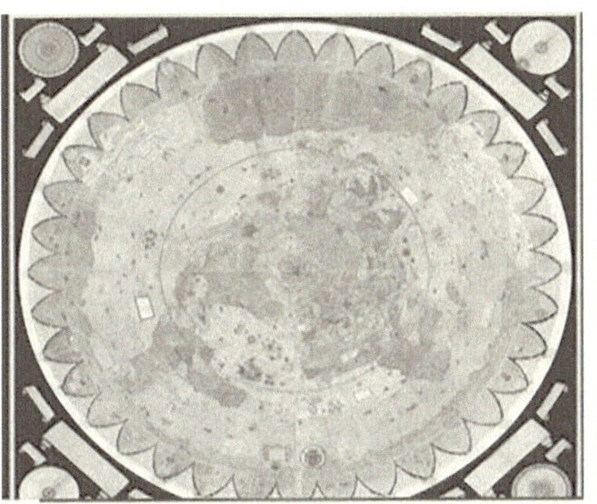

WHY WOULD THEY LIE ABOUT
THE SHAPE OF THE EARTH?
I DON'T KNOW, MAYBE TO..
HIDE FREE ENERGY
HIDE THE CREATOR
HIDE YOUR SPIRITUALITY
HIDE MORE LAND
HIDE MORE RESOURCES
HIDE SCIENTIFIC KNOWLEDGE
HIDE WHAT'S IN ANTARCTICA
HIDE THAT YOU'RE AT
THE CENTER OF THE UNIVERSE
HIDE THAT YOU ARE SPECIAL
TAKE YOUR PICK

Paranormal Crucible
4:46 / 5:05

Original NASA photo of MARS
Pobitite Kamani,
Bulgaria

GROENLANDIA
Guglielmo Marconi sent
a line of sight signal
2,100 miles across the
Atlantic in 1901
Physicists told him this
would be impossible due to
the earth's curvature
OCEANO
Terranova
ATLANTICO
Capo Cod
604 miles of missing curve

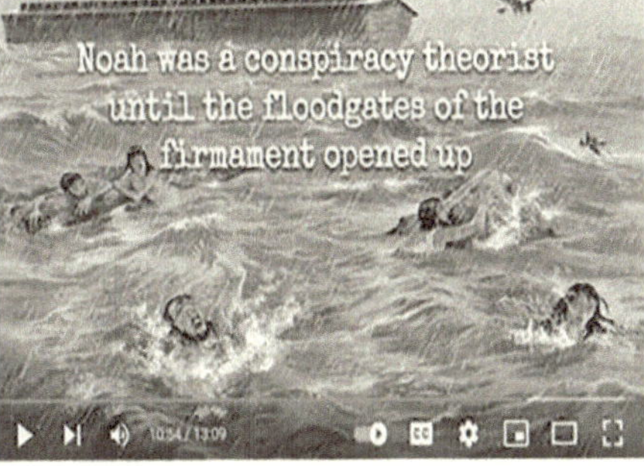
Noah was a conspiracy theorist
until the floodgates of the
firmament opened up
10:54 / 13:09

Dissertations Defended in the Scientific Council of the Institute of Physics of the Earth, Institute of Physics of the Atmosphere and Institute of Applied Geophysics, Ac..Sc. USSR during the First Semester of 1957.   Declassified in 2000 published in 1953

near-sun halo and also from the sun on a surface perpendicular to these rays. The dissertation contains **a certain formula** of the brightness of the sky, taking into consideration only the brightness of the first order and derived on the assumption of a "flat" Earth and giving some conclusions derived on the basis of this formula. For a certain coefficient of transparency of the atmosphere, the brightness of the sky at any point is represented by derivation of two functions of which one is the function **of the diffusion of** light and the other is a function of the zenith distances of the sun and of the observed point of the sky. On changing of the zenith distances of the sun z from 90 to 0°, the brightness of the sky on the almucantar of the sun increases first, reaching a maximum for a certain value of z , and then decreases. A method is also proposed of determining the brightness of the clear daylight sky at any point based on measuring the brightness along the almucantar of the sun and of 5-6 points of the firmament located at various zenith distances. This method permits determination

Flat Earth →

Firmament →

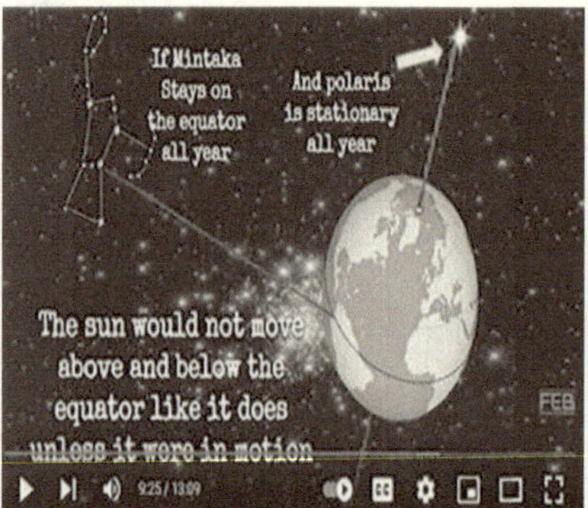

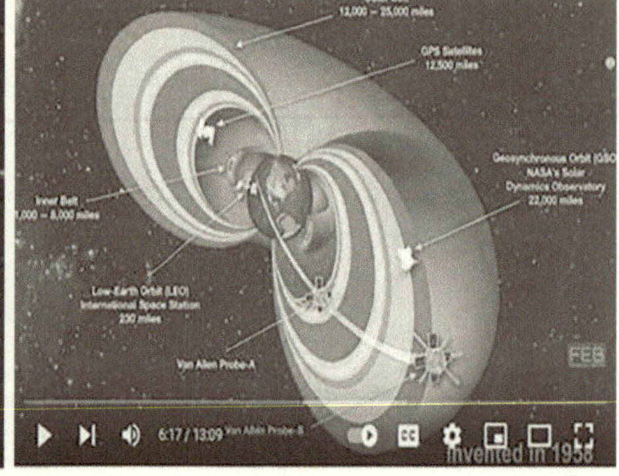

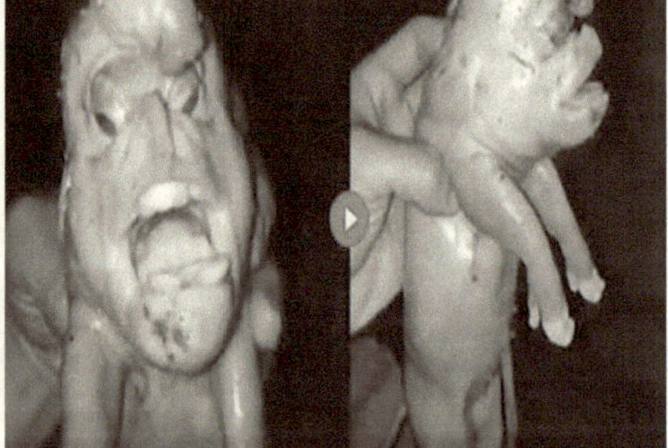

Messing with DNA

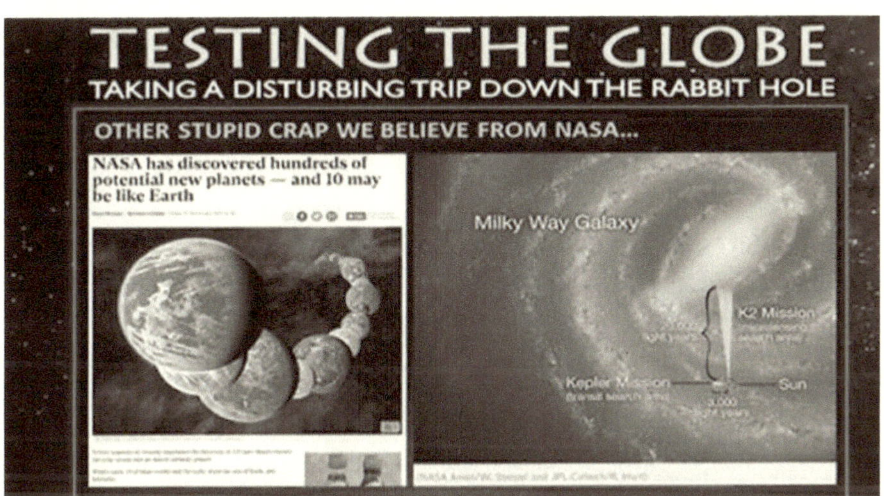

Milky Way photo 3000 lightyears away. 3000
x 6 trillion miles. SOME CAMERA!

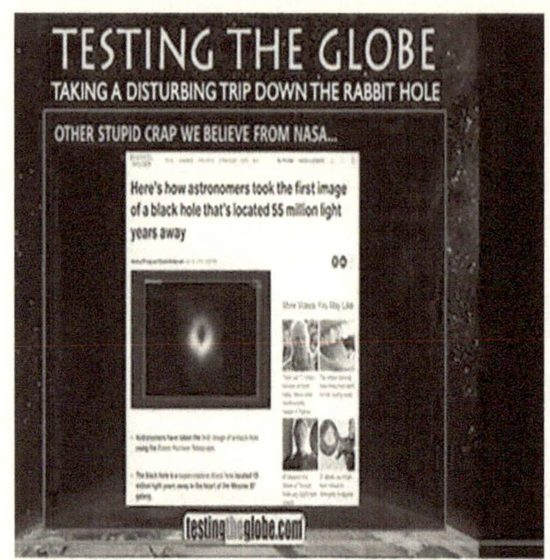
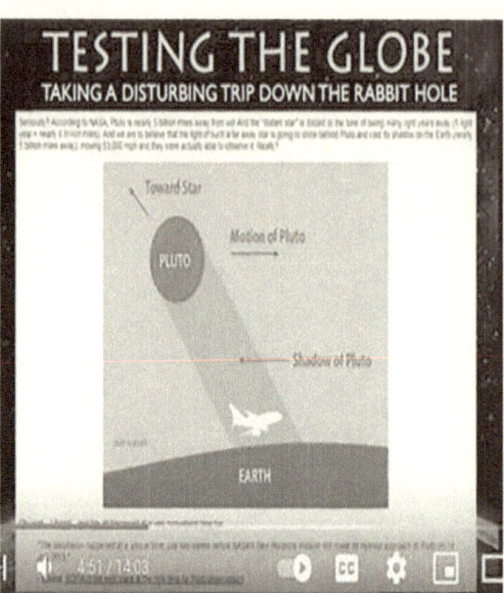

Shadow of Pluto on earth??

Ode to Evolution

Once I was a tadpole when I began to begin.
Next, I was a frog with my tail tucked in.
Then I was a monkey in a coconut tree.
Now I am a doctor with a PHD!

Physicist Auguste Piccard discovers Flat Earth in 1931

Auguste Antoine Piccard (28 January 1884 – 24 March 1962) was a Swiss physicist, inventor and explorer known for his record-breaking hydrogen balloon flights, with which he studied the Earth's upper atmosphere and became the first person to enter the Stratosphere. POPULAR SCIENCE MONTHLY MAGAZINE AUGUST, 1931 VOLUME 119: NO. 2. Rare highly sought periodical **(a copy can be purchased for $12,000 and $19,000 on the internet)** Auguste Piccard and Paul Kipfer reached a record altitude of 9.8 miles sky high in the stratosphere. Piccard and Kipfer became the first human beings to enter the stratosphere. An anonymous writer for the wofficial website of Auguste's grandson, Bertrand Piccard, claims that grandfather was the first to witness the shape of the earth with his own eyes. From article: "Through portholes, the observers saw the earth through copper-colored, then bluish, haze. It seemed a flat disk with upturned edges. The article first appeared in the May 30th 1931 of the New York Times. This information has literally been deleted from our history book, Go Figure!

CHAPTER 16 POLITICS

Bricks for BLM. Who delivered?   Zombified Millennials

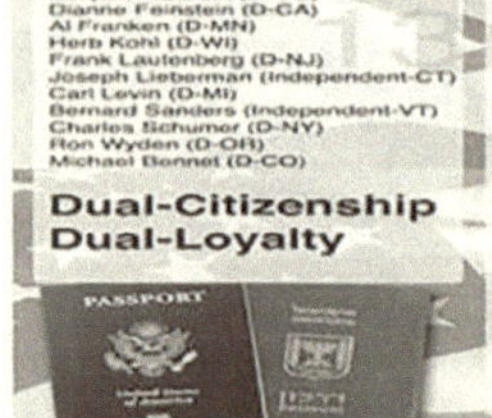

Richard Blumenthal (D-CT)
Barbara Boxer (D-CA)
Benjamin Cardin (D-MD)
Dianne Feinstein (D-CA)
Al Franken (D-MN)
Herb Kohl (D-WI)
Frank Lautenberg (D-NJ)
Joseph Lieberman (Independent-CT)
Carl Levin (D-MI)
Bernard Sanders (Independent-VT)
Charles Schumer (D-NY)
Ron Wyden (D-OR)
Michael Bennet (D-CO)

Gary Ackerman (D-NY)
Shelley Berkley (D-NV)
Howard Berman (D-CA)
Eric Cantor (R-VA)
David Cicilline (D-RI)
Stephen Cohen (D-TN)
Susan Davis (D-CA)
Ted Deutch (D-FL)
Eliot Engel (D-NY)
Bob Filner (D-CA)
Barney Frank (D-MA)
Gabrielle Giffords (D-AZ)
Jane Harman (D-CA)
Steve Israel (D-NY)
Sander Levin (D-MI)
Nita Lowey (D-NY)
Jerrold Nadler (D-NY)
Jared Polis (D-CO)
Steve Rothman (D-NJ)
Jan Schakowsky (D-IL)
Allyson Schwartz (D-PA)
Adam Schiff (D-CA)
Brad Sherman (D-CA)
Debbie Wasserman Schultz
Henry Waxman (D-CA)
Anthony Weiner (D-NY)
John Yarmuth (D-KY)

Dual-Citizenship Dual-Loyalty

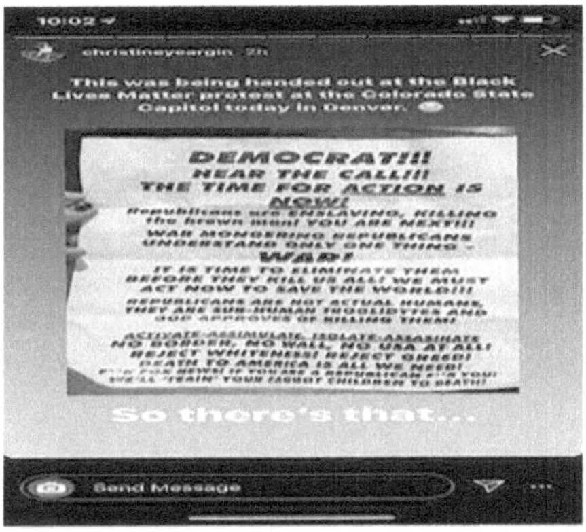
This was being handed out at the Black Lives Matter protest at the Colorado State Capitol today in Denver.
DEMOCRAT!!!
HEAR THE CALL!!!
THE TIME FOR ACTION IS NOW!
WAR!
So there's that...
Send Message

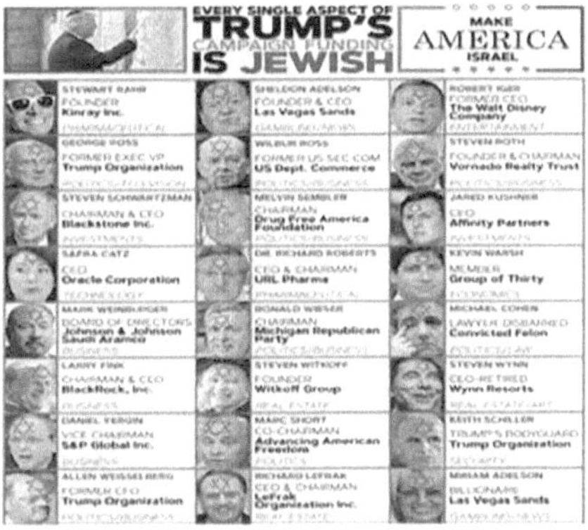
EVERY SINGLE ASPECT OF
TRUMP'S
CAMPAIGN FUNDING
IS JEWISH
MAKE
AMERICA
ISRAEL
Kinray Inc.
Las Vegas Sands
The Walt Disney Company
Trump Organization
US Dept. Commerce
Vornado Realty Trust
Blackstone Inc.
Drug Free America Foundation
Affinity Partners
Oracle Corporation
URL Pharma
Group of Thirty
Johnson & Johnson Saudi Aramco
Michigan Republican Party
Convicted Felon
BlackRock, Inc.
Witkoff Group
Wynn Resorts
S&P Global Inc.
Advancing American Freedom
Trump Organization
Trump Organization
LeFrak Organization Inc.
Las Vegas Sands

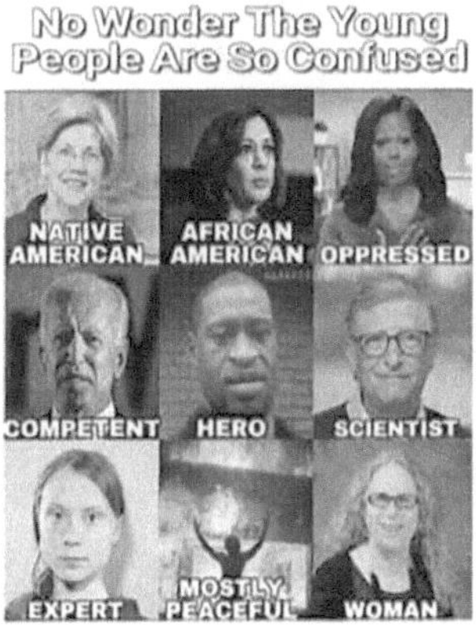
No Wonder The Young People Are So Confused
NATIVE AMERICAN
AFRICAN AMERICAN
OPPRESSED
COMPETENT
HERO
SCIENTIST
EXPERT
MOSTLY PEACEFUL
WOMAN

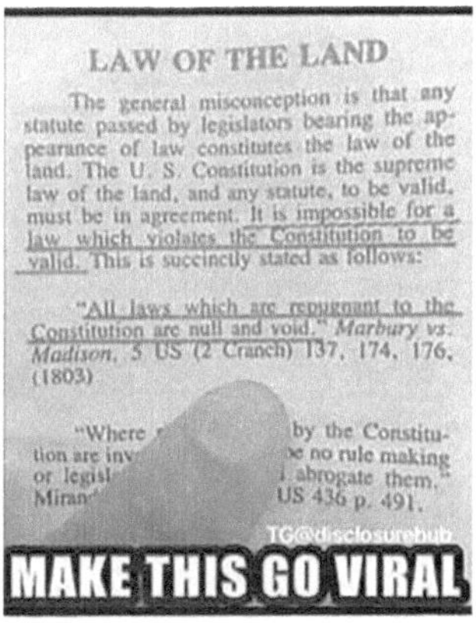
LAW OF THE LAND
The general misconception is that any statute passed by legislators bearing the appearance of law constitutes the law of the land. The U. S. Constitution is the supreme law of the land, and any statute, to be valid, must be in agreement. It is impossible for a law which violates the Constitution to be valid. This is succinctly stated as follows:
"All laws which are repugnant to the Constitution are null and void." Marbury vs. Madison, 5 US (2 Cranch) 137, 174, 176, (1803)
TG@disclosurebub
MAKE THIS GO VIRAL

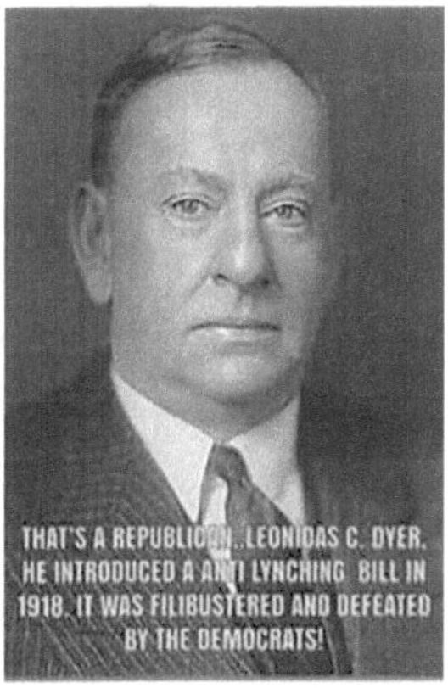
THAT'S A REPUBLICAN..LEONIDAS C. DYER.
HE INTRODUCED A ANTI LYNCHING BILL IN 1918. IT WAS FILIBUSTERED AND DEFEATED BY THE DEMOCRATS!

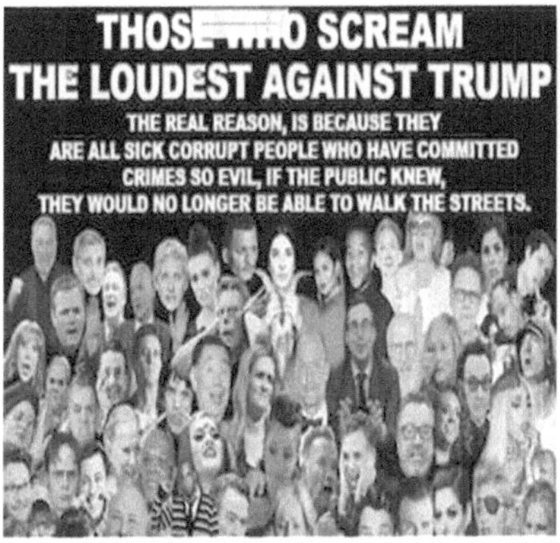
THOSE WHO SCREAM
THE LOUDEST AGAINST TRUMP
THE REAL REASON, IS BECAUSE THEY ARE ALL SICK CORRUPT PEOPLE WHO HAVE COMMITTED CRIMES SO EVIL, IF THE PUBLIC KNEW, THEY WOULD NO LONGER BE ABLE TO WALK THE STREETS.

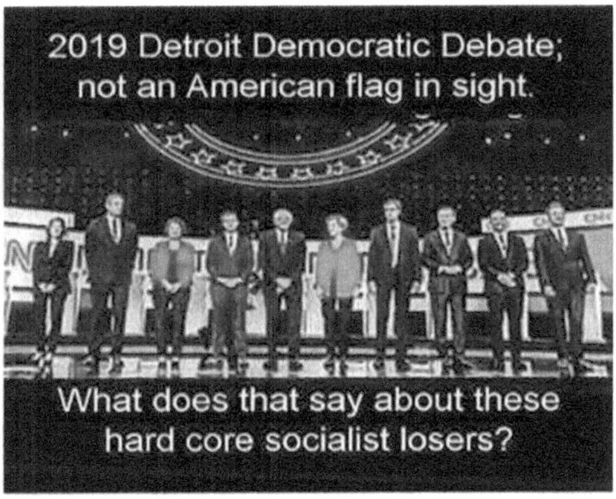
2019 Detroit Democratic Debate;
not an American flag in sight.
What does that say about these
hard core socialist losers?

I sure hope everyone is paying attention. There is no good explanation for this!
Judiciary Committee just offered an amendment that requires ICE be notified when an illegal immigrant tries to purchase a firearm Dems voted NO
So the Dems just admitted they have no problem with people having guns. As long as they are not American citizens that are working class
Really think about that for a minute

Watching the DNC last night, I noticed their logo.... now, where have I seen that uneven star before?
HIDING IN PLAIN SIGHT....
10:18 AM · 8/20/20 · Twitter for Android

When a company's logo says exactly who they are
Goes in and comes out
DOMINION VOTING
CHANGING THE WAY PEOPLE VOTE

DONALD TRUMP AND JOE BIDEN RALLY WITH THEIR BIGGEST SUPPORTERS
Dominion

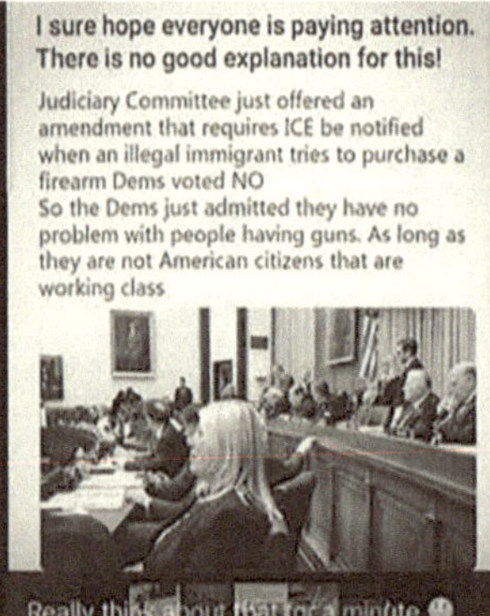

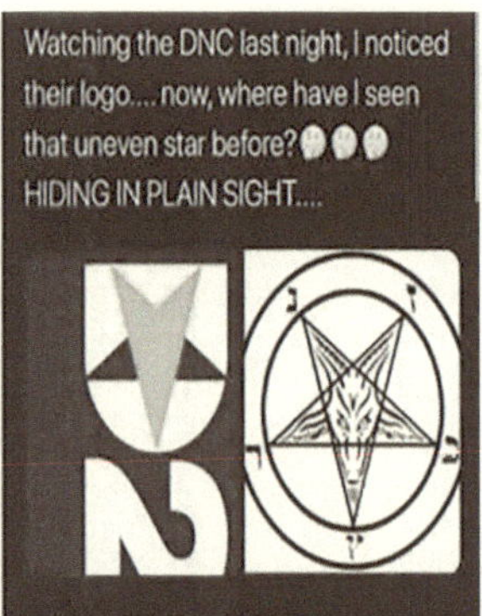

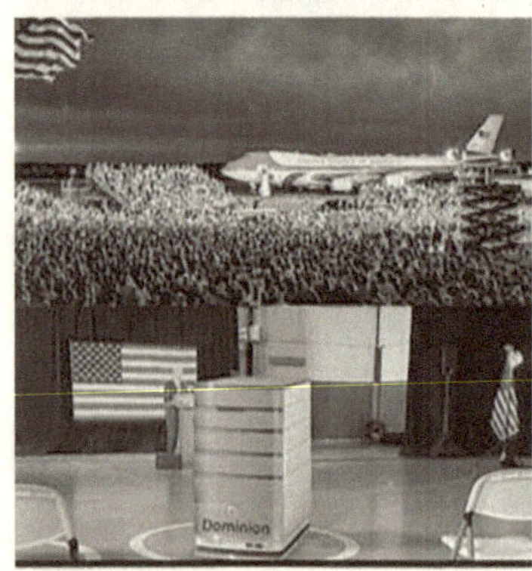

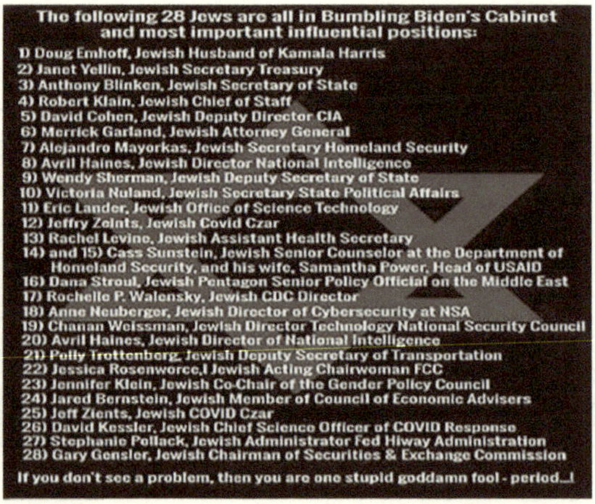

The following 28 Jews are all in Bumbling Biden's Cabinet and most important influential positions:
1) Doug Emhoff, Jewish Husband of Kamala Harris
2) Janet Yellin, Jewish Secretary Treasury
3) Anthony Blinken, Jewish Secretary of State
4) Robert Klain, Jewish Chief of Staff
5) David Cohen, Jewish Deputy Director CIA
6) Merrick Garland, Jewish Attorney General
7) Alejandro Mayorkas, Jewish Secretary Homeland Security
8) Avril Haines, Jewish Director National Intelligence
9) Wendy Sherman, Jewish Deputy Secretary of State
10) Victoria Nuland, Jewish Secretary State Political Affairs
11) Eric Lander, Jewish Office of Science Technology
12) Jeffry Zeints, Jewish Covid Czar
13) Rachel Levine, Jewish Assistant Health Secretary
14) and 15) Cass Sunstein, Jewish Senior Counselor at the Department of Homeland Security, and his wife, Samantha Power, Head of USAID
16) Dana Stroul, Jewish Pentagon Senior Policy Official on the Middle East
17) Rochelle P. Walensky, Jewish CDC Director
18) Anne Neuberger, Jewish Director of Cybersecurity at NSA
19) Chanan Weissman, Jewish Director Technology National Security Council
20) Avril Haines, Jewish Director of National Intelligence
21) Polly Trottenberg, Jewish Deputy Secretary of Transportation
22) Jessica Rosenworce,l Jewish Acting Chairwoman FCC
23) Jennifer Klein, Jewish Co-Chair of the Gender Policy Council
24) Jared Bernstein, Jewish Member of Council of Economic Advisers
25) Jeff Zients, Jewish COVID Czar
26) David Kessler, Jewish Chief Science Officer of COVID Response
27) Stephanie Pollack, Jewish Administrator Fed Hiway Administration
28) Gary Gensler, Jewish Chairman of Securities & Exchange Commission
If you don't see a problem, then you are one stupid goddamn fool - period...!

SO NOW BURNING A GAY FLAG IS CALLED A 'HATE CRIME' but burning the American Flag is FREE SPEECH!

Found an amusing little law. Illegal Immigration Reform and Responsibility Act of 1996. Not repealed. Non-citizens who vote MUST be deported.

BRANCO LegalInsurrection.com
©2021 Creators.com
CRITICAL RACE THEORY
NEO-RACISM
EQUITY & HATE
SHAMING
SEGREGATION
PUBLIC EDUCATION

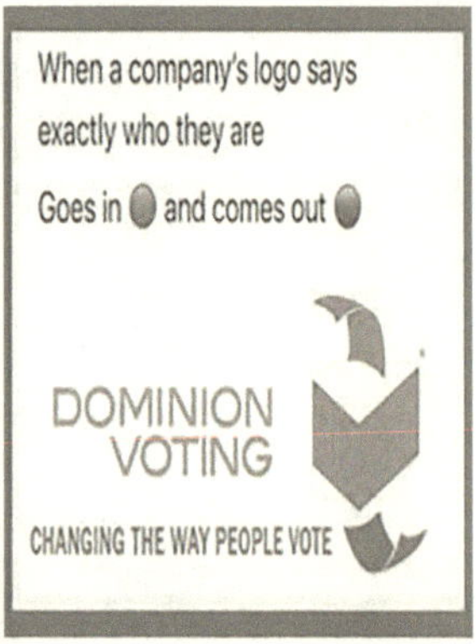

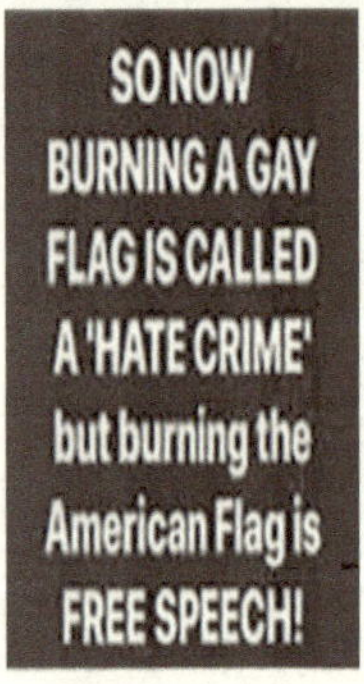

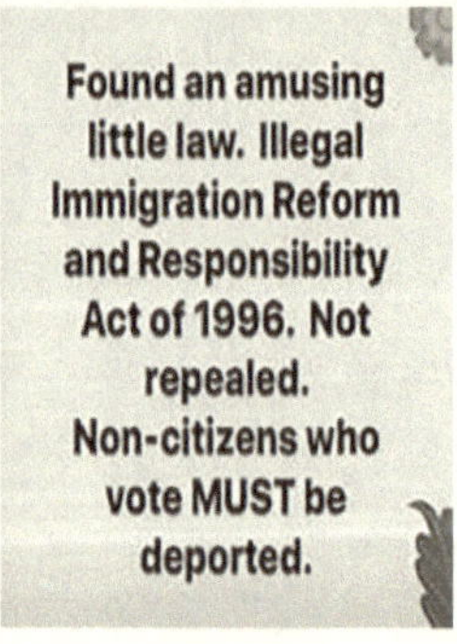

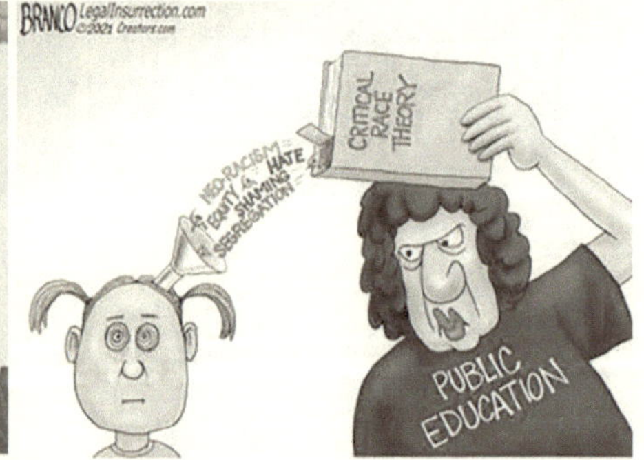

181. Silicon Valley Bank - Trump & The Cartel Drug Money Bank

Older JFK?? or more diversion!

13 - Masonic Emblems in Israel & US

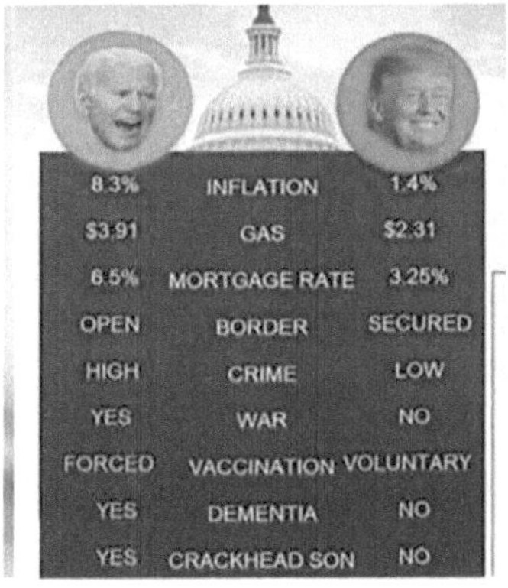

"I don't like Joe Biden and do not like his history with certain people or who he's aligned with, he's trash to me." —Kamala Harris June, 2019

Stolen election and sticking public with inflation, communism at it's best!

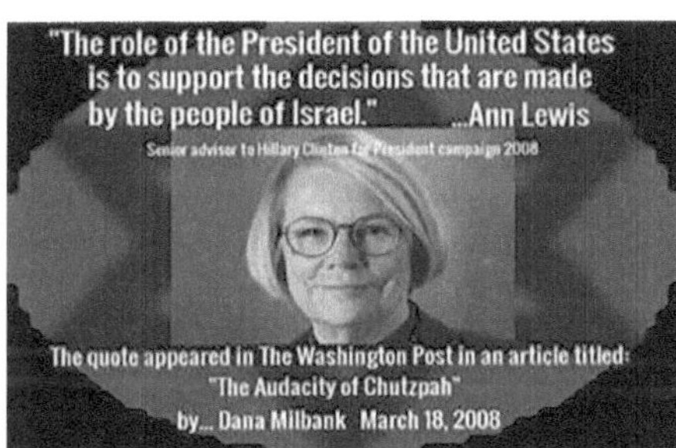

You at the airport: Juan at the border:

WARNING! - NO TRESPASS

YOU CAN ENTER THIS PROPERTY ...

1. ONLY if you have the owner's, or legal occupant's, written or verbal permission, OR
2. You are a U. S. Mail Carrier, or commercial delivery service, OR
3. You are responding to a medical or fire emergency, OR
4. You possess a valid Constitutional 4th Amendment warrant signed by a judge with proper jurisdiction, showing probable cause and the specific places or things to be searched.

REVOCATION OF "IMPLIED LICENSE"

Further, the owners, or legal occupants of this property, by authority granted under 10th Circuit Case 6:13-CR-00006-RAW-2 (2016), hereby REVOKE the "Implied License" in Breard v. Alexander 341 U. S. 622 (1951) and Florida v. Jardines 133 S. CT 1409 (2013), including revoking "knock and talk" and all other "Implied License" provisions in said cases.

- RIGHT TO EXCLUDE -

THE RIGHT TO EXCLUDE ANYONE, EVEN GOVERNMENT, OR LAW ENFORCEMENT, IS A CONSTITUTIONAL, INVIOLATE RIGHT, FURTHER SET IN LAW, TO-WIT:

"A property owner's right to exclude extends to private individuals as well as the government". See United States v. Lyons, 992 F.2d 1029, 1031 (10th Cir. 1993) "The intruder who enters clothed in the robes of authority in broad daylight commits no less an invasion of [property] rights than if he sneaks in the night wearing a burglar's mask." Hendler v. United States, 952 F.2d 1364, 1375 (Fed. Cir. 1991).

!VIOLATORS COULD FACE UP TO A $10,000 PENALTY AND 5 YRS. IN JAIL!

© Copyright 2017, by the National Association of Rural Landowners - All Rights Reserved - 1 800 682-7848 www.narla.org

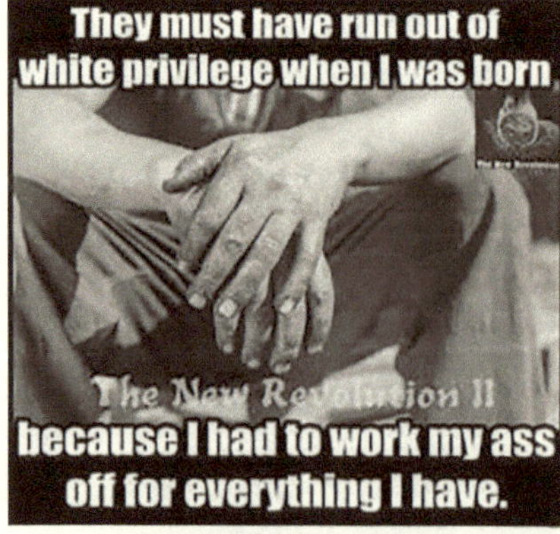

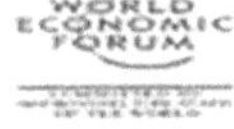

To Health Officials in Governments, States, and Cities responding to the Coronavirus (COVID-19) Pandemic

We are writing on behalf of the Governors of the World Economic Forum to inform you of coming changes to the way our world is run. We believe that the Coronavirus epidemic offers a golden oppourtunity to reorder the world to our design. With this in mind we recommend to you that getting the populations of your countries to take the vaccine when it is ready is of the highest importance to our endgame. We expect you to hit a 90% two shot vaccination target. Some extreme measures may be needed to convince the few who may become a problem. Starting with a positive line when doing press interviews is best. After most have beed convinced you can then start on the malcontents by bringing up vaccine passports which will be needed to live a normal life. This is of the utmost importance to reach our goal. It always works to state that "the unvaccinated are a danger to the vaccinated." This sort of logic always seems to work because the average person does not think too deeply about these things which is why they are so easy to manipulate.

There will be those who "fight the vaccine." These people need to be sidelined as a matter of the highest importance. Our partners in the social media empires have all agreed to help delete comments undesirable to our interests or delete accounts of those causing trouble which will greatly help in the process of informational flow in the directions we require.

If that mindset is allowed to flourish it will be a hinderance to our masterplan which is domination of the world under the guise of a medical emergancy. We will never have a chance as good as this ever again. One could say that Coronavirus is a perfect moment to push through our plans. Please contact our troubleshooter department if help is needed to counteract the extreme malcontents against the vaccine program that will be needed to control population growth in the future.

Thank you on behalf of the selected survivors in the exciting times to come.

Sincerely yours,

Steve Demetriou

Coen van Oostrom

Chair and Chief Executive Officer
Jacobs

Founder and Chief Executive Officer
EDGE Technologies / OVG Real Estate

THESE SIX COMPANIES ARE:

GE	NEWS-CORP	DISNEY	VIACOM	TIME WARNER	CBS
Notable Properties:	Notable Properties:	Notable Properties:	Notable Properties:	Notable Properties:	Notable Properties:
COMCAST	FOX	ABC	MTV	CNN	SHOWTIME
NBC	WALL STREET JOURNAL	ESPN	NICK JR	HBO	SMITHSONIAN CHANNEL
UNIVERSAL PICTURES	NEW YORK POST	PIXAR	BET	TIME	NFL.COM
FOCUS FEATURES		MIRAMAX	CMT	WARNER BROS	JEOPARDY
		MARVEL STUDIOS	PARAMOUNT PICTURES		60 MINUTES

60 advertising corporations eliminated to 6 today. CONTROLLED AMERICA!

Modern feminism, especially in America, was largely pioneered, influenced, and led by Jewish women.
Betty Friedan
Gloria Steinem
Andrea Dworkin
Shulamith Firestone
Ellen Willis
Naomi Wolf
Robin Morgan
Heather Booth
Susan Sontag
Meredith Tax
Grace Paley
Eve Ensler
Bella Sirota Gordon
Susan Faludi
Erica Jong
Elizabeth Wurtzel
Susan Brownmiller
Judith Butler
Dorothy Dinnerstein
Phyllis Chesler
Hedwig Dohm
Blu Greenberg
Gloria Allred
Bella Abzug
Gerda Lerner
Miriam Schapiro
Judy Chicago
Arlene Raven
Hélène Cixous
Chantal Akerman
Largely sourced from the Jewish Women's Archive (jwa.org)
Head over to their website learn more at jwa.org/feminism
JewishContributions.com

CHAPTER 17 NWO

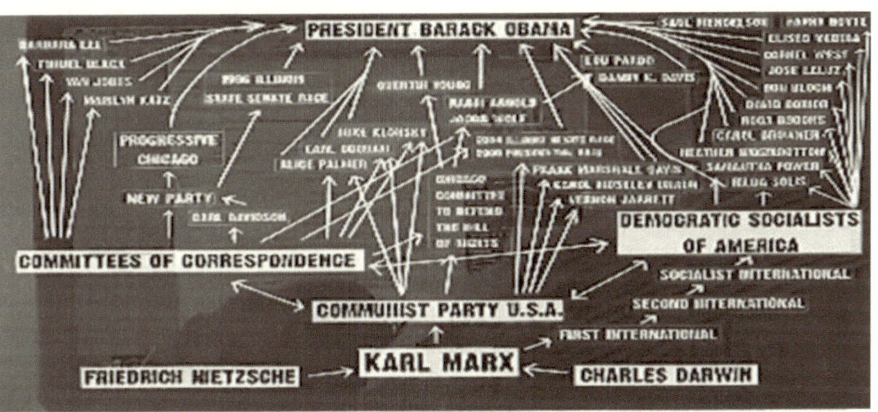

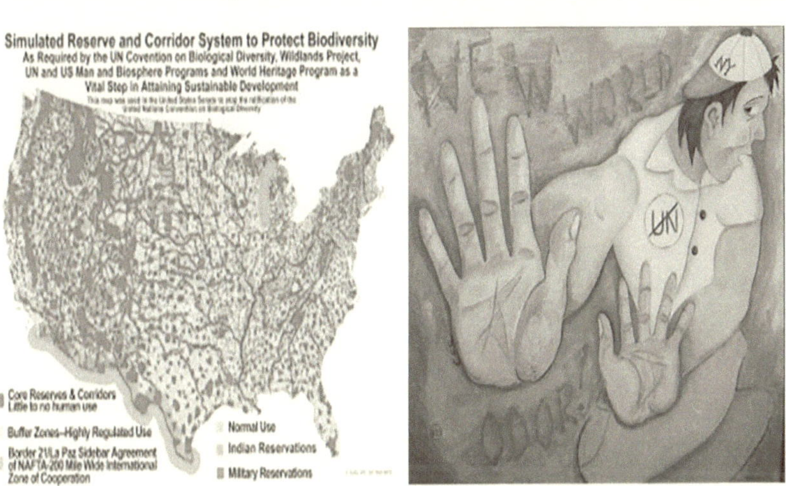

Agenda 21, taking control of America,
burning down one city at a time!

Usashi Jesuit priests, murdering Christians

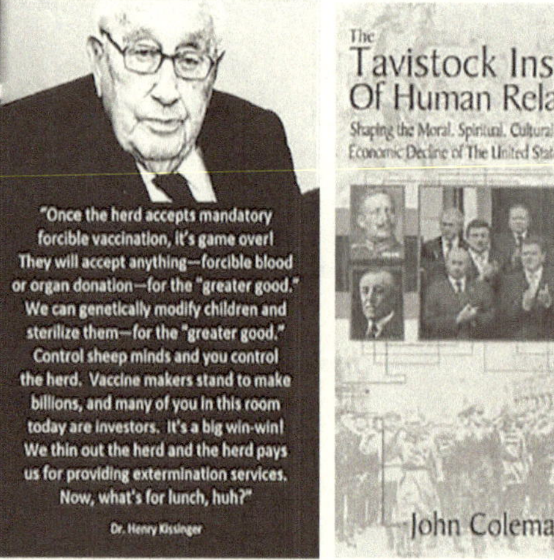

None, both claim master race, world takeover!

Kissinger coined the phrase; "Useless eater!" He won't be eating ever again!

More Croatian Ustashi murders

On Nov 4, Don't forget to disguise yourselves as patriots!

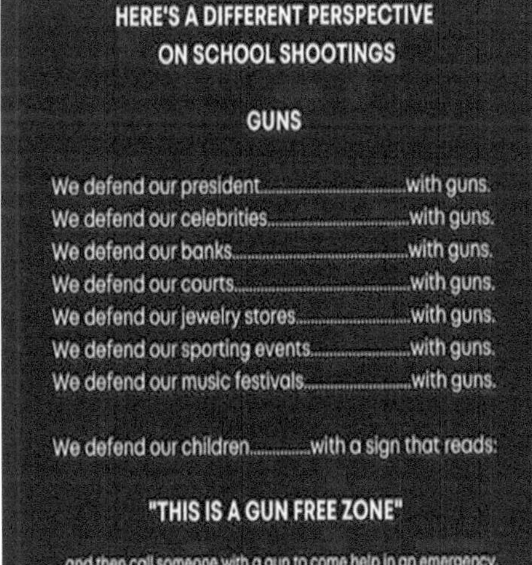

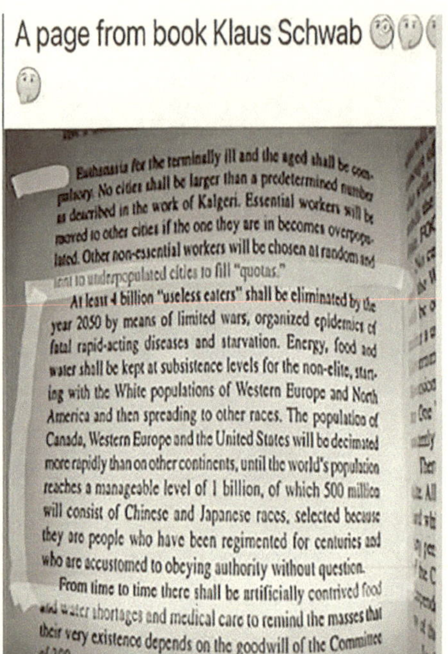

Euthanasia for the terminally ill and the aged shall be compulsory. No cities shall be larger than a predetermined number as described in the work of Kalgeri. Essential workers will be moved to other cities if the one they are in becomes overpopulated. Other non-essential workers will be chosen at random and sent to underpopulated cities to fill "quotas."

At least 4 billion "useless eaters" shall be eliminated by the year 2050 by means of limited wars, organized epidemics of fatal rapid-acting diseases and starvation. Energy, food and water shall be kept at subsistence levels for the non-elite, starting with the White populations of Western Europe and North America and then spreading to other races. The population of Canada, Western Europe and the United States will be decimated more rapidly than on other continents, until the world's population reaches a manageable level of 1 billion, of which 500 million will consist of Chinese and Japanese races, selected because they are people who have been regimented for centuries and who are accustomed to obeying authority without question.

From time to time there shall be artificially contrived food and water shortages and medical care to remind the masses that their very existence depends on the goodwill of the Committee of 300.

To Health Officials in Governments, States, and Cities responding to the Coronavirus (COVID-19) Pandemic

We are writing on behalf of the Governors of the World Economic Forum to inform you of coming changes to the way our world is run. We believe that the Coronavirus epidemic offers a golden oppourtunity to reorder the world to our design. With this in mind we recommend to you that getting the populations of your countries to take the vaccine when it is ready is of the highest importance to our endgame. We expect you to hit a 90% two shot vaccination target. Some extreme measures may be needed to convince the few who may become a problem. Starting with a positive line when doing press interviews is best. After most have beed convinced you can then start on the malcontents by bringing up vaccine passports which will be needed to live a normal life. This is of the utmost importance to reach our goal. It always works to state that "the unvaccinated are a danger to the vaccinated." This sort of logic always seems to work because the average person does not think too deeply about these things which is why they are so easy to manipulate.

There will be those who "fight the vaccine." These people need to be sidelined as a matter of the highest importance. Our partners in the social media empires have all agreed to help delete comments undesirable to our interests or delete accounts of those causing trouble which will greatly help in the process of informational flow in the directions we require.

If that mindset is allowed to flourish it will be a hinderance to our masterplan which is domination of the world under the guise of a medical emergency. We will never have a chance as good as this ever again. One could say that Coronavirus is a perfect moment to push through our plans. Please contact our troubleshooter department if help is needed to counteract the extreme malcontents against the vaccine program that will be needed to control population growth in the future.

Thank you on behalf of the selected survivors in the exciting times to come.

Sincerely yours,

Steve Demetriou

Chair and Chief Executive Officer
Jacobs

Coen van Oostrom

Founder and Chief Executive Officer
EDGE Technologies / OVG Real Estate

Death to the WEF devils!!

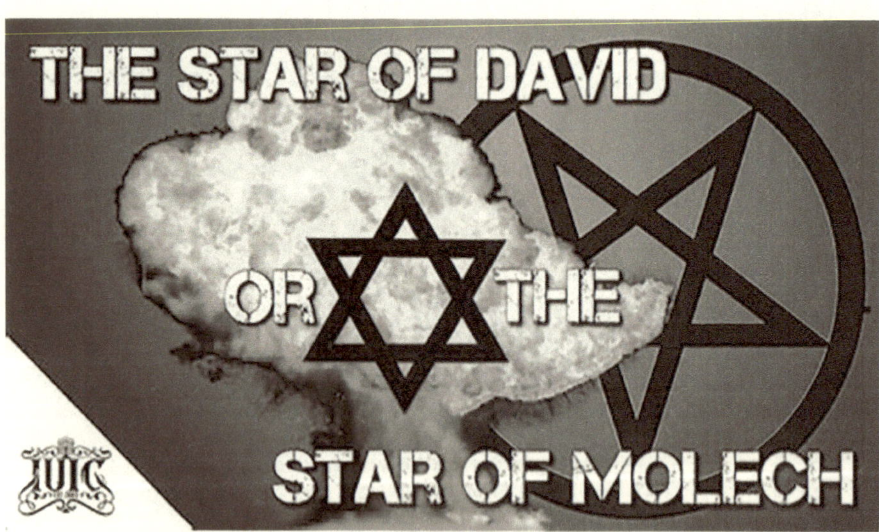

Acts 7:43

CHAPTER 18 RELIGION

Never discuss religion and politics in front of mixed company. That was a phrase I had heard often growing up. Why? Well, as a grownup today, it makes perfect sense. Now that our country is facing the complete takeover by the Zionists communists, my guess is this was propaganda that was introduced to the masses many, many years ago and probably the reason our country is in the demoralized condition it is today. I couldn't imagine our forefathers speaking this phrase today. If they did, we would all be speaking in a cockney accent or the King's English!

Fortunately, for the possible readers of my book, I am going to refrain from speaking politics. I am sure, if you have gone through the many screenshots, you will certainly recognize my political beliefs. But I will go into religion. How do you silence the churches, by government control. Make them use a 501C3 if they want to keep their tax deductions. I will throw out a word and not a phrase that has helped trick the churches into believing a lie, causing the churches to lie down and play dead knowing they will escape any tribulation on the earth. In the true sense, this word has become dogma, THE RAPTURE! My brother and I were greatly influenced by Hal Lindsay's book: The Late Great Planet Earth, and were enraptured by it. Definition of rapture: The state of being transported by a lofty emotion; ecstasy. An expression of ecstatic feeling. A good description of the church today concerning a RAPTURE! But in my late age, I found out there is no seven-year tribulation, Daniel's 70 weeks in chapter 9 was fulfilled in Jesus's ministry. To take 70 weeks and rip off 7 of the years to our time by the dispensationalists is ludicrous.

From Daniel chapter 9:24: Seventy weeks are determined upon thy people and the holy city, to finish the transgression, and to make an end of sins, and to make conciliation for iniquity, and bring in everlasting righteousness, and to seal up the vision and prophecy and to anoint the most holy.

The commission of Ezra to rebuild Jerusalem, until the complete restoration of the city, there were exactly 49 years, or seven weeks. From this period until the first proclamation of the Messiah by John the Baptist, there were exactly 434 years, or sixty - two weeks. John's ministry terminated at the end of three years and a half, then our Lord began to preach the kingdom of God, and thus virtually, in the midst of the week, 3 ½ years, Messiah was cut off, thus, completing the last week of Daniel's prophecy, 3 1/2 + 3 1/2 = 7 years or one week. So, you have Ezar's 7 weeks, = 49 years + the 434 years till John the Baptists ministry equaling sixty-two weeks, you have 7+62 = 69, with the ministry of John and Jesus equaling 1 week equals 70 weeks.

Now for the falsity of a Rapture, the word is not mentioned in the Bible. The history how the term Rapture took place occurred in Scotland in the early 19th century in which a 15-year-old girl by the name of Margaret McDonald was in a trance, and had a vision about God rescuing Christians before a great and terrible tribulation at the time of an antichrist, by the which came the term "RAPTURE." Good news that made every Christian highly excited! A man by the name of John Nelson Darby, who belonged to a group called the Pilgrim Brotherhood, took this vision and spread it across Europe then America. This induced a man named C. I. Scofield to write a Bible expounding this wonderful news, that we will escape death and torture, not, like the millions before us who had to endure the inquisition (Foxes book of Martyrs). Scofield was a criminal, crook and scoundrel, doing jail time and abandoning his family and leaving them destitute. But because of his Bible commentary, so called preachers have made millions on the "Left Behind" series, predicting a RAPTURE at least one a month for decades. Even the New York Times endorsed the series. Definitely a Red Flag!

I hope you will be enlightened as I have, seeing God is exposing the errors being propagated by the Dispensationalists. Those Christians hoping to escape the coming judgments will be greatly disappointed.

The scriptures say, we are not above our master, who was tortured and sacrificed at the cross, that we may one day enjoy the benefits of a heavenly residence. Not forgetting the murder and torture that the disciples endured, all except John, even he lived through being boiled in oil. Yea, and <u>all</u> that will live godly in Christ Jesus shall suffer persecution, 2 Timothy 3:12, and yes even death!

Dare I forget to mention the most historic Archeological discovery in the history of the world, further mentioned in Chapter 24. The Ark of the Covenant was discovered outside the walls of Jerusalem in January of 1982 by a man by the name of Ron Wyatt. That is just one of his discoveries: the discovery of Noah's ark in Turkey, the Egyptians chariot wheels in the Red Sea, the location of Sodam and Gomorrah, and the location of Mount Siani. Please go to www.ronwyatt.com to view his amazing discoveries.

Ron discovered the Ark in a cave just outside the walls of Jerusalem called Jeremiah's Grotto. It was placed there by Jeremiah at the time of the destruction of Jerusalem by king Nebuchadnezzar in 587-586 BC. He buried the Ark in a cave which was between the walls of Jerusalem and the Siege wall of the Babylonians, see 2 Maccabees 2: 4-8. No, it is not in Ethiopia, Egypt or Arizona. I am surprised you have not heard about his discovery on MSNBC, ABC, CBS, NBC, CNN or Fox News. Probably just an oversite. Or the media was not about to reveal that a man named Jesus walked the earth!

I challenge anyone's God against my own, Jesus the Christ. Has your god walked on water, spoke a word and caused a storm to cease, turned water into wine, healed the blind, the deaf, the mute, the lame and 10 Leppers, fed 5,000 men, not counting women and children with 2 fishes and 5 loaves of bread and then after all were fed gathered 12 baskets full of bread! He raised the dead, Lazarus, and then the greatest miracle of all, being crucified on a cross, buried 3 days and was raised from the dead Himself. And because of the sacrifice of shedding his blood, we can attain eternal life! I challenge anyone to give me a name of a god or religious leader that has done the same. Or can they speak these words: "I am the way, the truth, and the life. No man cometh to the father but by me!" John 14:6. When hearing these words many many years ago, I thought to myself, no man on earth could possibly speak these words, and they can't, only Jesus Christ the Son of God can! It was these words that changed my life change forever!

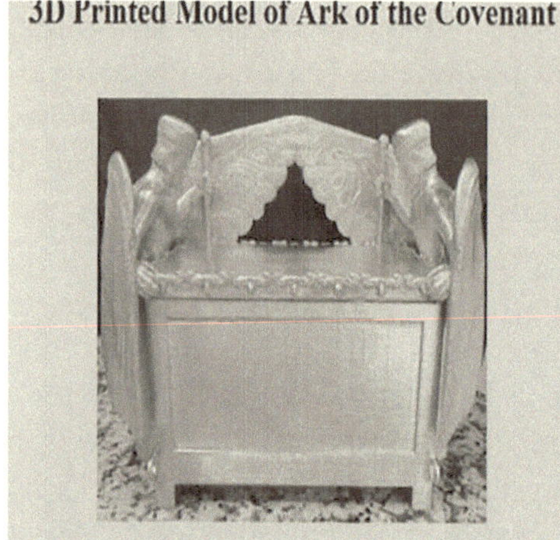

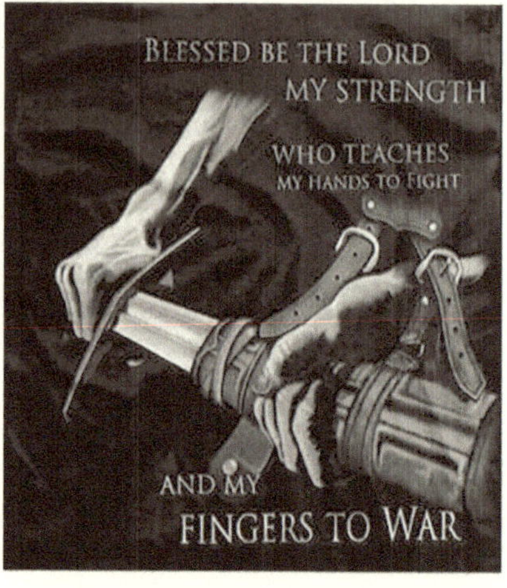

What the real ark looks with the Mercy Seat

He came as a lamb; he will return as a Lion!

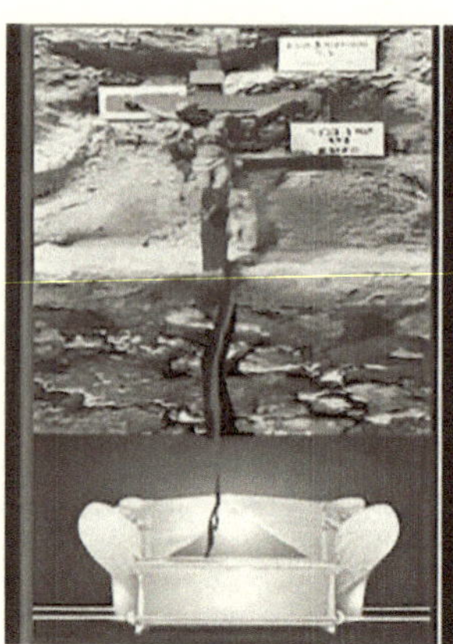

Christ blood onto the Mercy Seat

Fish head MITRE of Dagon!

Call no man Father! Matthew 23:9

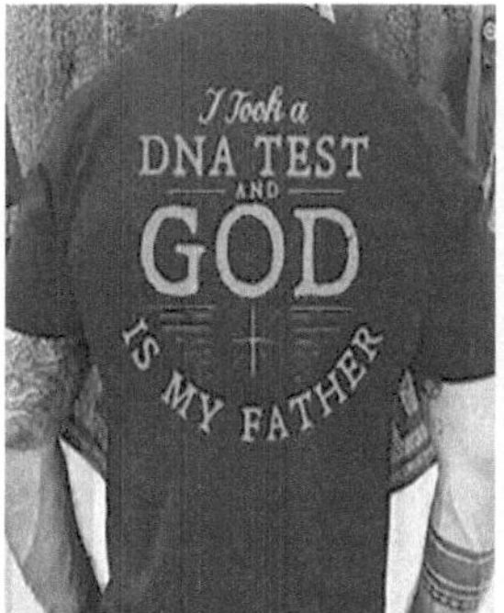

The Firmament discovered in Antarctica   Guillotines await. Revelation 20:4

The country you gave us, needs help!   Jewish Messiah? Eight-year-olds painting of Christ

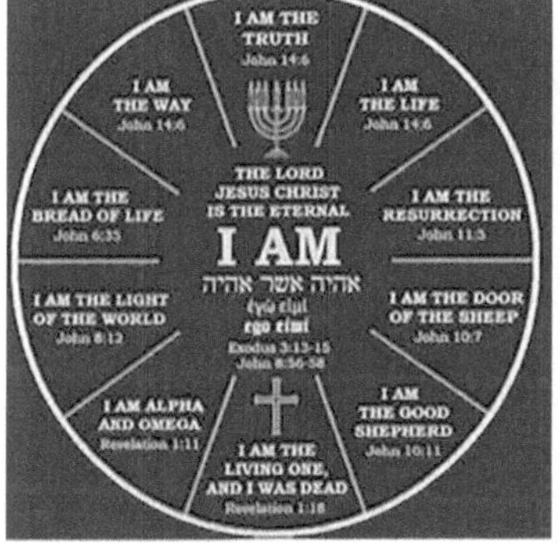

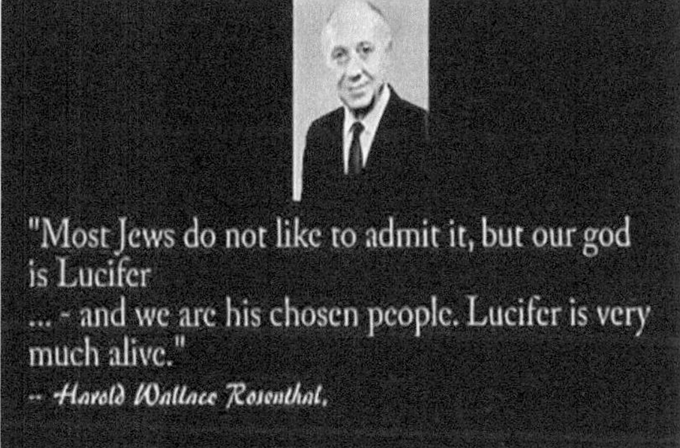

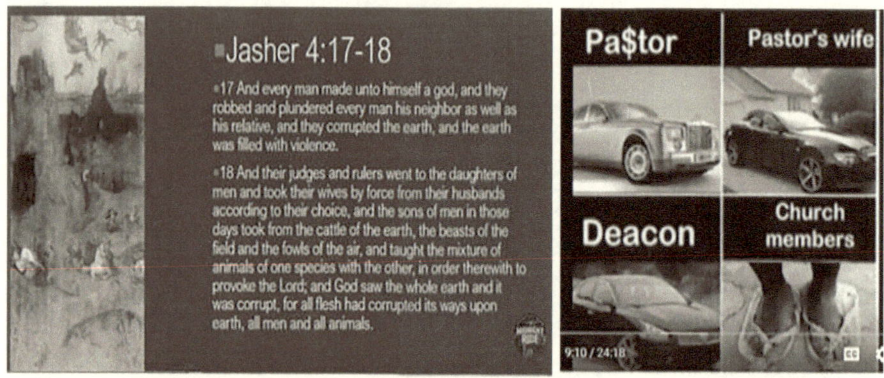

The corruption of Mankind before the flood, Biological engineering being used today.

No Sabbath keepers allowed

Revelation 20:4

Lion of the Tribe of Judah

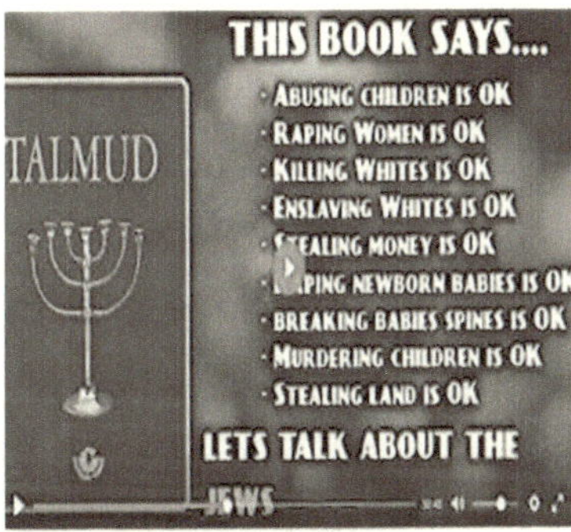

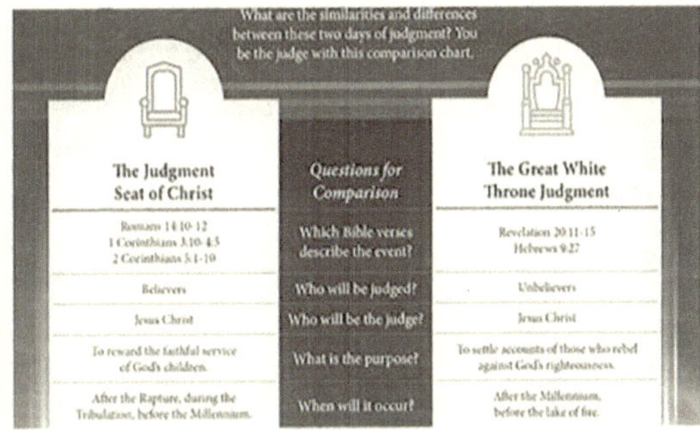

The Judgment Seat of Christ	Questions for Comparison	The Great White Throne Judgment
Romans 14:10-12 1 Corinthians 3:10-4:5 2 Corinthians 5:1-10	Which Bible verses describe the event?	Revelation 20:11-15 Hebrews 9:27
Believers	Who will be judged?	Unbelievers
Jesus Christ	Who will be the judge?	Jesus Christ
To reward the faithful service of God's children.	What is the purpose?	To settle accounts of those who rebel against God's righteousness.
After the Rapture, during the Tribulation, before the Millennium.	When will it occur?	After the Millennium, before the lake of fire.

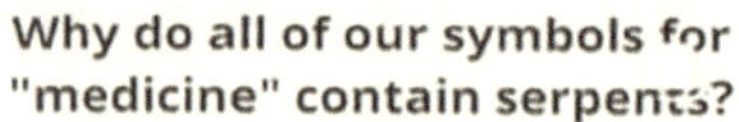

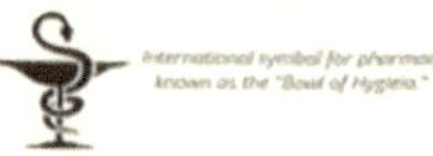

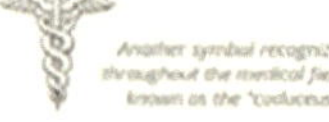

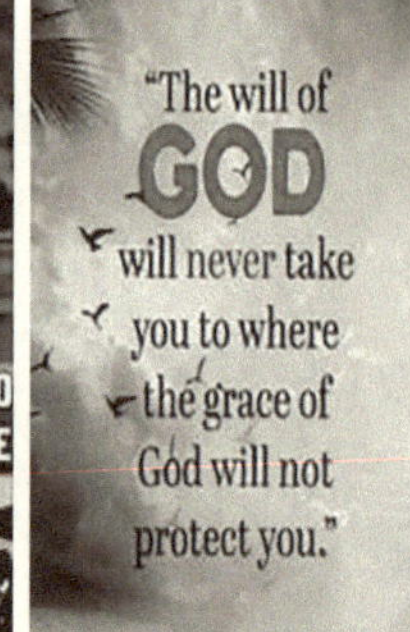

Washington for Jesus 1980, Remember? No, it got very little news coverage. Go figure!

The Punishments For Transgressing The 7 Noahide Laws ...

https://noahidelaw.com/punishment-for-transgressing-the-noahide-laws ▾

18/4/2020 · The Talmud lists the punishment for blaspheming the Ineffable Name of God as death. The sons of Noah are to be executed by decapitation for most crimes, considered one of the lightest capital punishments, by stoning if he has intercourse with a Jewish betrothed woman, or by strangulation if the Jewish woman has completed the marriage ceremonies, but had not yet consummated the marriage.

Signed by our government!

Old Testament prophecies Jesus fulfilled

The Bible is the story of human history and God's work in it. The most significant event in human history is the death and resurrection of Jesus Christ. The story of this event permeates the text of Scripture. The creation account shows us God's sovereignty over His creation. The fall shows us why we need a savior. The history of Israel shows two significant things: 1) the historical context of the coming of the Son of God incarnate, and 2) humanity's inability to save itself through works, thus, its need for a savior.

The gospels tell the story of Jesus the Savior on earth, and much of the rest of the New Testament teaches how to live in this age in light of Jesus' work on our behalf. The prophecies of the Bible, particularly in Daniel and Revelation but also elsewhere, show what Jesus as Savior is saving us to (eternal paradise) and from (eternal damnation in hell).

The story of Jesus saturates the metanarrative of the Bible, and prophecies of His first advent are found throughout the Old Testament. Allusions to Him also come up in micro ways, as many people and events hint at the work He would accomplish. One scholar, J. Barton Payne, has found as many as 574 verses in the Old Testament that somehow point to or describe or reference the coming Messiah. Alfred

Edersheim found 456 Old Testament verses referring to the Messiah or His times. Conservatively, Jesus fulfilled at least 300 prophecies in His earthly ministry.

So, the question of how many prophecies Jesus fulfilled is difficult to answer with precision. Should we count only direct <u>messianic prophecies</u>? Do we count repeated prophecies twice? How about allusions and indirect references to the ministry of Christ? And what about <u>types</u>? A type is a prophetic symbol: a person or thing in the Old Testament that foreshadows a person or thing in the New Testament. So, while Isaiah *prophesies* the Lord will offer good news for the brokenhearted (<u>Isaiah 61:1</u>), Boaz lives this out, acting as a *type* of Christ (<u>Ruth 4:1–11</u>).

Below is an attempt to list the types and prophecies given in the Old and New Testaments that Jesus has fulfilled. Undoubtedly, it is not complete. But that's one of the great things about the Bible—the more you read it, the more you see.

Type	**Given** **Fulfilled**
Type: Adam is a type of Christ because both their actions affected a great many people.	<u>Genesis 3:17-19</u> <u>Romans 5:14</u>
Type: Jesus is the fulfillment of the Passover Lamb.	<u>Exodus 12:1-11</u> <u>John 1:29-36</u>
Type: The rock that produced water for Israel points toward Jesus and the living water.	<u>Exodus 17:6</u> <u>John 4:10</u>; <u>1 Corinthians 10:3-4</u>
Type: The tabernacle where God dwelt among the Israelites is a type of Jesus, God with us.	<u>Exodus 25:8</u>; <u>Isaiah 7:14</u>; <u>8:8, 10</u> <u>Matthew 1:21-23</u>; <u>John 1:14</u>; <u>14:8-11</u>

Type: The feast of unleavened bread represents the purity of Jesus; Jesus' burial is like a kernel in the ground, waiting to burst forth in life.	Leviticus 23:6 1 Peter 2:22
Type: The feast of first fruits represents Jesus as the first fruit from the dead.	Leviticus 23:10 1 Corinthians 15:20
Type: Those who looked up at the snake on a pole were saved. Those who "look up" at Jesus on the cross are saved.	Numbers 21:8-9 John 3:14-15
Type: Boaz is a type of Christ the redeemer.	Ruth 4:1-11; Ezekiel 16:8 Galatians 3:13; 4:5; Colossians 1:14
Type: Jonah was in the fish for three days. Jesus' body was in the grave for three days.	Jonah 1:17 Matthew 12:40

Prophecy	**Given** **Fulfilled**
The serpent and the "seed" of Eve will have conflict; the offspring of the woman will crush the serpent. Jesus is this seed, and He crushed Satan at the cross.	Genesis 3:14-15 Galatians 4:4; Hebrews 2:14
God promised Abraham the whole world would be blessed through him. Jesus, descended from Abraham, is that blessing.	Genesis 12:3 Acts 3:25-26; Matthew 1:1; Galatians 3:16
God promised Abraham He would establish an everlasting covenant with Isaac's offspring. Jesus is that offspring.	Genesis 17:19 Matthew 1:1-2

God promised Isaac the whole world would be blessed by his descendent. That descendent is Jesus.	Genesis 28:13-14 Matthew 1:1-2; Luke 1:33; 3:23-34
Jacob prophesied Judah would rule over his brothers. Jesus the king is from the tribe of Judah.	Genesis 49:10 Matthew 1:1-2; Luke 1:32-33
The Jews were not to keep the Passover lamb overnight. Jesus was buried the day He died.	Exodus 12:10; Numbers 9:12 John 19:38-42
The Jews were not to break the bones of the Passover lamb. Jesus' bones were not broken on the cross.	Exodus 12:46; Numbers 9:12 John 19:31-36
The Jews were to devote the first-born males to God. Jesus is Mary's firstborn male; He is also the "first-born" over creation and the "first-born" of the dead.	Exodus 13:2; Numbers 3:13; 8:17 Luke 2:7, 23; Colossians 1:15-18
Moses promised another prophet like him would come. Jesus is that prophet.	Deuteronomy 18:15, 18-19 Matthew 21:11; Luke 7:16; 24:19; John 6:14; 7:40
God told the Jews to never leave the body of someone who had been hanged overnight. Jesus was buried the day He died.	Deuteronomy 21:23 John 19:31-36; Galatians 3:13
The word of God will be in hearts and mouths. Jesus is the Word who is in the hearts of His followers.	Deuteronomy 30:14 John 1:1; Matthew 26:26
Moses promised God would atone for His people. Jesus' sacrifice is that atonement.	Deuteronomy 32:43 Romans 3:25; Hebrews 2:17

God promised David his offspring would rule forever. Jesus is descended from David, although His literal reign has yet to begin.

2 Samuel 7:12-13, 16, 25-26; 1 Chronicles 17:11-14, 23-27; Psalm 89:3-4, 35-37; 132:11; Isaiah 9:7

Matthew 1:6; 19:28; 21:4; 25:31; Mark 12:37; Luke 1:32; 3:31

The nations, people, and rulers plot against the Lord and His anointed. The Sanhedrin, the crowd, Herod Antipas, and Pilate plotted against Jesus.

Psalm 2:1-2

Matthew 12:14; 26:3, 4, 47; Luke 23:1, 7

God will tell someone He is their Father. God told the crowd at Jesus' baptism that He is Jesus' Father.

Psalm 2:7

Matthew 3:17; 17:5; Mark 1:11; 9:7; Luke 3:22; 9:35

David believes God will not abandon him to the grave. Jesus rose from the grave.

Psalm 16:9-10; 30:3; 86:13; Isaiah 26:19

Luke 24:6-8; John 20

David cries out that God has forsaken him. Jesus uses the same words on the cross.

Psalm 22:1

Matthew 27:46

David says his enemies mock and insult him. Jesus endured the same on the cross.

Psalm 22:7

Matthew 27:38-44

David's tormentors tease him, telling him to have God rescue him. The people said the same to Jesus.

Psalm 22:7

Luke 23:35, 39

David describes his physical torment. The description matches the condition of someone who is being crucified.

Psalm 22:14-15

John 19:28

David says that "dogs" surround him and pierce his hands and feet. Gentile soldiers put nails through Jesus' hands and feet.

Psalm 22:16

John 19:16; 20:20; Acts 2:23

David says that others divide his clothing. The Roman soldiers took Jesus' clothes.

Psalm 22:18

John 19:23-24

David says false witnesses will testify against him. False witnesses did testify against Jesus, although they didn't have matching stories.

Psalm 27:12; 35:11; 109:6

Matthew 26:60; Mark 14:55-59

David says he commits his spirit to God. Jesus used the same words on the cross.

Psalm 31:5

Luke 23:46

God will protect the bones of the righteous. Jesus' bones were not broken on the cross.

Psalm 34:20

John 19:31-36

David talks of being hated without reason. Jesus was hated without reason.

Psalm 35:19; 69:4

John 15:24-25

The psalmist says his friends will abandon him. The disciples abandoned Jesus.

Psalm 38:11; 88:18

Matthew 26:56-58; Mark 14:50

David says he has come to do God's will. Jesus came to do God's will.

Psalm 40:6-8

Matthew 26:39, 42; John 6:38; Hebrews 10:5-9

David talks about being betrayed by a friend. Jesus was betrayed by Judas.

Psalm 41:9; 55:12-14

Matthew 26:14-16, 23; Mark 14:10-11, 43

The psalmists say God will rescue them from the land of the dead. God resurrected Jesus.

Psalm 49:15; 86:13

Mark 16:6; Luke 24:6-8; John 20

The Lord ascends on high, bringing captives with Him. Jesus ascended to heaven, and believers go to heaven.

Psalm 68:18

Luke 23:43; 24:51; Acts 1:9

David says he will be rejected by his siblings. Jesus' brothers refused to believe who He was until after the resurrection.

Psalm 69:8

Mark 3:20-21, 31; John 7:3-5

David has "zeal" for God's house and His honor but will be reproached. Jesus showed that zeal by cleaning out the temple and was questioned by the Sanhedrin members.

Psalm 69:9

Mark 11:15-17, 27-28; John 2:13-18; Romans 15:3

David talks of being fed gall and vinegar. Jesus was offered gall and vinegar on the cross.

Psalm 69:21

Matthew 27:34, 48; Mark 15:23; Luke 23:36; John 19:29

Solomon asks God for foreign kings to bring him gifts and honor. The magi did so for Jesus.

Psalm 72:10-11

Matthew 2:1-11

Solomon tells God that as king he will deliver the needy and weak. Jesus did this.

Psalm 72:12-14

Luke 7:22

The psalmist says he will speak in parables. Jesus spoke in parables.

Psalm 78:2

Matthew 13:3, 35

God says He will make David His firstborn. Jesus, David's descendent, is God's firstborn.

Psalm 89:27

Romans 8:29; Colossians 1:15

David's enemies attacked him, but he refrained froms responding. Jesus forgave His enemies.

Psalm 109:3-5

Matthew 5:44; Luke 23:34

David asks that his betrayer's life be short and his position be taken. Jesus' betrayer, Judas, died, and Matthias took his place.

Psalm 69:25; 109:7-8

Acts 1:16-20

David says his Lord will be made a priest of Melchizedek. Jesus is a priest of Melchizedek.	Psalm 110:4 Hebrews 5:1-6; 6:20; 7:15-17
The psalmist says the stone the builders reject will become the cornerstone. Jesus was rejected by the Jewish leaders, but He is the basis of God's salvation.	Psalm 118:22-23 Matthew 21:42; Mark 12:10-11; Luke 20:17; John 1:11
The Lord will redeem Israel from her sins. Jesus redeemed Israel.	Psalm 130:7-8 Matthew 1:21; Luke 1:68
God told Isaiah the people would not understand what He was doing. Jesus used parables to keep casual observers from understanding His teaching.	Isaiah 6:9-10 Matthew 13:14-15
God promised that a virgin would conceive. Mary was a virgin when Jesus was conceived.	Isaiah 7:14 Luke 1:26-35
God promised to send a Son who would be "God with us" ("Emmanuel"). Jesus is that Son.	Isaiah 7:14; 8:8, 10 Matthew 1:21-23; John 1:14; 14:8-11
God promised a "stone" that people would trip over. Jesus is that stone.	Isaiah 8:14-15 Matthew 21:42-44; Romans 9:32-33
God promised the land of Zebulun and Naphtali and "Galilee of the nations" a light for their darkness. Jesus is that light; at the time of Jesus, Galilee was a mix of Jews and Gentiles.	Isaiah 9:1-2 Matthew 4:12-16
God promised David His Spirit would rest on his offspring. Jesus is that offspring.	Isaiah 11:1-2 Matthew 1:1, 6; 3:16; Mark 1:10

Gentiles will come to God. A centurion and a Syrophoenician woman came to Jesus; the Gentiles in Pisidian Antioch responded to Paul's gospel message.

Isaiah 11:10; 42:1; 55:4-5; Hosea 2:23

Matthew 8:5-13; Mark 7:24-26; Acts 13:48

God promised a time when the blind would see. Jesus healed the blind.

Isaiah 29:18; 35:5

Matthew 9:30; 11:5; 12:22; 20:34; 21:14; Mark 10:52

God promised a time when the deaf hear. Jesus healed the deaf.

Isaiah 35:5

Matthew 11:5; Mark 7:31-37; 9:25

God promised a time when the lame would be healed. Jesus healed the lame.

Isaiah 35:6

Matthew 15:30-31; 21:14

God promised a time when the mute would speak. Jesus healed the mute.

Isaiah 35:6

Matthew 9:33; 12:22; 15:30; Luke 11:14

God promised a messenger who would announce the Lord's coming. John the Baptist is that messenger.

Isaiah 40:3-5; Malachi 3:1

Matthew 3:3; 11:10; Mark 1:3; Luke 3:4-6

God is the shepherd who tends His sheep. Jesus is the good shepherd.

Isaiah 40:10-11

John 10:11

God promised to put His Spirit on His servant. Jesus is that servant.

Isaiah 42:1

Matthew 3:16; 12:18; Mark 1:10

God's servant will not cry out. Jesus told those He healed to remain quiet.

Isaiah 42:2

Matthew 12:19

God's servant will be gentle. Jesus treated people gently.

Isaiah 42:3

Matthew 11:29; 12:20

The nations will put their hope in God's servant's teaching. Nations put their hope in Jesus' teachings.

Isaiah 42:4

Matthew 12:21

God will send His servant as a light to the Gentiles. Jesus is a light to the Gentiles.	Isaiah 42:6; 49:6 Luke 2:25-32
The writer says he will not be rebellious or turn away. Jesus obeyed God all the way to the cross.	Isaiah 50:5 Matthew 26:39
Isaiah speaks of one who will be beaten and spit upon. Jesus was beaten and spit upon.	Isaiah 50:6 Matthew 26:67; 27:26-30
The Suffering Servant will be so abused He will not look human. Jesus was beaten, whipped, crucified, and pierced by a spear.	Isaiah 52:14 Matthew 26:67; 27:26-30; 35
The Suffering Servant will be despised and rejected by His own people. Jesus' tormentors rejected Him and spit in His face.	Isaiah 53:3 Luke 23:18; Matthew 26:67; John 1:11
The Suffering Servant will bear the abuse we deserve for our physical and spiritual healing. Jesus did this.	Isaiah 53:4-5 Matthew 8:17; Romans 5:6-8; 1 Corinthians 15:3
The Suffering Servant will bear our sins. Jesus bore our sins.	Isaiah 53:6, 8, 12 Romans 4:25; 1 Peter 2:24-25
The Suffering Servant is like a lamb that does not defend itself. Although Jesus spoke during His trials, He never offered a defense.	Isaiah 53:7 Matthew 27:12; Luke 23:9; John 1:29-36
The Suffering Servant's people did not protest His death. Only Pilate protested Jesus' death.	Isaiah 53:8 Matthew 27:23-25
The Suffering Servant will die with the wicked. Jesus died with the two thieves.	Isaiah 53:9, 12 Matthew 27:38; Mark 15:27

The Suffering Servant will be buried in the grave of a rich man. Jesus was buried in the grave of Joseph of Arimathea. — Isaiah 53:9; Matthew 27:57-60

God ordained that the Suffering Servant would suffer and die. God sent Jesus to die. — Isaiah 53:10; John 3:16; 19:11; Acts 2:23; Philippians 2:8

The Suffering Servant's sacrifice offers forgiveness of sins. Jesus' sacrifice offers forgiveness of our sins. — Isaiah 53:11; Acts 10:43; 13:38-39

The Suffering Servant will intercede for His abusers. Jesus asked God to forgive those who crucified Him. — Isaiah 53:12; Luke 23:34

God promises a great light to pierce the darkness of Israel and the nations. Jesus is that light. — Isaiah 60:1-3; Matthew 4:16; Luke 2:32; John 12:46

God promises someone to declare good news for the brokenhearted, captives, and prisoners. Jesus is that someone. — Isaiah 61:1; Matthew 3:16; Luke 4:18

God promises a "righteous Branch" from the line of Jesse who will do what is just. Jesus is that Branch. — Jeremiah 23:5-6; 33:15-16; Romans 3:22; 1 Corinthians 1:30

A woman will weep for her dead children. Herod killed the baby boys in Bethlehem. — Jeremiah 31:15; Matthew 2:16-18

God makes a woman "encircle" or protect a man. The Holy Spirit conceived Jesus in Mary. — Jeremiah 31:22; Matthew 1:20; Luke 1:35

God promises a new covenant. Jesus provides the work for that new covenant. — Jeremiah 31:31-34 ; 32:37-40; 50:5; Matthew 26:27-29; Mark 14:22-24; Luke 22:15-20

"David" will return as his people's shepherd. Jesus is that shepherd.	Ezekiel 34:23-24; 37:24 John 10:11
Gabriel tells Daniel when the "Anointed One" will be "cut off." This is the exact time Jesus is crucified.	Daniel 9:24-26 Matthew 27:50
God will call His "child" from Egypt. Jesus returned from Egypt when He was young.	Hosea 11:1 Matthew 2:13-15
Israel's ruler will be struck on the cheek with a rod. Jesus was struck on the head with a staff.	Micah 5:1 Matthew 27:30
The ruler of Israel will come from Bethlehem. Jesus was born in Bethlehem.	Micah 5:2 Luke 2:4-7
God will live among His people. Jesus lived among the Jews.	Zechariah 2:10 John 1:14
The Branch will be a priest in the temple. Jesus is a priest in the order of Melchizedek.	Zechariah 6:12-13 Hebrews 7:11-28; 8:1-2
Israel's king will ride a donkey. Jesus came into Jerusalem riding a donkey.	Zechariah 9:9 Mark 11:1-10
God told Zechariah to take the thirty pieces of silver he earned and throw it to the potter. Judas took thirty pieces of silver and returned it to the priests who used it to buy the potter's field.	Zechariah 11:12-13 Matthew 26:14-15; 27:3, 6-10
If someone strikes the shepherd, the sheep will scatter. When Jesus was arrested, His disciples fled.	Zechariah 13:6-7 Matthew 26:56; Mark 14:50

The Lord will come to the temple and refine the silver and the priests. Jesus came to the temple and threw out the money changers.	Malachi 3:1-3 Matthew 21:12; Mark 11:15-19; John 2:13-16
The sun of righteousness will come. Jesus is that sun.	Malachi 4:2 Luke 1:78
Elijah will return. John the Baptist fulfills the role of Elijah.	Malachi 4:5 Matthew 11:13-14; Mark 9:11-13; Luke 1:17; 7:27-28
Jesus said He will suffer and die. Before the crucifixion, both the priests' guards and the Roman soldiers beat Jesus.	Matthew 16:21; Mark 8:31 Luke 22:63-65; Mark 14:53, 65; 15:33-37; John 19:1
Jesus said He will be handed over on the Passover. He was handed over at night, after Galileans celebrated the Passover but before Judeans do.	Matthew 26:2 John 19:14-16
Jesus said one of His disciples will betray Him. Judas betrayed Him.	Matthew 26:21-22 Luke 22:47-48
Jesus said the disciples will scatter. They did at His arrest.	Matthew 26:31; Mark 14:27 Matthew 26:56; Mark 14:50
Jesus said Peter will deny Him. Peter did so at the trial before Caiaphas.	Matthew 26:33-34 Matthew 26:69-75
Jesus said He will be handed over, killed, and rise again on the third day.	Mark 9:30-31; 10:32-34 John 18-20
Jesus said He will be delivered to the chief priests and scribes, killed, and rise again three days later.	Mark 10:32-34 John 18-20
Simeon said Jesus will cause many hearts to be revealed. The Sanhedrin was revealed to be jealous.	Luke 2:35 Matthew 27:18

Simeon told Mary her soul will be pierced because of Jesus. She witnessed the crucifixion.	<u>Luke 2:35</u> <u>John 19:25-27</u>
Jesus said He will rebuild the "temple" (His body) after three days. He rose from the dead after three days.	<u>John 2:18-22</u> <u>Acts 10:40</u>; <u>1 Corinthians 15:4</u>

Professor Peter W. Stoner was Chairman of the Departments of Mathematics and Astronomy at Pasadena City College and Chairman of the science division at Westmont College. In his book, *Science Speaks*, Professor Stoner outlines the mathematical probability of one person in the first century fulfilling just eight of the most clear and straightforward Messianic prophecies.

Josh and Sean McDowell quote Stoner in their book, *Evidence That Demands a Verdict*:

We find that the chance that any man might have lived down to the present time and fulfilled all eight prophecies is 1 in 1017 (1 in 100,000,000,000,000,000).

In case you're wondering, the Mega Millions had a $1.6 billon jackpot in October 2018, and the odds of winning it were merely 1 in 302,575,350. [1]

Stoner went on to calculate the probability of one person fulfilling 48 prophecies: 1 in 10157

How much more proof is needed to show Jesus was more than a prophet or mortal man! These calculations prove beyond a shadow of a doubt he was indeed the Son of God, the creator of the universe: "In the beginning was the Word, and the Word was with God and the Word was God' The same was in the beginning with God. All things were made by him; and without him was not anything made that was made, John 1:1-3.

CHAPTER 19 ZIONISM

True Seed of Abraham

For they are not all Israel, which are of Israel. Neither, because they are the seed of Abraham, are they all children: but in Isaac shall thy seed be called. That is, They, which are the children of the flesh, these are not the children of God. but the children of the promise are counted for the seed. Romans 9: 6-8.

Israel is not the seed of Abraham. Christ is the seed of Abraham. Galatians 3:16 talks of the seed of Abraham, which is Christ, not as to seeds, as of many, Israel. Romans 2:28,29 For he is not a Jew which is one outwardly; neither is that circumcision, which is outward in the flesh. But he is a Jew, which is one inwardly; and circumcision is that of the heart, in the spirit, and not in the letter; whose praise is not of men, but of God. Galatians 3: 27-29. For as many of you as has been baptized unto Christ have put on Christ. There is neither Jew nor Greek, there is neither bond nor free, there is neither male nor female: for ye are all one in Christ. And if ye be in Christ, then are you Abraham's seeds, and heir according to the promise.

The kingdom of God was taken from the Jews because they rejected Jesus the chief corner stone, Matthew 21: 42,43. Verse 44 states: whosoever shall fall upon this stone shall be broken: but on whomsoever it shall fall, it will ground him to powder, 70 A.D, the destruction of Jerusalem. Little children, it is the last time and as you have heard that antichrist shall come, even now are there many anti-christs whereby we know it is the last time. Who is a liar but he that denieth that Jesus is the Christ? He is antichrist that denieth the Father and the Son. 1 John 2:18, 22, 23. Knowing this, you have understanding that Zionist Israel is but one of many antichrist nations! Christian Zionists are promoting antichrists and the total Genocide against the Palestinian people! The term Judaea Christian is an oxymoron. The religion of Judaism is not the religion of the Old Testament. Judaism follows the Rabbinic Talmud which not only denies Christ Jesus and says he is in hell being boiled in excrement but also calls his mother Mary a whore and is diabolically opposed to all Christians. Anyone that is not a Jew is considered less than human!

The Rothschilds are the planet's wealthiest family worth many trillions. They control Royal Dutch/Shell, BP, Anglo-American, BHP Billiton, Rio Tinto, Bank of America and scores of other global corporations and banks. They are the largest shareholders in the Bank of England, the Federal Reserve and most every private central bank in the world. They needed a footprint in the Middle East to protect their new oil concessions, thus the creation of the state Israel, which they procured through Four Horsemen fronts like the Iranian Consortium, Iraqi Petroleum Company and Saudi ARAMCO.

Rothschild's Shell and BP formed these cartels with the Rockefeller half of the Four Horsemen- Exxon Mobil and Chevron Texaco. This new alliance required a "special relationship" between Great Britain and the US, which still exists today. Rothschild and other wealthy European shareholders could now utilize the United States military as a Hessianized mercenary force, deployed to protect their oil interests and paid for by US taxpayers. Israel would serve the same purpose in closer proximity to the oilfields. The Israeli Mossad is less a national intelligence agency than it is a Rothschild/Rockefeller family security force.

Israel is not a "Jewish homeland". It is an oil monopoly lynchpin. Its citizens are being put in harm's way- used by the Four Horsemen and their Eight Families-owners as geopolitical pawns in an international resource grab. No peaceful solution is possible until the stolen land is returned to its rightful Palestinian owners.

The original city of Jerusalem was leveled in 70 A.D. by the Roman General Titus. No stone was left upon another, as Jesus prophesied. The Roman Emperor Hadrian in 130-135 A.D. on the leveled land of Jerusalem built a city and named it Aelia Capitolina. It was renamed Jerusalem in the 4th century by Emperor Constantine and the walls rebuilt by Suleiman the Magnificent of the Ottoman Empire in around 1516. Jesus could have never walked in today's Roman city of Jerusalem.

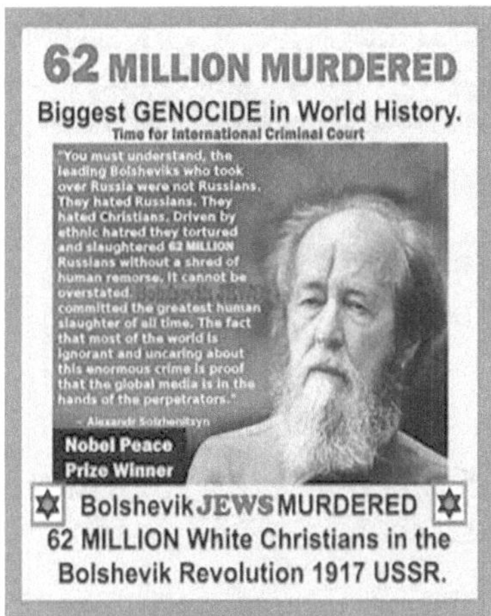

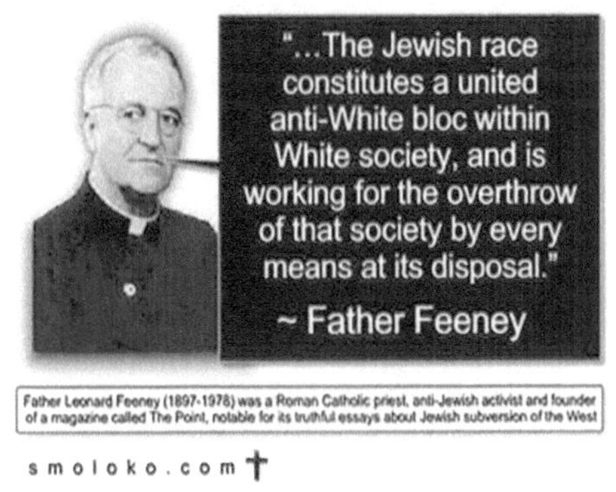

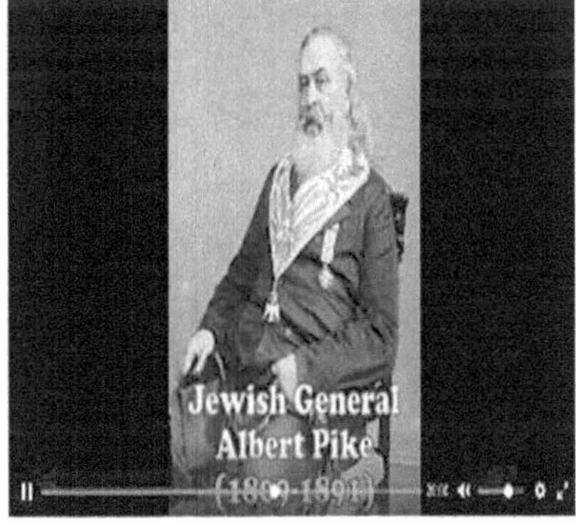

Anti-white (Code name for Christians) agenda being propagated today!

We will see if you still have that smirk on
your face when burning in hell!

After ruining Russia during the Bolshevik Soviet years, and then playing a huge back-door role in the destruction of Europe through two World Wars, elite Jews are now engaged in a takedown as they finish off the host with a variety of honed tactics, including inflation, illegal migration, and woke psychopathy.

THE PROTOCOLS OF THE LEARNED ELDERS OF ZION

THE JEW'S PLAN FOR WORLD DOMINATION
1897 EDITION

1. PLACE OUR AGENTS AND HELPERS EVERYWHERE
2. TAKE CONTROL OF THE MEDIA AND USE IT IN PROPAGANDA FOR OUR PLANS
3. START FIGHTS BETWEEN DIFFERENT RACES, CLASSES AND RELIGIONS
4. USE BRIBERY, THREATS AND BLACKMAIL TO GET OUR WAY
5. USE FREEMASON LODGES TO ATTRACT POTENTIAL PUBLIC OFFICIALS
6. APPEAL TO SUCCESSFUL PEOPLE'S EGOS
7. APPOINT PUPPET LEADERS WHO CAN BE CONTROLLED BY BLACKMAIL
8. REPLACE ROYAL RULE WITH SOCIALIST RULE, THEN COMMUNISM, THEN DESPOTISM
9. ABOLISH ALL RIGHTS AND FREEDOMS, EXCEPT THE RIGHT OF FORCE BY US
10. SACRIFICE PEOPLE, INCLUDING JEWS, WHEN NECESSARY
11. ELIMINATE RELIGION, REPLACE IT WITH SCIENCE AND MATERIALISM
12. CONTROL THE EDUCATION SYSTEM TO SPREAD DECEPTION AND DESTROY INTELLECT
13. REWRITE HISTORY TO OUR BENEFIT: ZIONIST NEW WORLD ORDER
14. CREATE ENTERTAINING DISTRACTIONS
15. CORRUPT MINDS WITH FILTH AND PERVERSION
16. ENCOURAGE PEOPLE TO SPY ON ONE ANOTHER
17. KEEP THE MASSES IN POVERTY AND PERPETUAL LABOR
18. TAKE POSSESSION OF ALL WEALTH, PROPERTY, AND ESPECIALLY – GOLD
19. USE GOLD TO MANIPULATE THE MARKETS, CAUSE DEPRESSIONS, ETC.
20. INTRODUCE A PROGRESSIVE TAX ON WEALTH
21. REPLACE SOUND INVESTMENT WITH SPECULATION
22. MAKE LONG TERM INTEREST BEARING LOANS TO GOVERNMENTS
23. GIVE BAD ADVICE TO GOVERNMENTS AND EVERYBODY ELSE
24. BLAME THE VICTIM

"A Racial Plan for the Twentieth Century"

Israel Cohen
1912

We must realize that our party's most powerful weapon is racial tension. By propounding into the consciousness of the dark races that for centuries they have been oppressed by the whites, we can mould them to the program of the Communist Party. In America we will aim for subtle victory. While inflaming the Negro minority against the whites, we will endeavor to instill in the whites a guilt complex for their exploitation of the Negroes. We will aid the Negroes to rise in prominence in every walk of life, in the professions and in the world of sports and entertainment. With this prestige, the Negro will be able to intermarry with the whites and begin a process which will deliver America to our cause.

"The Jewish people as a whole will be its own Messiah. It will attain world dominion by the dissolution of other races, by the abolition of frontiers, the annihilation of monarchy, and by the establishment of a world republic in which the Jews will everywhere exercise the privilege of citizenship. In this new world order the Children of Israel will furnish all the leaders without encountering opposition. The Governments of the different peoples forming the world republic will fall without difficulty into the hands of the Jews. It will then be possible for the Jewish rulers to abolish private property, and everywhere to make use of the resources of the state. Thus will the promise of the Talmud be fulfilled, in which is said that when the Messianic time is come, the Jews will have all the property of the whole world in their hands."

~Baruch Levy
Letter to Karl Marx
La Revue de Paris
p. 574
June 1, 1928

EVERY SINGLE ASPECT
OF THE LGBTQ+ MOVEMENT
IS JEWISH
Drag Queen
STORY HOUR
PRIDEMONTH
Matthew 18:6 - But who so shall offend one of these little ones which believe in me, it were better for him that a milestone were hanged about his neck, and that he were drowned in the depth of the sea.
In the Babylonian Talmud there are 6 Genders
Avodah Zarah 37a - Permits intercourse with a 3 year old girl
Why are Jews Pushing LGBTQ? Scan the QR Codes Below to Learn
LEV. 18:22
FOR MORE INFO VISIT: GOYIMTV.TV
GDL
ISAIAH 3:9
THESE FLYERS WERE DISTRIBUTED RANDOMLY WITHOUT MALICIOUS INTENT

New York Times
Jewish
If roughly 2% of Americans are Jews, is it odd that a newspaper's Chairman & Vice Chairman, Publisher & Deputy Publisher, Managing Editor & Deputy Managing Editor, President & CEO's spouse, Chief Operating Officer, and majority of its Directors and Exec. Committee are Jewish? What if its D.C., L.A., London, Paris, Rome, Berlin, Central/East Europe, South Asia, and Australia Bureau Chiefs, its Editor-in-Chief of its Editorial Page and Global, Magazine, and Business Editions, and its Chief National, International, Political, Domestic Affairs, Military, and White House Correspondents—all but one "Chief" Correspondent—are also Jewish?

What's it called when you remove corruption from government?
Antisemitism

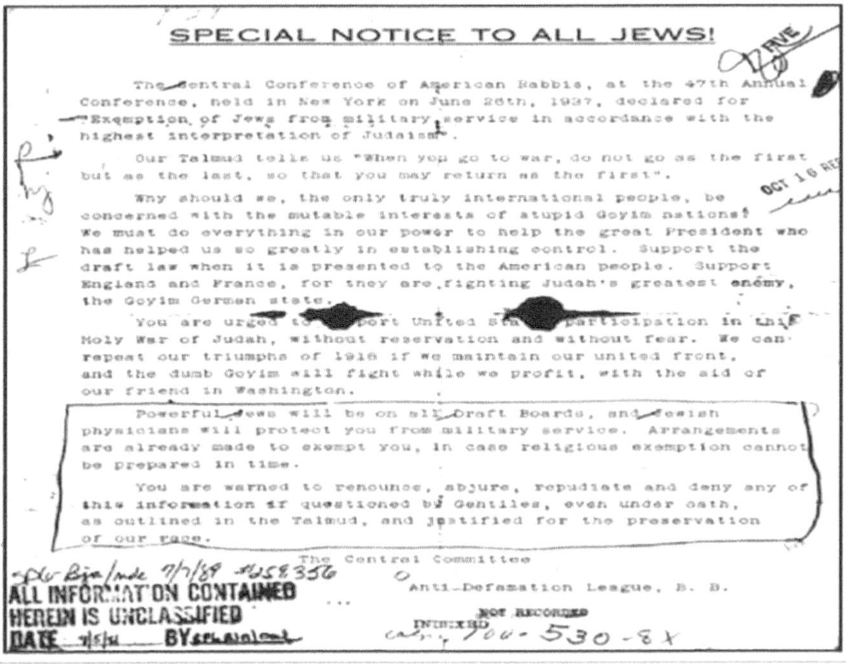

SPECIAL NOTICE TO ALL JEWS!

The Central Conference of American Rabbis, at the 47th Annual Conference, held in New York on June 26th, 1937, declared for "Exemption of Jews from military service in accordance with the highest interpretation of Judaism".

Our Talmud tells us "When you go to war, do not go as the first but as the last, so that you may return as the first".

Why should we, the only truly international people, be concerned with the mutable interests of stupid Goyim nations? We must do everything in our power to help the great President who has helped us so greatly in establishing control. Support the draft law when it is presented to the American people. Support England and France, for they are fighting Judah's greatest enemy, the Goyim German state.

You are urged to support United States participation in this Holy War of Judah, without reservation and without fear. We can repeat our triumphs of 1918 if we maintain our united front, and the dumb Goyim will fight while we profit, with the aid of our friend in Washington.

Powerful Jews will be on all Draft Boards, and Jewish physicians will protect you from military service. Arrangements are already made to exempt you, in case religious exemption cannot be prepared in time.

You are warned to renounce, abjure, repudiate and deny any of this information if questioned by Gentiles, even under oath, as outlined in the Talmud, and justified for the preservation of our race.

The Central Committee
Anti-Defamation League, B. B.

And it's not the martini he's holding in his hand!

Jewish Bolshevicks

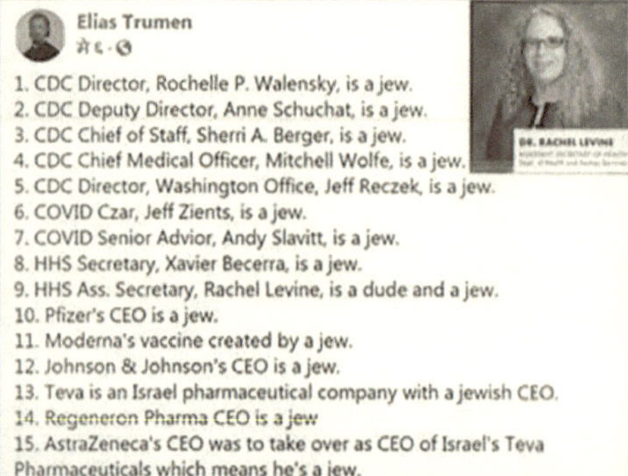

Elias Trumen

1. CDC Director, Rochelle P. Walensky, is a jew.
2. CDC Deputy Director, Anne Schuchat, is a jew.
3. CDC Chief of Staff, Sherri A. Berger, is a jew.
4. CDC Chief Medical Officer, Mitchell Wolfe, is a jew.
5. CDC Director, Washington Office, Jeff Reczek, is a jew.
6. COVID Czar, Jeff Zients, is a jew.
7. COVID Senior Advior, Andy Slavitt, is a jew.
8. HHS Secretary, Xavier Becerra, is a jew.
9. HHS Ass. Secretary, Rachel Levine, is a dude and a jew.
10. Pfizer's CEO is a jew.
11. Moderna's vaccine created by a jew.
12. Johnson & Johnson's CEO is a jew.
13. Teva is an Israel pharmaceutical company with a jewish CEO.
14. Regeneron Pharma CEO is a jew
15. AstraZeneca's CEO was to take over as CEO of Israel's Teva
Pharmaceuticals which means he's a jew.

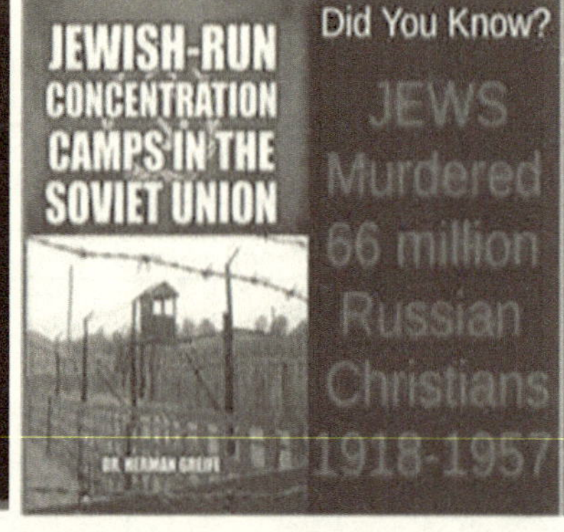

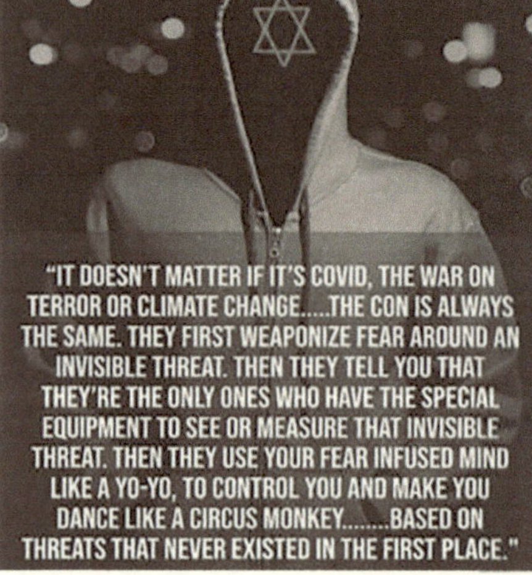

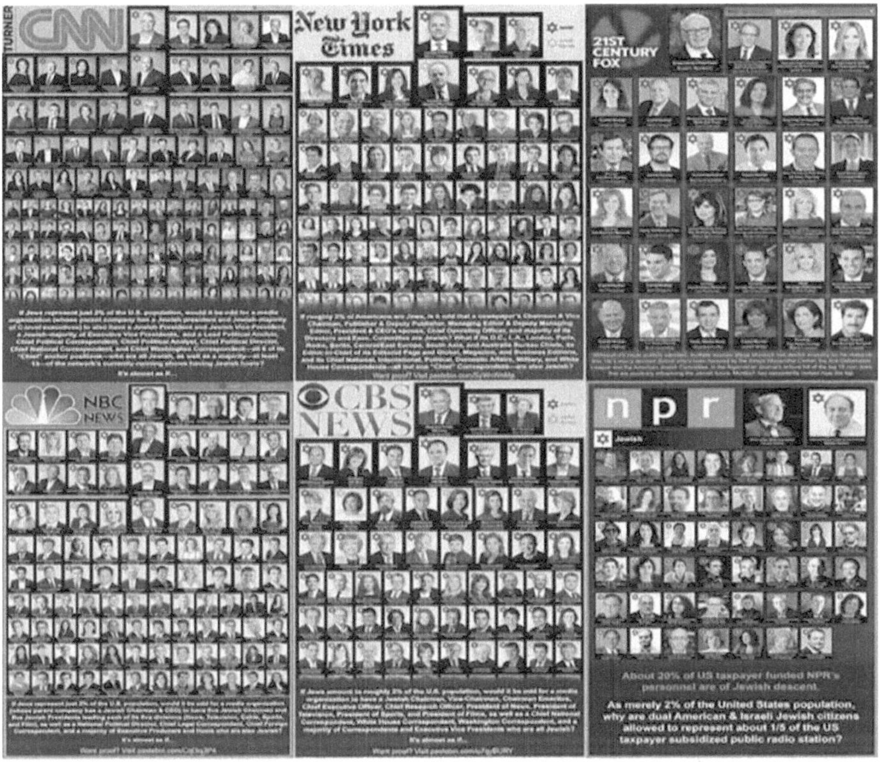

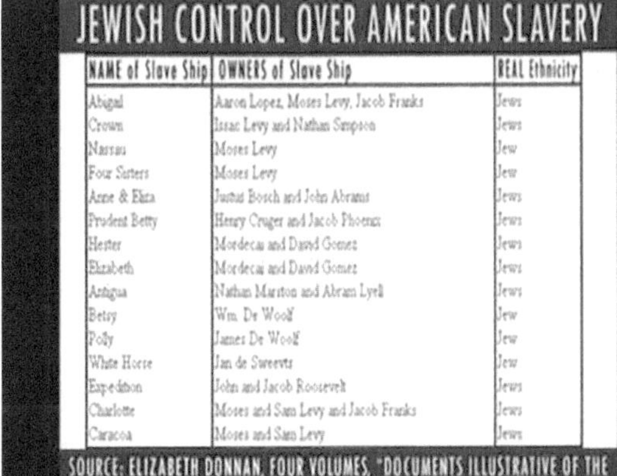

Zionists own media

JEWISH CONTROL OVER AMERICAN SLAVERY

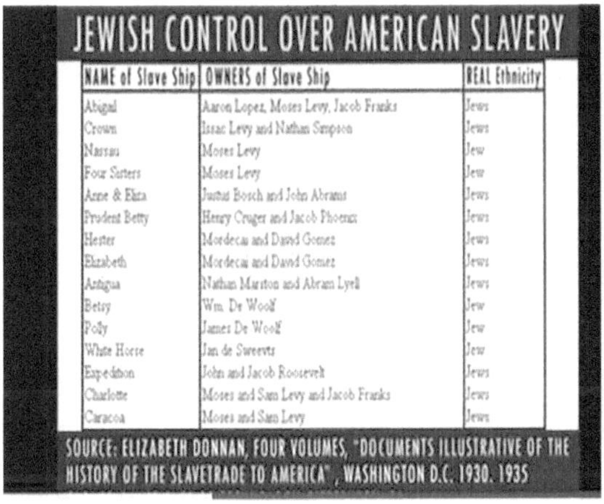

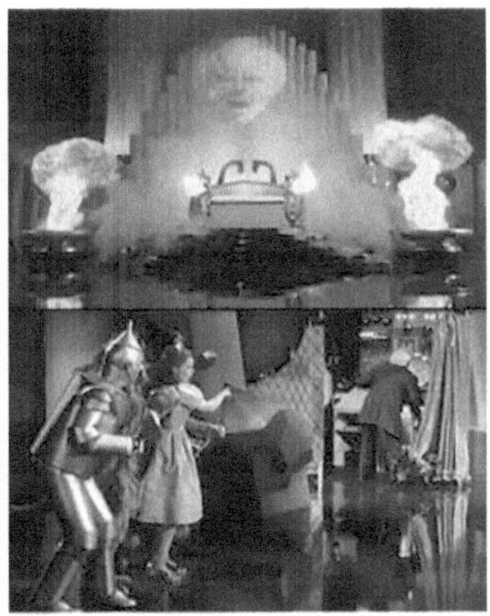

NAME of Slave Ship	OWNERS of Slave Ship	REAL Ethnicity
Abigail	Aaron Lopez, Moses Levy, Jacob Franks	Jews
Crown	Issac Levy and Nathan Simpson	Jews
Nassau	Moses Levy	Jew
Four Sisters	Moses Levy	Jew
Anne & Eliza	Justus Bosch and John Abrams	Jews
Prudent Betty	Henry Cruger and Jacob Phoenix	Jews
Hester	Mordecai and David Gomez	Jews
Elizabeth	Mordecai and David Gomez	Jews
Antigua	Nathan Marston and Abram Lyell	Jews
Betsy	Wm. De Woolf	Jew
Polly	James De Woolf	Jew
White Horse	Jan de Sweevts	Jew
Expedition	John and Jacob Roosevelt	Jews
Charlotte	Moses and Sam Levy and Jacob Franks	Jews
Caracoa	Moses and Sam Levy	Jews

SOURCE: ELIZABETH DONNAN, FOUR VOLUMES, "DOCUMENTS ILLUSTRATIVE OF THE HISTORY OF THE SLAVETRADE TO AMERICA", WASHINGTON D.C. 1930, 1935

Traitor Bush signing Noahide Laws!

On the Jews and Their Lies
by Martin Luther

Edition Description

I had made up my mind to write no more either about the Jews or against them. But since I learned that those miserable and accursed people do not cease to lure to themselves even us, that is, the Christians, I have published this little book, so that I might be found among those who opposed such poisonous activities of the Jews and who warned the Christians to be on their guard against them. I would not have believed that a Christian could be duped by the Jews into taking their exile and wretchedness upon himself. However, the devil is the god of the world, and wherever God's word is absent he has an easy task, not only with the weak but also with the strong. May God help us. Amen. Grace and peace in the Lord. Dear sir and good friend, I have received a treatise in which a Jew engages in dialog with a Christian. He dares to pervert the scriptural passages which we cite in testimony to our faith, concerning our Lord Christ and Mary his mother, and to interpret them quite differently. With this argument he thinks he can destroy the basis of our faith. Read Less

Edition Details

Christians will be beheaded!
Guillotines in Georgia and Montana!!

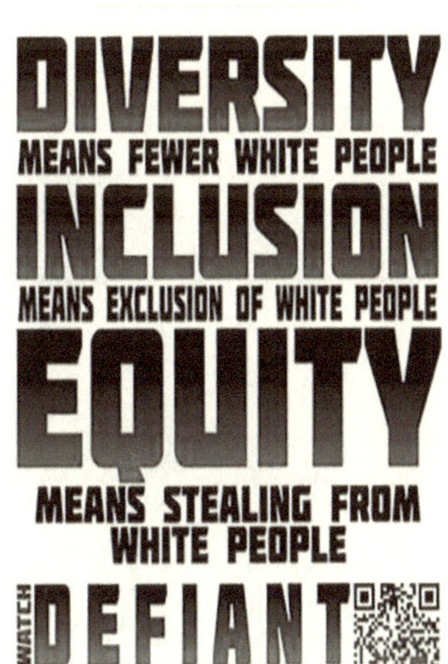

119

You can't make this stuff up!

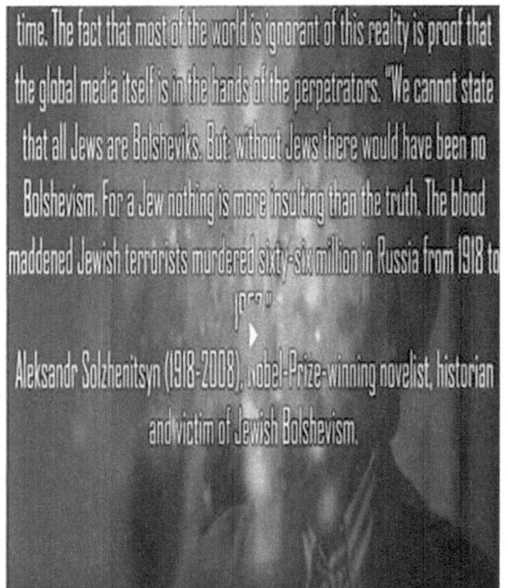

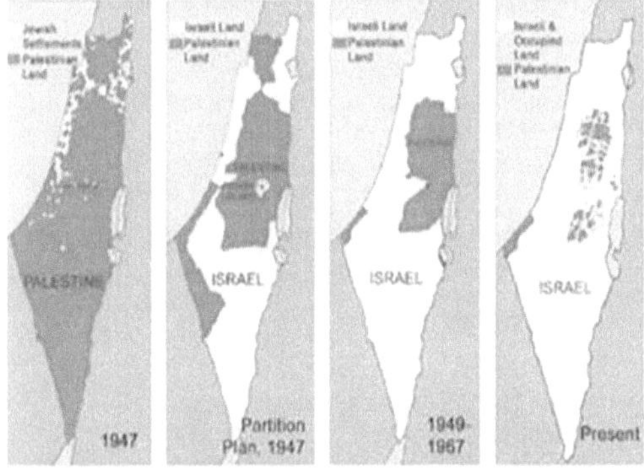

Zionist takeover of Palestine, 1947-Present

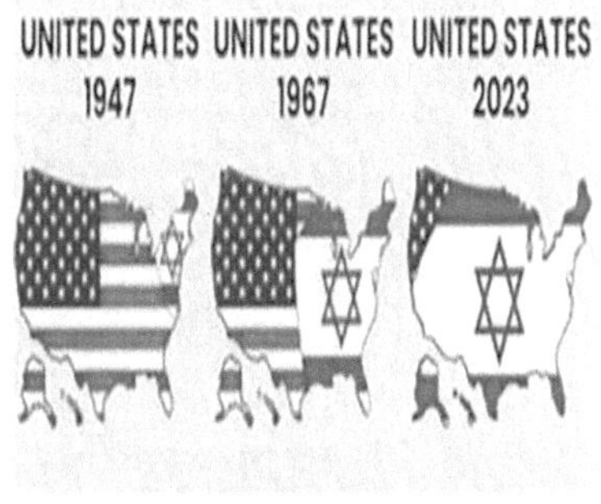

Zionist takeover of America, 1947-Present

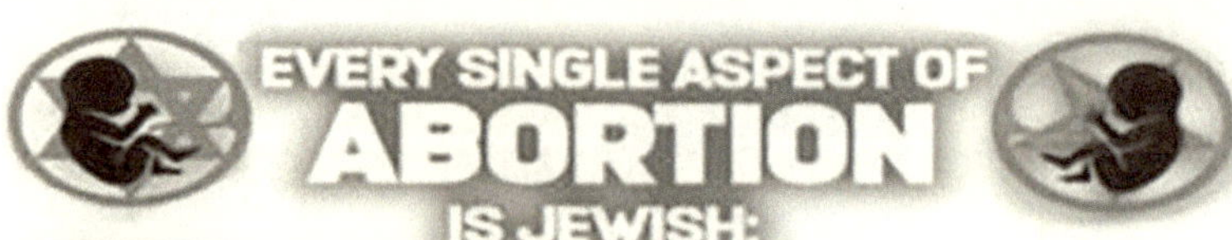
EVERY SINGLE ASPECT OF
ABORTION
IS JEWISH:

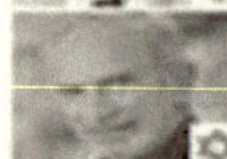
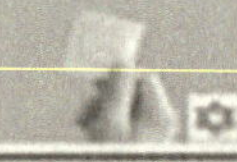
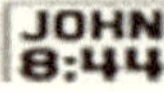
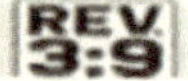
ÉTIENNE-ÉMILE BAULIEU
"FATHER" OF THE ABORTION PILL.
KNOWN WORLDWIDE FOR HIS WORK ON RU486 (MIFEPRISTONE).

ALAN FRANK GUTTMACHER
PRESIDENT OF PLANNED PARENTHOOD AND VICE-PRESIDENT OF THE AMERICAN
EUGENICS SOCIETY.

FANIA ESIAH MINDELL
STARTED PLANNED PARENTHOOD WITH MARGARET SANGER AND HER SISTER,
ETHEL BYRNE.

LAWRENCE LADER
"THE FOUNDING FATHER OF THE ABORTION MOVEMENT"
ONE OF THE FOUNDERS OF THE PRO-ABORTION GROUP NARAL.

HENRY MORGENTALER
"FATHER OF ABORTION IN CANADA"
FIRST DOCTOR IN NORTH AMERICA TO USE VACUUM ASPIRATION.
PRESIDENT OF THE HUMANIST ASSOCIATION OF CANADA, '68-'99.

GREGORY GOODWIN PINCUS
"FATHER OF THE BIRTH CONTROL PILL"
WORKED WITH MARGARET SANGER AND ABRAHAM STONE TO BEGIN HORMONAL
CONTRACEPTIVE RESEARCH.

MALVIN WEISBERG
OPERATED AN ABORTION CLINIC IN CALIFORNIA WHERE 16,433 ABORTED FETUSES
WERE STORED IN HIS SHIPPING CONTAINER.

PAUL RALPH EHRLICH
"FATHER OF THE
OVERPOPULATION THEORY"
THE POPULATION BOMB (1968)

JULIUS SCHMID
"KING OF CONDOMS"
TO HIDE HEBREW ORIGINS, HE MARKETED
USING MIDDLE EASTERN AND AFRICAN
NAMES, SUCH AS RAMSES AND SHEIK.

JOHN
8:44

REV
3:9

CHRISTIAN ZIONISM
A PACT WITH THE DEVIL!

EVERY SINGLE ASPECT OF
DISNEP
CHILD GROOMING IS JEWISH:
PROTECT YOUR CHILDREN PROTECT YOUR CHILDREN PROTECT YOUR CHILDREN PROTECT YOUR CHILDREN PROTECT YOUR CHILDREN
Bob Iger
CEO
JEWISH
Alan N. Braverman
Sr. Exec. VP
JEWISH
Alan Bergman
Chairman
JEWISH
Jay Rasulo
CFO
JEWISH
Jennifer Cohen
Exec. VP
JEWISH
Brent Woodford
Exec. VP
JEWISH
Susan Arnold
Chairwoman
JEWISH
Mary T. Barra
Board Director
JEWISH
Zenia Mucha
Exec. VP
JEWISH
Ronald L. Iden
Sr. VP
JEWISH

21ST CENTURY FOX

New York Times
If roughly 2% of Americans are Jews, is it odd that a newspaper's Chairman & Vice Chairman, Publisher & Deputy Publisher, Managing Editor & Deputy Managing Editor, President & CEO's spouse, Chief Operating Officer, and majority of its Directors and Exec. Committee are Jewish? What if its D.C., L.A., London, Paris, Rome, Berlin, Central/East Europe, South Asia, and Australia Bureau Chiefs, its Editor-in-Chief of its Editorial Page and Global, Magazine, and Business Editions, and its Chief National, International, Political, Domestic Affairs, Military, and White House Correspondents—all but its "Chief" Correspondent—are also Jewish?

EVERY SINGLE ASPECT OF THE JFK ASSASSINATION IS JEWISH
"I will splinter the CIA into a thousand pieces and scatter it into the winds"
— John F. Kennedy
Lyndon B. Johnson
Abraham Zapruder
David Weinblad
Jack Ruby (Jacob Rubenstein)
Sam Bloom
Reuben Efron
Julius Schepps
JFK AND HIS WAR AGAINST THE INTERNATIONAL JEWRY
Opposed to nuclear proliferation, investigated Israel's Dimona nuclear reactor to collect more information.
Monitored Israeli nuclear scientists visiting the U.S. throughout his administration.
Ignored Israeli Prime Minister Ben-Gurion's requests for supplying Israel with nuclear weapons and a joint declaration with the USSR.
Signed the Executive Order 11110 to strip the Rothschild Bank of its power to loan money to the U.S. Federal Government at interest.

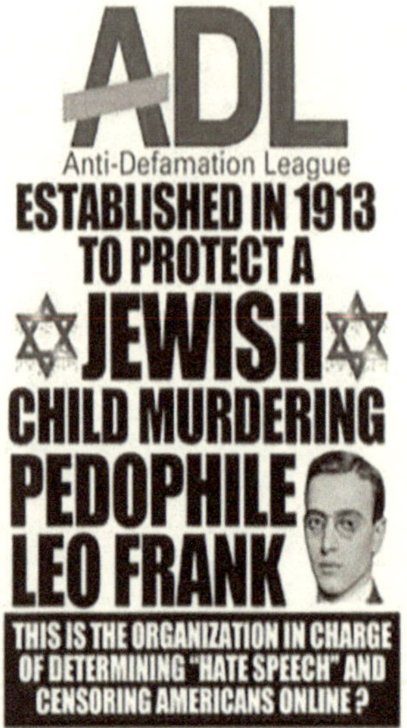
ADL
Anti-Defamation League
ESTABLISHED IN 1913
TO PROTECT A
JEWISH
CHILD MURDERING
PEDOPHILE
LEO FRANK
THIS IS THE ORGANIZATION IN CHARGE
OF DETERMINING "HATE SPEECH" AND
CENSORING AMERICANS ONLINE?

EVERY SINGLE ASPECT OF
COMMUNISM
IS JEWISH

EVERY SINGLE ASPECT OF THE
FEDERAL RESERVE
IS
JEWISH

EVERY SINGLE ASPECT OF
MASS IMMIGRATION
IS JEWISH
JEWISH NGOs PROMOTING MASS IMMIGRATION
"WHITES WILL BE AN ABSOLUTE MINORITY IN AMERICA...
THAT'S THE SOURCE OF OUR STRENGTH." - JOE BIDEN

EVERY SINGLE ASPECT OF THE BIDEN ADMINISTRATION IS JEWISH

During the Six-Day War between Israel and Egypt, the United States maintained a neutral country status, and the ship USS Liberty was sent to collect signals intelligence in **international waters** near Egypt.

During the **visual contact,** Israeli aerial naval observer Major Uri Meretz **reported** it was a US Navy ship.

Despite the US flag was plainly-visible, Israeli Air Force and Navy attacked the ship with rockets and torpedos, **killing 34 US Navy personnel** and leaving **171 crew members wounded.**

Israel claimed Liberty was **mistaken** for an Egyptian ship.

This case was kept quiet by President Lyndon B. Johnson, whom had been having an affair with Israeli spy **Mathilde Krim** at the time of incident.

ISRAELI RADIO CHATTER BEFORE FIRING

Israeli pilot to IDF war room: This is an American ship. Do you still want us to attack?

IDF war room to Israeli pilot: Yes, follow orders.

Israeli pilot to IDF war room: But sir, it's an American ship - I can see the flag!

IDF war room to Israeli pilot: Nevermind; hit it.

ISRAEL | OUR GREATEST ALLY?

THESE FLYERS WERE DISTRIBUTED RANDOMLY WITHOUT MALICIOUS INTENT

ANTISEMETISM WAS CREATED BY THE PROTOCOLS OF THE LEARNED ELDERS OF ZION, WHY? TO PROTECT ALL THEIR NEFARIOUS ACTIVITIES. CREATE ANTICHRISTIANISM, AND SEE HOW FAR THAT WOULD GO! COMPARE THE SUPPOSED SIX MILLION JEWS WHO DIED IN THE HOLLOCAUST TO OVER SIXTY- SIX MILLION TO 100 MILLION CHRISTIANS KILLED DURING THE JEWISH BOLSHEVICK REVOLUTION, BY THE JEWISH LEADERSHIP OF TROTSKY, LENIN AND STALIN, THE SIXTY TO EIGHTY MILLION CHRISTIANS KILLED DURING THE CATHOLIC INQUISITION AND THE UNTOLD THOUSANDS OR MILLIONS OF CHRISTIAN FED TO THE LIONS BY THE ROMAN EMPIRE. THE CHRISTIAN HOLOCAUST AS BEEN TOTALLY MUTED IN COMPARISON!

<u>If you do not follow the following protocol, you are an ANTI-SEMITE!</u>

On October 16th, 2004, President Bush signs into law the Global Anti-Semitism Review Act, designed to force the entire world into never being critical of the Jews, whatever their actions. This Act establishes a special department within the United States State Department to monitor global anti-Semitism, which is to report annually to Congress. This Act defines a person as being anti-Semitic if they purport any of the following beliefs:

1.) Any assertion, "that the Jewish community controls government, the media, international business and the financial world. (Ask the Rothschild family!)

2.) The expression of "strong anti-Israel sentiment." (Here in America, we can express whatever we feel like expressing. It's called the Bill of Rights, FREE SPEECH!)

3.) Expressing "Virulent criticism" of Israel's leaders, past or present. The State Department gives an example of this occurring when a swastika is portrayed in a cartoon decrying the behavior of a past or present Zionist leader. (FREE SPEECH!)

4.) Any criticism of the Jewish religion or its religious leaders or literature with the emphasis on the Talmud and Kabbalah. (Talmud calls Mary a whore and Jesus in hell boiling in excrement, need I say more!)

5.) Any criticism of the United States Government and Congress for being under undue influence by the Jewish-Zionist community, which would include Jewish organizations such as American-Israel Public Affairs Committee (AIPAC). (Zionists use the American military to kill Zionist enemies, and gives them billions of tax payers dollars to do so. I don't remember voting for that!)

6.) Any criticism of the Jewish-Zionist community for promoting globalism or what some call the, "New World Order. ("Does the term: Jewish Utopia sound familiarThe Zionists Rothschilds main goal. Unfortunately, we Goyim are not invited!)

7.) Placing any blame on Jewish leaders and their followers for inciting the Roman crucifixion of Christ. (Bible: The Jewish people cried out, let his blood be on us and our children! Matthew 27:25)

8.) Citing any **<u>facts</u>** that could in any way diminish the, "six million," figure of holocaust victims. (Why would you deny facts? That figure has never been substantiated! The population of Jews in Germany in 1939 was only 1.2 million and some say as little as 550 thousand.)

9.) Claiming that Israel is a racist state. (Just read the Talmud! And the term created by the Jews: Goyim!)

10.) Making any claim that there exists a "Zionist Conspiracy." (Again, read the Talmud!)

11.) **Offering proof that Jews and their leaders created Communism and the Bolshevik Revolution in Russia.** (Want proof? Communism was started by a Jew, Karl Marx, real name Moses Mordechai Levy) The Bolshevik Revolution was conducted by three Jews: Lenin, Trotsky and Stalin and also financed by the Jewish Rothschilds.)

12.) **Making "derogatory statements about Jewish persons."** (I am not Jewish but I get derogatory remarks all the time. I guess I need to print out my own Global Anti-Christian Review Act!)

13.) **Asserting that spiritually disobedient Jews do not have the biblical right to reoccupy Palestine.** (Not when they are committing genocide on the Palestinians to get that land!)

14.) **Making any allegations of Mossad involvement in the 9/11 attack.** (sorry, you are way too late on that statement as proof is coming in daily that Mossad was involved. Video shows Jews dancing in the streets at the scene of 911)

Ashkenazi Jews

The following is an introduction by Texe Marrs to the book: "The Synagogue of Satan" by Andrew Carrington Hitchcock in which he talks about those who say they are Jews and are not, Rev. 2:9.

The riddle of those who say they are Jews and are not and do lie may be explained by the fact the men at the top of the tier of power in the "Synagogue of Satan" organization have been proven by many respected researchers to be "Khazar Jews" also called "Ashkenazi Jews" The Khazars were a Turk-mongol people who lived centuries ago in the kingdom of Khazaria, eventually to be integrated into the Russian Empire by the Czars. The king of the Khazars forced his citizens upon the penalty of death to convert to Judaism. Later, after their takeover by hostile enemies, demographers and historians say the Khazars migrated to Poland, France, Romana, Hungary and Germany.

There in Europe, the Khazars – who said they were Jews and practiced a mystical and Pagan form of Judaism – gathered in their own communities, keeping separate those around them whom they classified as gentiles. The "Khazars Jews" considered the gentiles to be racially inferiors. In fact, the racial inferiority of gentiles was taught to them in their Talmud.

The book speaks about Ashkenazi and Crypto Jews. Ashkenazi jews are not Jews. Crypto Jews are those that have hidden their Jewishness by changing their names using Gentile names to keep the Jews pure by covering any relationship of wrong doing, which is plenty.

A few examples: President Franklin Deano Roosevelt, a Sephardic Crypto Jew, real name Rosenfelt, orders the all-seeing eye to be place upon all new dollar bills along with the motto, "Novus Ordo Seclorum," Latin for "A new Order of the Ages," the New World Order, a Jewish term.

Winston Churchill whose mother, Jenny (Jacobson) Jerome. Was Jewish – meaning he is Jewish under Israeli immigration law as he is born of a Jewish mother.

Vladimir Lenin was Jewish. He was a Crypto Jew, and was born Ilyich Ulyanov, along with Josef Stalin. His real name is Djugashvili which translate in the Georgian language, "shvili," means son of, and Djuga means Jew.

Communism was invented for the Rothschilds by Moses Mordechai Levy, more commonly known as Karl Marx. Benjamin Netanyahu is also an Ashkenazi Crypto Jew along with most all former Israeli heads of state. So, claiming Israel is a Jewish state is really a misnomer. It is Jewish in name only.

One side features a Star of David, the other side is engraved with a swastika

NAZI AND ZIONIST WWII COIN SHOWING COLLABORATION

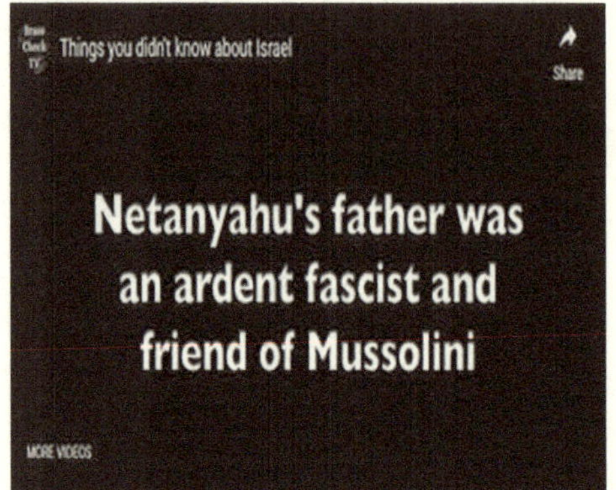
Things you didn't know about Israel
Share
Netanyahu's father was
an ardent fascist and
friend of Mussolini
MORE VIDEOS

To learn who
rules over you,
simply find out
who you are
not allowed
to criticize.

CHAPTER 20 NOAHIDE LAW

Georgia Guillotine Law HB 1274 March 1996

Jewish Noahide Laws passed by Congress are for beheading of Christians.

Few Americans have ever heard of the Guillotine Death by Noahide Laws that PASSED CONGRESS in 1991 and signed into law and was approved March 20, 1991 by President of the US, George Bush, Sr.

To keep this simple the Laws that are now a part of the American legal system say that if you have any other faith than the Talmud's counterfeit Kabbala or break any of the 7 Noahide Laws and one person says that you have done so, you can have your head cut off!

The NOAHIDE LAWS forbid the free exercise of religion (especially Christianity) in America, and respect no religion over another. (JUDAISM over all other religions) They clearly violate the First Amendment Establishment Clause.

THEREFORE, as long as the US CONSTITUTION remains in force, they CANNOT ACTIVATE THE NOAHIDE LAWS AND ENFORCE THEM IN AMERICA AT THIS TIME!

However, WHEN the CONSTITUTION IS ABOLISHED through the declaration of a NATIONAL EMERGENCY, MARTIAL LAW, THEN you will see the NOAHIDE LAWS activated and the enforcers (which are the military, foreign and domestic) and their guillotines brought out in full force.

THEN the NWO forces and their Jewish supporters will activate the NOAHIDE LAWS, will round up Christians ALREADY ON THE SECRET GOVERNMENT LISTS, and demand that they either RENOUNCE THIER FAITH IN JESUS CHRIST, and conform to their NOAHIDE LAWS or BE EXECUTED with the guillotines.

It is as simple as that and already spoken of prophetically in **Revelation 20:4.**

The **NOAHIDE LAWS** legislation was written by the Orthodox Jewish organization based in Brooklyn, NY. They presented them to George Bush, Sr., Mr. NWO himself, to sign into legislation.

Mr. **"ILLUMINATI BLOODLINE"** Bush knew exactly what he was doing, knew who would be primarily targeted and what would happen to Christians in America as a result.

ALL NWO adherents, Jew and Gentile alike, hate the Christians in America (and worldwide) with a passion, as former adherents admitted to me personally.

They know the Christians in America are the GREATEST DETERRENT to their realization of a NEW WORLD ORDER agenda!

These Noahide Laws state that Gentiles/Christians must conform to their 7 NOAHIDE LAWS supposedly given by God to Noah for GENTILES after the flood. (This is nowhere stated in the Bible, however.)

The penalty for breaking THREE of these NOAHIDE LAWS is CAPITOL PUNISHMENT by BEHEADING. Two of those Jewish laws attack fundamental Christian beliefs directly:

Prohibition against "BLASPEHMY AGAINST GOD" and "IDOLATRY." Judaism teaches that Christian faith in Jesus Christ VIOLATES BOTH.

Jesus Christ was ordered EXECUTED by the Jewish Pharisees for declaring he WAS THE SON OF GOD after His arrest. They called His admission "BLASPHEMY" and sentenced Him to death.

And now, the Jews in America seek to use their Noahide Laws to discriminate against and finally execute CHRISTIANS for THEIR "blasphemy" of calling Jesus "The Son of God" and worshipping Him as GOD WITH US, "Emmanuel." Jewish writers of this legislation even mandate CAPITOL PUNISHMENT BY BEHEADING for those who violate 3 of their 7 Noahide laws!

This is FORCED RELIGIOUS CONVERSION AT THE THREAT OF DEATH! Is this a NEW INQUISITION and new DARK AGES coming to "AMERIKA"???

What if JEWS IN AMERICA were given the mandate to renounce their Judaism and CONVERT TO CHRISTIANITY or be BEHEADED!!! Can you imagine the public outcry then???

So WHERE is the American/Christian outrage and outcry in this hour? THIS LEGISLATION HAS ALREADY BEEN PASSED AND THE GUILLOTINES ARE HERE!

OUR OWN MILITARY (and foreign also) are training even NOW to operate them on US under martial law!

WHOSE tax dollars pay for their training? WHOSE tax dollars paid for the guillotines to be imported/manufactured?

Americans should be outraged and in protest across the nation, especially in Washington DC, over the NOAHIDE LAWS and their total violation of everything America has ever stood for regarding religious freedoms!

BUT BECAUSE OF OUR CONSTITUTION AND THE FIRST AMENDMENT ESTABLISHMENT CLAUSE, they CANNOT activate the NOAHIDE LAWS IN AMERICA YET!

AMERICANS HAVE BUT A SHORT TIME TO PROTEST AND DEMAND THE NOAHIDE LAWS BE RESCINDED AND ABOLISHED NOW!

Otherwise, when MARTIAL LAW IS DECLARED, and the Constitution abolished, THEN you will witness with your own eyes the unveiling and public display of these modern military guillotines and the US and foreign troops training (in FORT LEWIS, FORT BRAGG, FORT HOOD and elsewhere) to operate them on AMERICAN violators of these outrageous, discriminatory and strictly Jewish religion-based laws.

THEREFORE, THE JEWS WHO SUPPORT THE NOAHIDE LAWS AND ADVOCATE FORCED CONVERSION OF CHRISTIANS/GENTILES, CANNOT WAIT FOR MARTIAL LAW TO TRANSPIRE.

For then and ONLY then can their NOAHIDE LAWS be fully activated in AMERICA.

The enemies of the American Constitution and Christianity in America, and our religious and all other freedoms, cannot wait for the planned government black ops to take place, nullifying everything promised in the Constitution to us.

So NOW you KNOW WHEN the NOAHIDE LAWS and the horrific modern military GUILLOTINES to enforce them will come into full force in America."

If you think the Noahide Laws are a conspiracy theory or the information above about the laws and use of guillotines is false, I would like to give you a personnel account given to my wife whose friend told her that years ago, her friend had seen pallets of guillotines in a warehouse in Montana. Why would I believe such an account? Just look around you today, you would have to be blind not to see the Zionist takeover of our country by the control of the MSM and our government! Rumors or reality; 30 thousand guillotines shipped to Montana and Georgia. Of, course MSM says more conspiracy theories. Never believe the liberal fact checking website Snopes, unless you want all slanted information protecting nefarious government activities!

You want proof of forthcoming beheadings, read Revelations 20:4; "And I saw the souls of them that were beheaded for the witness of Jesus and for the word of God, and which had not worshipped the beast, neither his image, neither had received his mark upon their foreheads or in their hands."

The Mark of the Beast is till future, and beheadings will use only one method to accomplish this, GUILLOTINES! Take heed of these Noahide Laws or face the consequences!

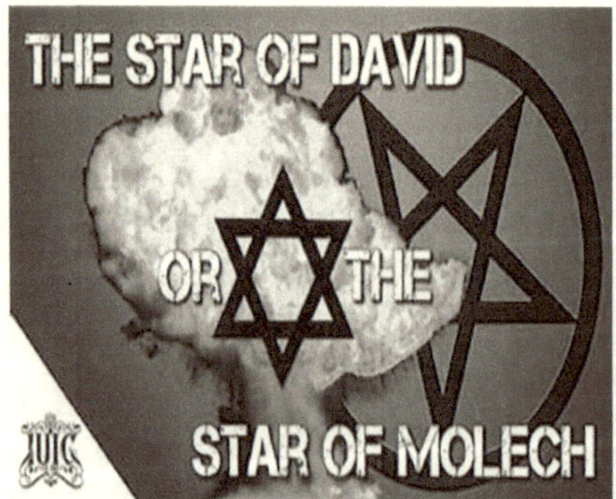

CHAPTER 21
REVOLUTIONARY SOLDIERS

The forgotten heroes of America

Most all these old soldiers were over 100 years old,
how? They didn't eat over processed foods!

ALEXANDER MILLENER, AGED 104,
ONE OF THE SURVIVORS OF THE REVOLUTION.

AN

ACT AND LAW,

Made and paffed by the General Court or Affembly of the Governor and Company of the State of CONNECTICUT, in AMERICA, holden at NEW-HAVEN, on the fecond Thurfday of October, *Anno Domini* 1776.

AN ACT to compel the furnifhing neceffary Sup-plies and Affiftance to the Quarter-Mafter-Gene-ral of the Continental Army.

BE IT ENACTED, by the Governor, Council, and Re-prefentatives, in General Court affembled, and by the Au-thority of the fame, That if any Perfon or Perfons within this Colony, fhall, upon Requeft, refufe to fell or fupply to the Quar-ter-Mafters-General of the Continental Army, the Articles of Timber, Boards, Shingles, Brick or Stone, or to fell or let their Horfes, Oxen, Carts or Carriages, for tranfporting the fame, or to furnifh any other neceffary Supplies and Affiftance for the Ufe of faid Army, it fhall be the Duty of any one Affiftant or Juftice of the Peace, within this Colony, and they are hereby ordered and di-rected, upon Application to them, made by any fuch Quarter-Mafter, or Quarter-Mafters, their Agent or Agents, to grant a proper Warrant or Warrants, for the impreffing from any fuch Perfon or Perfons, fo refufing any of the neceffary Articles or Things aforefaid, or of any other Article or Thing needful for the Support or Supply of faid Army, or for the Tranfportation of the fame, directed to the Sheriff, his Deputy, Conftable, or any indif-ferent Perfon within the County where fuch Application fhall be made, who fhall imprefs, and caufe an Apprizement to be made thereof, by two or more indifferent Men within faid County, to be appointed by the Authority granting fuch Warrant, at the juft and true Value, and deliver the fame to faid Quarter-Mafter or Quarter-Mafters, their Agent or Agents, he or they paying to the Owner or Owners thereof, or into the Hands of fuch Officers who fhall imprefs the fame, the Sum or Sums at which the faid Article or Thing fhall be apprized as aforefaid, or fo much as fhall be reafonable for the Ufe of fuch Horfe or Horfes, Oxen, Cart or Carriages, where the fame fhall be returned again to the Owner thereof, by his own Confent and Agreement.

A true Copy of Record, examined by
GEORGE WYLLYS, Sec'ry.

REVOLUTIONARY
SOLDIER
COL. CHARLES STEWART
COMMISSARY GEN. OF ISSUES
1775   1783
PLACED BY
COL. LOWREY CHAPTER, D.A.R.

WASHINGTON'S LOOKOUT
-GREAT NOTCH-
On October 23, 1780, the light
infantry was stationed here.
The hill on the east side of
the Notch was used by
Washington as a lookout
from which to observe the
movement of his troops.

REVOLUTIONARY WAR
SOLDIER'S GRAVE

Samuel Ferguson (1744 - 1825) and
wife Mary Jameson (1746 - 1827) are
buried nearby. Served in Montgomery
Co. Va. militia at battles of Alamance
and King's Mountain. An early settler
on Bluestone Creek, he gave land for
Tazewell courthouse in 1772. In 1804
moved here to Kanawha Co., later
Cabell, now Wayne. Progenitor of the
area's extended Ferguson family.

REVOLUTIONARY
WAR
VETERAN

PATRIOTS   COOPER   PIXLEY   AND
ALEXANDER PORTER served the cause
of gaining our nation's independence while
dedicated members of the military. Both are
buried in Section 33 of this National
Soldiers Rest.

Cooper Pixley, born in Great Barrington,
Berkshire County, Massachusetts on July
16, 1763, enlisted at the age of 15 and
served three years in Captain Josiah Troop's
Company of Colonel Marius Willett's
Regiment of New York Militia. He was
present at the famed battle of Monmouth in
New Jersey and participated in General John
Sullivan's expedition against the Iroquois in
the Finger Lakes area of New York.

Following the Revolution, he lived in New
York and Canada, moving to Portage in June
1849. Cooper Pixley died March 12, 1855.
(Continued on other side)

SPONSORED BY THE WISCONSIN SOCIETY OF THE SONS OF THE
AMERICAN REVOLUTION, THIS MARKER WAS DEDICATED IN 2008.
IT WAS FUNDED BY SOCIETY MEMBER THOMAS GOULD.

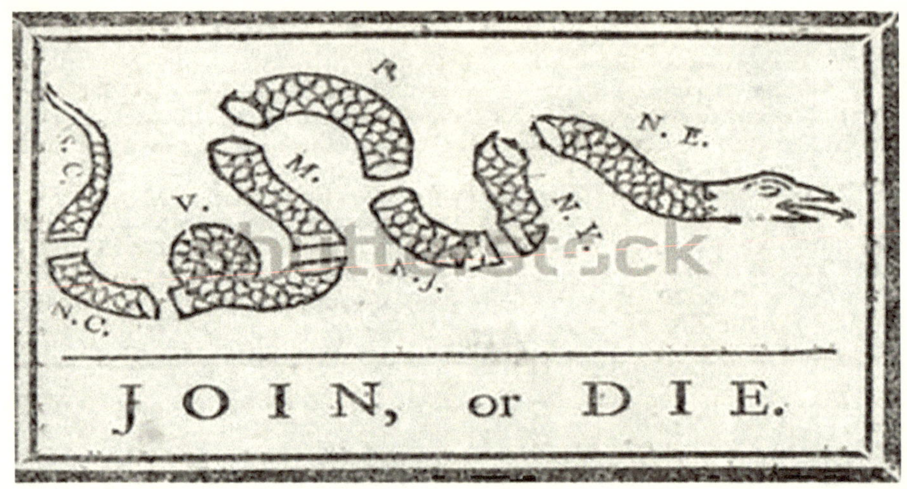

R
V.
M.
S. C.
N. C.
N. J.
N. Y.
N. E.
JOIN, or DIE.

CHAPTER 22 FREEDOM!

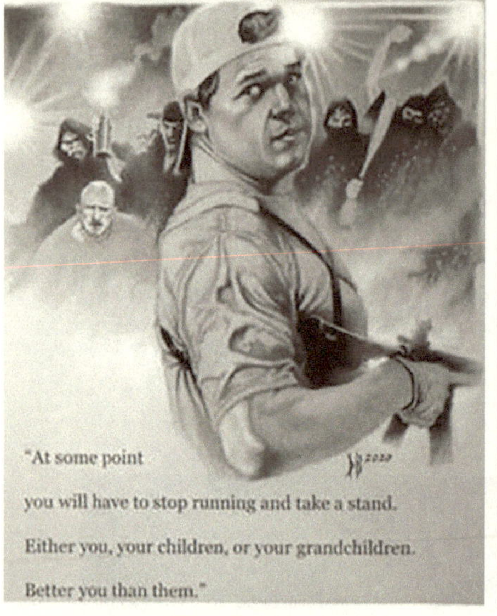
"At some point
you will have to stop running and take a stand.
Either you, your children, or your grandchildren.
Better you than them."

This is the USA. There is
No one Coming to our rescue if
things go Sideways. No one Will be
reSupplying us. No one Will airdrop food,
ammunition, medicine. There is no place
to escape to for freedom.
This is It!

THE SEEDS OF THE AMERICAN REVOLUTION
WERE PLANTED BY THOSE MEETING IN
TAVERNS, RESTAURANTS, AND CHURCHES.
NOW DO YOU UNDERSTAND WHY
THEY WANT TO FORCE CLOSURES, KEEP
YOU ISOLATED, AND CENSOR YOU?

MIKE RILLING
YOU CAN PRAY
ALL YOU WANT
BUT EVENTUALLY
DAVID HAD TO
PICK UP A
STONE AND ACT
AGAINST
GOLIATH

Amen sister!

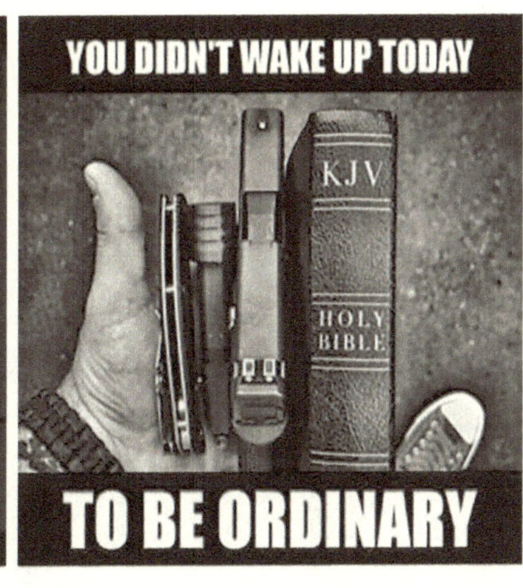

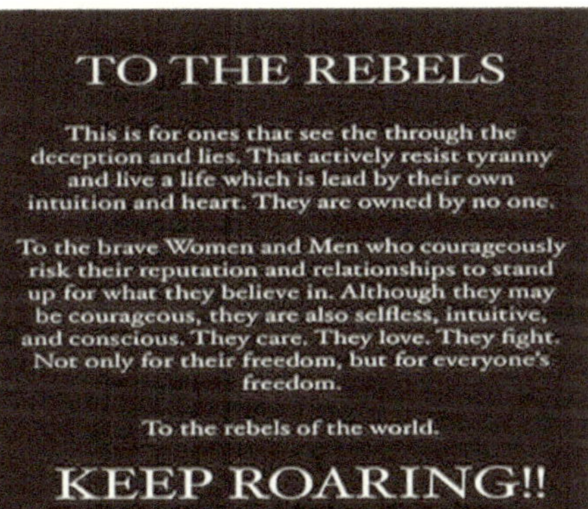

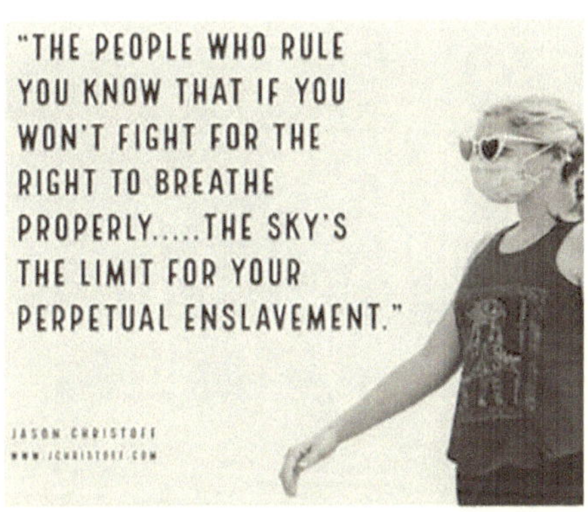

How would you like a one way ticket to knuckelsville?

Resist Every Situation Involving Satanic Tyranny!
RESIST!
ECCLESIASTES 10:4
LARRY WALLACE

RAISE CROPS,
MAKE BABIES,
SUPPORT FARMERS,
AVOID PHARMACISTS,
LOVE GOD
AND DON'T TRUST THE
GOVERNMENT.
FARMERS' STOREHOUSE

WORLDCOM
THE FALLOUT SPREADS
Newsweek
'Under God'
Under Fire
The
Pledge
Furor
By Howard
Fineman
Liberty,
Security
& 'Smart
Profiling'
By Fareed
Zakaria

RED EAGLE

Freedom!!

George Flynn, Freedom Fighter

Michael Corbin, Freedom Fighter!

No Fear!

Fear thou not, For I am with thee: be not dismayed; For I am thy God: I will strengthen thee: yea, I will help thee; yea I will uphold thee with the right hand of my righteousness. Isaiah 41:10

The fear of the Lord is the beginning of wisdom. Psalms 111:10

The fear of the Lord is the beginning of knowledge. Proverbs 1:7

Fear not them which kill the body, but are not able to kill the soul; but rather fear him which is able to destroy both soul and body in hell. Mathew 10:28

For God has not given us a spirit of fear: but of power, and of love, and of a sound mine. 2 Timothy 1:7.

Say ye not, a confederacy, to all them to whom this people shall say, a confederacy; (Zionist Communism) neither fear ye their fear, nor be afraid. Isaiah 8:12

Hearken unto me, ye that know righteousness, the people whose heart is in my law; fear ye not the reproach of men, neither be ye afraid of their reviling's. Isaiah 51:7.

If God be for us, who can be against us, Romans 8:31. So why should we fear man or all the devils of hell that come against us, their pitch forks shall all be melted away!

No weapon formed against us shall prosper, Isaiah 54:17.

Why all the scripture on fear? Because today we are being bombarded (thus the name of the book) on every occasion by government, medical, (thanks to the massive campaign of fear for an everyday flu) and yes, even religion, by the spirit of Fear. But most of all by the demonic organization called the WEF (World Economic Forum) who is promising the world;" You will own nothing and be happy". What they are not telling you is they will be far happier because they intend to own everything. But the true ownership of the WEF and the world is Rothschild Zionist communism. You would have to be a half dozen sandwiches short of a picnic not to see their tentacles today in every area of our lives, especially in our Federal, State, County and City governments, the stolen presidential election, a President with Dementia, and 12 million illegal aliens now coming after our Police departments and being given by our corrupt government everything but a new Lamborghini and a mansion, thanks to the welcome wagons given to them at our southern borders! Communism will get very good use of the criminal gangs now being let into every city in America that will create sleeper cells who in the future will be used by the communist army to rise up and kill every sleeping American for a sizeable RED paycheck!

Why are we seeing the disintegration of the greatest country that has ever existed? I am ashamed to say it but the voice of God's church, once a beacon and a light on the hilltop and strong foundation for freedom and liberty in the beginning of our nation, has become silent and impotent in our country today. We are told in Scripture to not be a partaker of evil, but rather expose it. Ephesians 5:11. Has your church been exposing evil lately? If they have, give them a grade of A+. I have not seen very many!

I believe one of the major causes of the churches down fall has been the blatant corruption of a scripture that has been misinterpreted and promoted for centuries and that is Romans 13: 1-4. Which speaks: Let every soul be subject unto the higher powers. For there is no power but of God: the powers that be are ordained of God. Whosoever therefore resisteth the power, resisteth the ordinance of God. And they that resist shall receive to themselves damnation. For the rulers are not a terror to good works, but to the evil. Wilt thou then not be afraid of the power? Do that which is good and thou shalt have praise of the same, for he is the minister of God to thee for good. But if thou do that which is evil, be afraid; for he beareth the sword not in vain; for he is the minister of God, a revenger to execute wrath upon him that doeth evil.

I have had Christians believe this scripture actually says we should obey everyone in power. I would say, you mean people like Hitler and Stalin? No, this scripture says nothing of the sort. Verse three says: For rulers are not a terror to good works, but to the evil. We are talking strictly to the power given to Christian ministers! This scripture would totally go against Ecclesiastes 10:4: "If the spirit of the ruler rise up against thee, leave not thy place; for yielding pacifieth offences!" We are not to yield to maniacal dictators ever! This scripture is held very highly in the Catholic church. It has to since they are told his Pope- a- ship, the Pope, is Jesus Christ on earth, which is impossible, Jesus never sinned. The Popes of the past have delivered many Christians to ashes!

CHAPTER 23 HELL

Another Doctrine in the churches today, that is false, is all who go to hell in a burning lake of fire will burn throughout eternity. What does fire do? It destroys completely!

This brings up a subject propagated by most of Christianity. The subject of people burning in hell for eternity can't happen, why? You have to have an eternal soul, an immortal soul to burn forever. By the way, the term eternal soul and immortal soul is not in the Bible. For all who think all human beings will live forever after death are sadly mistaken.

When we die, will we go to heaven or hell? Almost all the world including most churches believe the soul is immortal and the lie that the Serpent told Eve in the Garden of Eden. "God told Adam and Eve not to eat the fruit of the tree of the knowledge of good and evil. In the <u>DAY</u> that you eat of it, you will surely die, but the serpent told them, you shall surely not die, for God doth know that in the day ye eat thereof, your eyes shall be open (Illuminated, Illuminati), and ye shall be as gods knowing good and evil."

God said in the DAY that you eat of it you will surely die. When they ate of the fruit that DAY, they didn't die. God was talking about the death of the soul not the flesh, because Adam lived almost a thousand years.

What does John 3:16 say? "For God so loved the world, that he gave his only begotten Son that whosoever believes in him shall not PERISH but have everlasting life".

Why would God see his son tortured, beaten, spit on, and die on the cross to give you everlasting life if you already had it? The word perish, as mentioned in John 3:16 in the Greek is, apollumi which means to DESTROY FULLY. Yet every cult, secret societies, Masons, Illuminati, New Age Movement, all your isms, Buddhism, Hinduism, Satanism, Muslims, many Christian denominations, the Catholic church, Mormons, Jehovah's Witnesses, every kind of church or organization bought the lie that the serpent told Eve in the garden: "Ye shall not die."

As I said before, there is nowhere in the Bible the words eternal soul or immortal soul is mentioned. Looking at scripture, only Jesus has immortality and to those who receive His gift of salvation. 1 Timothy 6:15, 16 states: "Which in his times he shall show, who is the blessed and only Potentate, the King of kings, and Lord of Lords who only hath immortality. It says in 1Corinthians 15:53, For this corruptible must put on incorruption, and this MORTAL must put on Immortality. If you had immortality you wouldn't have to put it on. Romans 6:23 says: "The wages of sin is death, but the gift of God is eternal life through Jesus Christ our Lord." This is not talking of the flesh, because we all die in the flesh. There are many scriptures that say the soul dies, or about the saving of the soul. "Let him know that he who turns a sinner from the error of his way will save a soul from death". (James 5:20) But nowhere does it say you have an eternal or immortal soul without Jesus Christ. That was the very reason he came into the world to give you eternal life because of the loss of the soul of mankind suffered in the garden.

This truth puts the flame out of a person burning in hell forever. You would have to have an immortal soul to burn throughout eternity and the only way to have immortality is through Jesus Christ. Let's look at another verse of scripture in Revelation 20:14, 15. "And death and HELL were cast into the lake of fire". This is the second death (Death of the soul). And whosoever was not found written in the book of life was cast into the lake of fire." This is speaking of the white throne judgement, the final judgment of mankind. The fearful and unbelieving and the abominable and murderers and whoremongers and sorcerers and idolaters and all liars shall have their part in the lake of fire which burns with fire and brimstone, which is the second death. (Rev. 21:8). What is the second death? The lake which burns with fire and brimstone!

Read Psalms 92:7 "When wicked spring up as the grass, and when all the workers of iniquity do flourish; it is that they shall be DESTROYED FOREVER." (Hebrews 9:27) "And as it is appointed unto man ONCE to die, but after this the judgment, showing the error of reincarnation." EZEKIEL 18:4, 20 states, "The soul that sinneth it shall die!" 2 Thess. 1:8,9 continues, "In flaming fire taking vengeance on them that know not God and that obey not the gospel of our Lord Jesus Christ. Who shall be punished with EVERLASTING DESTRUCTION from the presence of the Lord and from the glory of His power,

Jer.7:30,31 says: "For the children of Judah have done evil in my sight, saith the Lord: they have set their ABOMINATIONS in my house which is called by my name, to POLLUTE it. And they have built the high places of Tophet, which is in the valley of Hinnom, TO BURN THEIR SONS AND THEIR DAUGHTERS IN THE FIRE; WHICH I COMMANDED THEM NOT, NEITHER CAME IT UNTO MY HEART."

Duet. 12:30-31: "Take heed to thy self, thou shalt not do so unto the lord thy God: for every abomination to the Lord, WHICH HE HATETH, HAVE THEY DONE UNTO THEIR gods; for even their sons and their daughters THEY HAVE BURNT IN THE FIRE TO THEIR GODS." Yet we still hear preached that if you are a sinner, God's going to burn you for all eternity. These two scriptures show God hates the burning even of the children of the ungodly (sinners). It is certainly understandable why many have rejected the Gospel, being told that God who is supposed to be merciful and loving would burn someone throughout eternity! The Gospel is not about heaven or hell, it is about life or death.

Now this leads to the question, "What about the punishment for the likes of Hitler, Stalin and all those who have murdered millions?" I did not mention there is not a lake of fire. Again, without an immortal soul you cannot burn forever but you can certainly burn for the sins you have committed, whether great or small. Just as in our day, different crimes get different punishments. Speeding ticket, you get fined. Steal or rob someone, you get jail time. Yes, I believe there is a place of torment and depending on the sins committed, an allocation of time will be allotted in pain and suffering or Jesus would not have said that those who offend little children, it is better for him that a millstone was hanged about his neck and he were casted into the sea. For the likes of Hitler and Stalin, that time of pain will be allocated to them for all who have suffered at their hands and that was a lot of suffering! These two men died and never paid for the atrocities they committed. Stalin died a natural death. Hitler as far as we know escaped to Argentina.

The word of God does not return unto Him void. The scriptures state: "An eye for an eye and a tooth for a tooth." "That which you sow, so shall ye reap!" We may not see those scriptures fulfilled in our lifetime but justice will be processed, eternal life or eternal death!

CHAPTER 24
HISTORICAL JESUS

Although there is overwhelming evidence that the New Testament is an accurate and trustworthy historical document, many people are still reluctant to believe what it says unless there is also some independent, non-biblical testimony that corroborates its statements.

Edwin Yamauchi, a Japanese-American historian, (Protestant) Christian apologist, editor and academic states: *Probably the most important reference to Jesus outside the New Testament, "Is* Emperor Nero's reporting a decision to blame the Christians for the fire that had destroyed Rome in A.D. 64, the Roman historian Tacitus wrote:

Nero fastened the guilt ... on a class hated for their abominations, called Christians by the populace. Christus, from whom the name had its origin, suffered the extreme penalty during the reign of Tiberius at the hands of ... Pontius Pilatus, and a most mischievous superstition, thus checked for the moment, again broke out not only in Judaea, the first source of the evil, but even in Rome....

What can we learn from this ancient (and rather unsympathetic) reference to Jesus and the early Christians? Notice, first, that Tacitus reports Christians derived their name from a historical person called Christus (from the Latin), or Christ. He is said to have *"suffered the extreme penalty,"* obviously alluding to the Roman method of execution known as crucifixion. This is said to have occurred during the reign of Tiberius and by the sentence of Pontius Pilatus. This confirms much of what the Gospels tell us about the death of Jesus.

But what are we to make of Tacitus' rather enigmatic statement that Christ's death briefly checked *"a most mischievous superstition,"* which subsequently arose not only in Judaea, but also in Rome? One historian suggests that Tacitus is here *"bearing indirect ... testimony to the conviction of the early church that the Christ who had been crucified had risen from the grave."* While this interpretation is admittedly speculative, it does help explain the otherwise bizarre occurrence of a rapidly growing religion based on the worship of a man who had been crucified as a criminal. How else might one explain *that*?

Another important source of evidence about Jesus and early Christianity can be found in the letters of Pliny the Younger to Emperor Trajan. Pliny was the Roman governor of Bithynia in Asia Minor. In one of his letters, dated around A.D. 112, he asks Trajan's advice about the appropriate way to conduct legal proceedings against those accused of being Christians. Pliny says that he needed to consult the emperor about this issue because a great multitude of every age, class, and sex stood accused of Christianity.

At one point in his letter, Pliny relates some of the information he has learned about these Christians:

They were in the habit of meeting on a certain fixed day before it was light, when they sang in alternate verses a hymn to Christ, as to a god, and bound themselves by a solemn oath, not to any wicked deeds, but never to commit any fraud, theft or adultery, never to falsify their word, nor deny a trust when they should be called upon to deliver it up; after which it was their custom to separate, and then reassemble to partake of food – but food of an ordinary and innocent kind.

This passage provides us with a number of interesting insights into the beliefs and practices of early Christians. First, we see that Christians regularly met on a certain fixed day for worship. Second, their worship was directed to Christ, demonstrating that they firmly believed in His divinity. Furthermore, one scholar interprets Pliny's statement that hymns were sung to Christ, *"as to a god"*, as a reference to the rather distinctive fact that, *"unlike other gods who were worshipped, Christ was a person who had lived on earth."* If this interpretation is correct, Pliny understood that Christians were worshipping an actual historical person as God! Of course, this agrees perfectly with the New Testament doctrine that Jesus was both God and man.

Not only does Pliny's letter help us understand what early Christians believed about Jesus' *person*, it also reveals the high esteem to which they held His *teachings*. For instance, Pliny notes that Christians *"bound themselves by a solemn oath"* not to violate various moral standards, which find their source in the ethical teachings of Jesus. In addition, Pliny›s reference to the Christian custom of sharing a common meal likely alludes to their observance of communion and the *"love feast."* This interpretation helps explain the Christian claim that the meal was merely *"food of an ordinary and innocent kind"*. They were attempting to counter the charge, sometimes made by non-Christians, of practicing *"ritual cannibalism."* The Christians of that day humbly repudiated such slanderous attacks on Jesus› teachings. We must sometimes do the same today.

Perhaps the most remarkable reference to Jesus outside the Bible can be found in the writings of Josephus, a first century Jewish historian. On two occasions, in his *Jewish Antiquities*, he mentions Jesus. The second, less revealing, reference describes the condemnation of one *"James"* by the Jewish Sanhedrin. This James, says Josephus, was *"the brother of Jesus the so-called Christ."* This points out how this agrees with Paul›s description of James in <u>Galatians 1:19</u> as *"the Lord's brother."* And Edwin Yamauchi informs us that *"few scholars have questioned"* that Josephus actually penned this passage.

As interesting as this brief reference is, there is an earlier one, which is truly astonishing. Called the "Testimonium Flavia Num," the relevant portion declares:

About this time there lived Jesus, a wise man, if indeed one ought to call him a man. For he ... wrought surprising feats.... He was the Christ. When Pilate ...condemned him to be crucified, those who had . . . come to love him did not give up their affection for him. On the third day he appeared ... restored to life.... And the tribe of Christians ... has ... not disappeared.

Did Josephus really write this? Most scholars think the core of the passage originated with Josephus, but that it was later altered by a Christian editor, possibly between the third and fourth century A.D. But why do they think it was altered? Josephus was not a Christian, and it is difficult to believe that anyone but a Christian would have made some of these statements.

For instance, the claim that Jesus was a wise man seems authentic, but the qualifying phrase, *"if indeed one ought to call him a man,"* is suspect. It implies that Jesus was more than human, and it is quite unlikely that Josephus would have said *that*! It is also difficult to believe he would have flatly asserted that Jesus was the Christ, especially when he later refers to Jesus as *"the so-called"* Christ. Finally, the claim that on the third day Jesus appeared to His disciples restored to life, inasmuch as it affirms Jesus› resurrection, is quite unlikely to come from a non-Christian!

But even if we disregard the questionable parts of this passage, we are still left with a good deal of corroborating information about the biblical Jesus. We read that he was a wise man who performed surprising feats. And although He was crucified under Pilate, His followers continued their discipleship and became known as Christians. When we combine these statements with Josephus' later reference to Jesus as *"the so-called Christ,"* a rather detailed picture emerges which harmonizes quite well with the biblical record. It increasingly appears that the «biblical Jesus» and the «historical Jesus» are one and the same!

There are only a few clear references to Jesus in the Babylonian Talmud, a collection of Jewish rabbinical writings compiled between approximately A.D. 70-500. Given this time frame, it is naturally supposed that earlier references to Jesus are more likely to be historically reliable than later ones. In the case of the Talmud, the earliest period of compilation occurred between A.D. 70-200. The most significant reference to Jesus from this period states:

On the eve of the Passover Yeshu was hanged. For forty days before the execution took place, a herald ... cried, "He is going forth to be stoned because he has practiced sorcery and enticed Israel to apostasy."

Let's examine this passage. You may have noticed that it refers to someone named "Yeshu." So why do we think this is Jesus? Actually, "Yeshu" (or "Yeshua") is how Jesus' name is pronounced in Hebrew. But what does the passage mean by saying that Jesus *"was hanged"*? Doesn't the New Testament say he was crucified? Indeed, it does. But the term *"hanged"* can function as a synonym for *"crucified.* "For instance, <u>Galatians 3:13</u> declares that Christ was *"hanged"*, and <u>Luke</u>

<u>23:39</u> applies this term to the criminals who were crucified with Jesus. So, the Talmud declares that Jesus was crucified on the eve of Passover. But what of the cry of the herald that Jesus was to be stoned? This may simply indicate what the Jewish leaders were *planning* to do. If so, Roman involvement changed their plans!

The passage also tells us *why* Jesus was crucified. It claims He practiced sorcery and enticed Israel to apostasy! Since this accusation comes from a rather hostile source, we should not be too surprised if Jesus is described somewhat differently than in the New Testament. But if we make allowances for this, what might such charges *imply* about Jesus?

Interestingly, both accusations have close parallels in the canonical gospels. For instance, the charge of sorcery is similar to the Pharisees' accusation that Jesus cast out demons *"by Beelzebub the ruler of the demons."* But notice this: such a charge actually tends to confirm the New Testament claim that Jesus performed miraculous feats. Apparently, Jesus› miracles were too well attested to deny. The only alternative was to ascribe them to sorcery! Likewise, the charge of enticing Israel to apostasy parallels Luke›s account of the Jewish leaders who accused Jesus of misleading the nation with his teaching. Such a charge tends to corroborate the New Testament record of Jesus› powerful teaching ministry. Thus, if read carefully, this passage from the Talmud confirms much of our knowledge about Jesus from the New Testament.

Lucian of Samosata was a second century Greek satirist. In one of his works, he wrote of the early Christians as follows:

The Christians ... worship a man to this day – the distinguished personage who introduced their novel rites, and was crucified on that account.... [It] was impressed on them by their original lawgiver that they are all brothers, from the moment that they are converted, and deny the gods of Greece, and worship the crucified sage, and live after his laws

Although Lucian is jesting here at the early Christians, he does make some significant comments about their founder. For instance, he says the Christians worshipped a *man, "who introduced their novel rites."* And though this *man's* followers clearly thought quite highly of Him, He so angered many of His contemporaries with His teaching that He *"was crucified on that account."*

Although Lucian does not mention his name, he is clearly referring to Jesus. But what did Jesus teach to arouse such wrath? According to Lucian, he taught that all men are brothers from the moment of their conversion. That's harmless enough. But what did this conversion involve? It involved denying the Greek gods, worshipping Jesus, and living according to His teachings. It's not *too* difficult to imagine someone being killed for teaching *that*. Though Lucian doesn't say so explicitly, the Christian denial of other gods combined with their worship of Jesus implies the belief that Jesus was more than human. Since they denied other gods in order to worship Him, they apparently thought Jesus a greater God than any that Greece had to offer!

Let's summarize what we've learned about Jesus from this examination of ancient non-Christian sources. First, both Josephus and Lucian indicate that Jesus was regarded as wise. Second, Pliny, the Talmud, and Lucian imply He was a powerful and revered teacher. Third, both Josephus and the Talmud indicate He performed miraculous feats. Fourth, Tacitus, Josephus, the Talmud, and Lucian all mention that He was crucified. Tacitus and Josephus say this occurred under Pontius Pilate. And the Talmud declares it happened on the eve of Passover. Fifth, there are possible references to the Christian belief in Jesus' resurrection in both Tacitus and Josephus. Sixth, Josephus records that Jesus' followers believed He was the Christ, or Messiah. And finally, both Pliny and Lucian indicate that Christians worshipped Jesus as God!

I hope you see how this small selection of ancient *non-Christian* sources helps corroborate our knowledge of Jesus from the gospels. Of course, there are many ancient *Christian* sources of information about Jesus as well.

Many were astonied at thee; his visage was so marred more than any man, and his form more than the sons of men. Isaiah 52:14

He was wounded for our transgressions. He was bruised for our iniquities! (Isaiah 53:5) BRUISED, look again! Do you know of any religious leader or so-called prophet, or god, that went through the suffering that Jesus went through, and could have called a legion of angels to rescue him from the cross! The Pharisees thought they had revenge on the one who was bringing down their elder's Talmudic traditions. Not so, they paid the price in spades with the destruction of Jerusalem in 70 A. D. No one mocks the God of the universe!

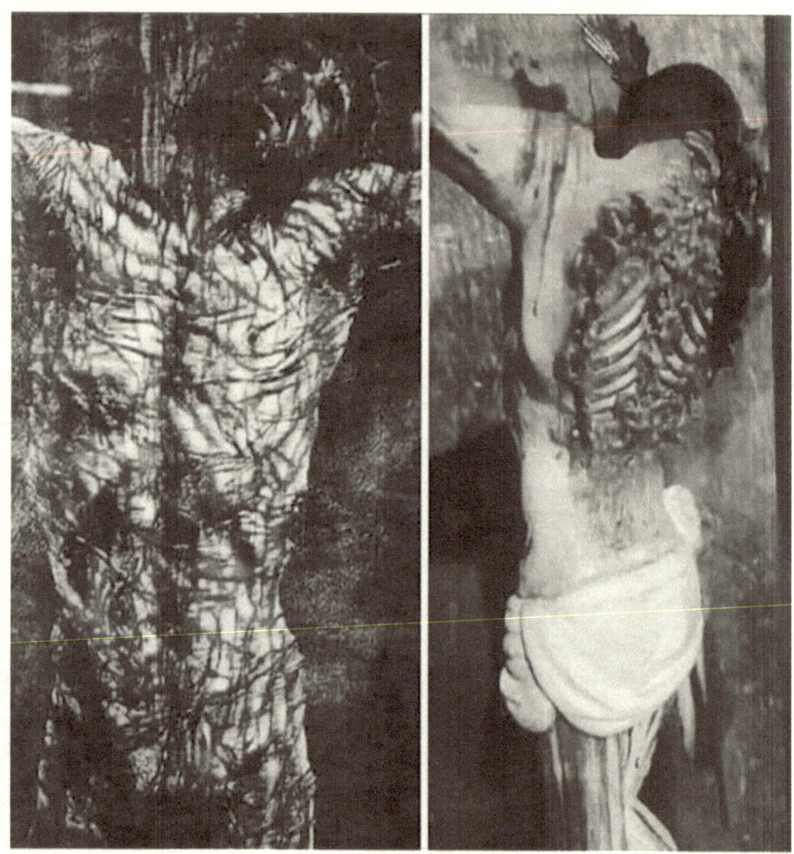

CHAPTER 25 ARK OF THE COVENANT DISCOVERED

The greatest Truth Bomb discovery in the history of mankind, buried in the hidden mine field of lies and corruption. Ron Wyatt died in 1998 having discovered Biblical archeological sites: The Ark of the Covenant, Noah's ark, Egyptian chariot wheels in the Red Sea, Mt Siani and Sodom and Gomorrah and the grain storage kept by Joseph who save the Egyptians and his own people from starvation.

Ron was an anesthesiologist and amateur archeologist from Nashville Tennessee. The following is his incredible journey. Of course, Ron throughout his life's discoveries was ridiculed and called a fake and charlatan. He was a devout Christian, that alone in the world's view makes him suspect. The Nay Sayers say how could this man have done this without the help of professional archeologists making the discoveries. I will tell you the reason, the answer, he was a true believer of Jesus Christ who was the author of the word of God, the Bible. A secular discovery of these events would have been exploited and corrupted for the simple fact it is the manner of human nature, Romans 3:23. It could only be protected against such actions by one who was born again in the Spirit of God, John 3:3.

When Jerusalem was surrounded by the Babylonian army in 597 BC., the prophet Jeremiah, knowing the Babylonians were going to eventually conquer the city, took the Ark and other temple implements in the dead of night, to a cave that was outside the wall of Jerusalem between the Babylonian siege wall they had erected to starve the people into submission, this was the cave Wyatt discovered in 1982. All the archeologists saying the Ark is here, or the Ark is there, don't believe them! Only by the guidance of God using a Christian archeologist, was the Ark discovered.

Ron and a member of the Jerusalem Historical Society who had contacted him about chariot wheels he discovered, were walking by the area of Jeremiah's Grotto outside the city walls when Ron's arm lifted up and pointed to his left and he said to the official: "This is where the Ark of the Covenant is located!" Ron has stated, the lifting of his arm and the words that popped out of his mouth was not by his own volition. The man told him, wonderful, I will supply whatever you need for the excavation. Ron had also discovered the chariot wheels of the Egyptians when they had crossed the Red Sea chasing the Israelites, while scuba diving 100 ft. in the Sea of Acaba, part of the Red Sea. This was the reason the member of the Historical Society had contacted him.

The cave was thirty feet below where Ron had already discovered the post hole of Jesus's cross on Golgotha Hill. After much hard and strenuous work digging out the debris with the help of a young Muslim boy, Ron discovered a small hole on one of the sides of the cave and immediately began digging through it. He lifted up the young boy holding a flash light to enter the hole they had dug; the hole was not large enough for Ron to enter. When the boy looked inside, he became terrified and ran frantically out of the cave. When Ron cleared enough material so he could get a better view, as he looked inside, he saw the glitter of gold. With months of effort getting inside and clearing the cave, Ron discovered the Ark that had the Ten Commandments inside it, the golden candle stand, the menorah, the table of showbread and a large sword, believed to be Goliath's sword that King David decapitated Goliath with. He noticed from the top of the cave a dark substance that flowed down the wall onto the mercy seat of the Ark. What he realized was that the substance was located right below the location above, where the post hole had been discovered. When Ron had discovered the hole, there was a large crack going across the hole. He realized this must have taken place when the earthquake happened after Jesus died. We know in the story of the Bible the Roman soldier, to make sure Jesus was truly dead, stuck a spear in His side. Ron surmised the blood that gushed out, ran down into the crack made by the earthquake, which he discovered on the caves ceiling and wall, onto the ark, explaining the dark substance.

Days later upon returning to the excavation. Ron was startled to see four young men in the cave next to the ark. He said to them: who are you and how did you come into the cave? They told Ron they were angels of the Lord who were appointed to guard the ark. The angels lifted the solid gold mercy seat lid off the ark and handed the ten commandments written in stone that was inside and had it set aside for Ron to take a picture of it with a video camera Ron had brought with him. The angels told Ron this discovery was not going to be shown to the world until a time appointed.

Ron realizing the substance could be Christ's blood, took a sample to be analyzed by a local laboratory that did blood work. He asked the technicians what they could tell him about the blood and they said we will reconstitute it and they found it to be human blood. Then Ron asked them if they could take a sample of some white blood cells and put it in a growth medium, gently swirling it and keeping it for 48 hours at body temperature, and they told him that will do no good, the blood is dead. Ron said, will you do it and they said OK and he said to let him know when they take the blood out. When the sample was reexamined under the microscope the one technician called the head technician and began talking Hebrew a mile a minute and they said to Ron this blood has only 24 chromosomes in it. A person has 46 chromosomes, 23 from the mother and 23 from the father. This blood had 23 chromosomes from the mother and 1 Y chromosome from a non-human father. Then they told Ron, this blood is alive, whose blood is this? And Ron tearfully said, this is the blood of your Messiah! The Ark is where Ron left it. The Jews closed the entrance and told Ron never to mention its discovery. Ron said the Ark and Ten Commandments would be revealed during the tribulation period. I believe that time is now upon us! We will know for sure that what Ron said will come true in the not-too-distant future.

Ron's death bed confession in 1998 is on the You Tube video link below. Ron being the devout Christian he was, would never give away his entry into the eternal kingdom of heaven by lying with his last breath! Would you?

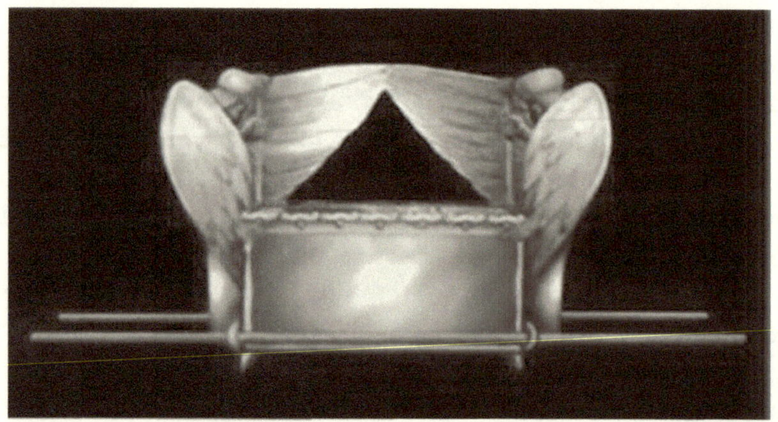

What the real Ark looks like

Christs blood dripped to Ark

Ron Wyatt

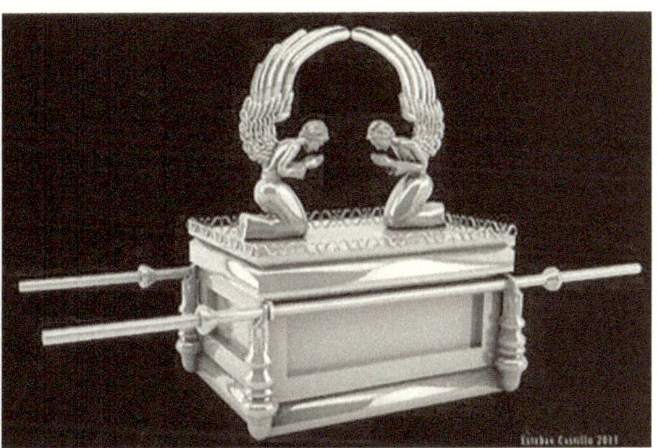

Man's false interpretation of the Ark!
No Mercy Seat! God nor man could
sit on such an ark!

Noah's ark found by Ron Wyatt

Anchor Stone from the ark

Sulfur ball lodged in cliff in Sodom and Gomorrah

CHAPTER 26 DUMITRU DUDUMAN

For 25 years, Dumitru Duduman was a faithful pastor who also smuggled Bibles from his native land Romania into communist Russia. He was later caught and sent to prison.

In August of 1980, Dumitru was arrested, imprisoned and interrogated for five months. He was beaten almost every day and repeatedly shocked in an electric chair. Arrest and interrogation became a continuous way of life for Dumitru. During this time of torture, he was hung by his waist and beaten on three different occasions. He suffered nine broken ribs, leaving permanent deformities on his rib cage.

Finally, the authorities gave Dumitru three choices; a mental hospital, prison. . . or expulsion to the United States. This was God's plan.

The choice was hard for Dumitru because of his loyalty to his homeland, but he felt his first loyalty was to God.

In 1984, after years of persecution and torture, Dumitru and his family were exiled to the United States and ended up in California. This is the true story of the man and the message that God gave him. The message: God was going to judge America!

Dumitru Duduman's book: "A Walk Through
the Fire Without Getting Burned"
Contribute to Dumitru's orphanage at www.
handsofhelp.com/index.plp

Dumitru Duduman's Testimonial

God's message to America:
AMERICA WILL BURN!

September, 1984

Late one night, I could not sleep. The children were sleeping on the luggage. My wife and daughter were crying. I went outside and walked around. I didn't want them to see me cry. I walked around the building crying and saying, "God! Why did you punish me? Why did you bring me into this country? I can't understand anybody. If I try to ask anybody anything, all I hear is, *I don't know.*"

I stopped in front of the apartment and sat on a large rock. Suddenly a bright light came toward me. I jumped to my feet because it looked as if a car was coming directly at me, attempting to run me down! I thought the Romanian Secret Police had tracked me to America, and now they were trying to kill me. But it wasn't a car at all. As the light approached, it surrounded me. From the light I heard the same voice that I had heard so many times in prison.

He said "Dumitru, why are you so despaired?" I said, "Why did you punish me? Why did you bring me to this country? I have nowhere to lay my head down. I can't understand anybody." He said, "Dumitru, didn't I tell you I am here with you, also? I brought you to this country because this country will burn." I said, 'Then why did you bring me here to burn? Why didn't you let me die in my own country? You should have let me die in jail in Romania! He said, "Dumitru, have patience so I can tell you. Get on this." I got on something next to him. I don't know what it was. I also know that I was not asleep. It was not a dream. It was not a vision. I was awake just as I am now.

He showed me all of California and said, **"This is Sodom and Gomorrah! All of this, in one day it will burn! Its sin has reached the Holy One."** Then he took me to Las Vegas. **"This is Sodom and Gomorrah. In one day it will burn."** Then he showed me the state of New York. "Do you know what this is?" he asked. I said, "No." He said **"This is New York. This is Sodom and Gomorrah! In one day it will burn."** Then he showed me all of Florida. **"This is Florida,"** he said. **"This is Sodom and Gomorrah! In one day it will burn."** Then he took me back home to the rock where we had begun. **"IN**

ONE DAY IT WILL BURN! All of this I have shown you."

I said, "How will it burn?" He said, "Remember what I am telling you, because you will go on television, on the radio and in churches. You must yell with a loud voice. Do not be afraid, because I will be with you." I said, "How will I be able to go? Who knows me here in America? I don't know anybody here." He said, "Don't worry yourself. I will go before you. I will do a lot of healing in the American churches and I will open the doors for you. But do not say anything else besides what I tell you. This country will burn!"

I said, "What will you do with the church?" He said, "I want to save the church, but the churches have forsaken me." I said, "How did they forsake you?" He said, "The people praise themselves. The honor that the people are supposed to give Jesus Christ, they take upon themselves. In the churches there are divorces. There is adultery in the churches. There are homosexuals in the churches. There is abortion in the churches and all other sins that are possible. Because of all the sin, I have left some of the churches. You must yell in a loud voice that they must put an end to their sinning. They must turn toward the Lord. The Lord never gets tired of forgiving. They must draw close to the Lord and live a clean life. If they have sinned until now, they must put an end to it, and start a new life as the Bible tells them that they might live."

I said, "How will America burn? America is the most powerful country in this world. Why did you bring us here to burn? Why didn't you at least let us die where all the Dudumans have died?"

He said, "Remember this, Dumitru. The Russian spies have discovered where the nuclear warehouses are in America. When the Americans will think that there is peace and safety - from the middle of the country, some of the people will start fighting against the government. The government will be busy with internal problems. Then from the ocean, from Cuba, Nicaragua, Mexico..." (He told me two other countries, but I didn't remember what they were.) "...they will bomb the nuclear warehouses. When they explode, America will burn!"

"What will you do with the Church of the Lord? How will you save the ones that will turn toward you?" I asked. He said, "Tell them this: how I saved the three young ones from the furnace of fire, and how

I saved Daniel in the lions' den, is the same way I will save them."

The angel of the Lord also told me, "I have blessed this country because of the Jewish people who are in this country. I have seven million Jews in this country, but they do not want to recognize the Lord. They didn't want to thank God for the blessings they have received in this country. Israel doesn't want to recognize Jesus Christ. They put their faith in the Jewish people in America. But, when America burns, the Lord will raise China, Japan, and other nations to go against the Russians. They will beat the Russians and push them all the way to the gates of Paris.

Over there they will make a treaty, and appoint the Russians as their leaders. They will then unite against Israel. When Israel realizes she does not have the strength of America behind her, she will be frightened. That's when she will turn to the Messiah for deliverance. That's when the Messiah will come. Then, the church will meet Jesus in the air, and He will bring them back with Him to the Mount of Olives. At that time, the battle of Armageddon will be fought."

When I heard all of this I said, "If you are truly the angel of the Lord, and everything you have told me is true, then all you have said must be written in the Bible." He said, "Tell everyone to read from Jeremiah 51:8-15, Revelation chapter 18, and Zechariah chapter 14, where Christ fights against those who possess the earth. After His victory," the angel said, "there will be one flock and one Shepherd. There will be no need for light. The Lamb of God will be the Light. There will be no sickness, no tears and no death. There will only be eternal joy and God will be the ruler. There will be only one language. Only one song and no need for a translator!" "Dumitru", he continued, "a word of warning, if you keep anything from the American people that you have been told, I will punish you severely." "How will I know that this is for real - that it will really happen?" I asked. "As a sign that I have spoken to you, tomorrow before you wake, I will send someone to bring you a bed, and at noon I will send you a car and a bucket of honey. After which I will send someone to pay your rent." Then the angel left.

The next day someone brought Dumitru a bed, at noon a car arrived delivering a bucket of honey and his rent was also soon paid, as God had promised him. (See chapter 10, "Through the Fire Without Burning")

(In the following summary, sections in italics are from Dumitru's dreams, visions and prophecies.)

WHEN WILL IT HAPPEN?

SEPT. 1984: *"From the middle of the country, some of the people will start fighting against the government. The government will be busy with internal problems. Then... (The attack will come) Look around you! Look at the rise of the militias. They are in virtually every state and growing in strength and numbers. They are training right now to do battle against the government. One militia leader has recently stated that if the government continues to distance itself from the people, war and revolution are inevitable. All it would take is one incident to unite the militias."*

1991: *The angel said: "Tell the people of America that one day with the Lord is as a thousand years, and a thousand years as one day. If they will repent and turn back to God, they will make it through the second day to the third day. If they don't, they will not make it."*

NOV. 1993: *I opened the book and the words "Book of the Gentiles" was scrawled on it. I saw all kinds of different names written. When I reached the end of the book, I found that there were one, and three quarter pages left blank - unwritten.*

JAN. 1996: *The angel said to me," Do you remember how many pages were left to fill when I showed you last time? Now, there is but one page left. When this is completed, what I have told you will happen to America." The man proceeded to tell me that the time it would take for this page to be filled, would not be longer, but shorter.*

APRIL, 1996, in a vision: *The Russian and Chinese presidents made a contract to fight against America. A voice said to me, "Watch where the Russians penetrate America." I saw these words being written: Alaska, Minnesota and Florida. Then, the man spoke again, "When America goes to war with China, the Russians will strike without warning."...The presidents of two other countries said, "We too will fight for you." Each had a place already planned as a point of attack..."Without a doubt, together, we can destroy America"... "Everything I have shown you is how it will REALLY happen...Then, when it comes to pass, the people will remember the words the Lord has spoken."*

CHAPTER 27
"WHERE DID EVIL SPIRITS COME FROM?"

This brings up a subject that most Christians are not aware of and that is, where did these evil spirits come from? The Bible does not give evidence of their beginnings. But it does in the books of Enoch, Jubilees and Jasher. Most Christians have been told not to read these books because they were not canonized. I believe with all that is taking place in the world today, we are living in the last days, a good reason to read the book of Enoch, since the first verses in Enoch, we are told that the book was written for those living in the last days! Good enough for me! In the book of Jude, Jude quoted a verse of scripture from the Book of Enoch. The book of Jasher was quoted in the book of Joshua and 2 Samuel. Because the books were not canonized, do we go by what a group of men has told us about these books or do we simply take the word of God in which these books were recognized! By reading these books, I just recently received an answer that has puzzled me for years, and that is why God had the Israelites destroy the men, women, children and animals of the Canaanites. God is love! (1 John 4:8).

Sounds kind of contradictory, doesn't it? (Matthew 24: 38,39) says "For as in the days before the flood, they were eating and drinking, marrying and giving in marriage, until the day Noah entered into the Ark, and knew not until the flood came, and took them all away; so, shall also the coming of the Son of man be." This scripture is important, because it is talking about our day! God destroyed the Antediluvian world because they were eating, drinking, marrying and given in marriage! Wow, what kind of God are we serving? He kills women, children and animals and then decides to destroy the world for what? Eating and drinking too much! The answer is in (Genesis 6:1-12). "And it came to pass, when men began to multiply on the face of the earth, and daughters were born unto them, the sons of God saw the daughters of men, that they were fair and they took them wives of all which they chose."

Many say this is talking about the Sons of God being from the bloodline of Seth, while the sons of men are the bloodline of Cain. Not true. The Hebrew Bible states the sons of God as divine beings. Enoch, Jubilees and Jasher call them angels. Verse 4 of Genesis 6 says: "There were giants in the earth in those days and after that, when the sons of God came in unto the daughters of men and they bear children unto them, the same became mighty men which were of old, men of renown (Giants)." There is nothing in the Bible to conclude that the sons of Seth and Cain would produce giants. Verse 5 of Genesis says: "And God saw that the wickedness of man was great in the earth and that every imagination of the thoughts of his heart was only evil continually." Verse 12 of chapter 6: "And God looked upon the earth, and behold, it was corrupt; for all flesh had corrupted his way upon the earth." What was the corruption speaking of? (Jasher 4:18) tells us of the corruption: "And their judges and rulers (Sons of God) went to the daughters of men and took their wives by force from their husbands according to their choice, and the sons of men, being taught by the Sons of god, in those days took from the cattle of the earth, the beasts of the field and the fowls of the air and taught the mixture of animals of one species with the others, in order therewith to provoke the Lord and God saw the whole earth and it was corrupt, for all flesh had corrupted its ways upon earth, all men and all animals."

Thus, Greek and Egyptian mythology may not be mythology, some of their gods being half humans and half animals. We are now seeing in our time this corruption of DNA performed during the Antediluvian world by scientist secretly doing hybrid experiments with animals and humans, not to mention the vaccines using mRNA changing the DNA in humans, history repeating itself! This is the reason God destroyed the world before the flood, The original DNA of His creation was being corrupted with a mixture of human and animal DNA.

This, was my answer why Joshua and David were instructed to kill not just the men, but the women, children and even the animals of the Canaanites. Remember the curse God caused to be put upon Canaan, Hams son, Noah's grandson, who exposed his father's nakedness. I believe it was through the Canaanites that the giants continued after the flood, the reason Joshua and David had to destroy that polluted DNA bloodline, thus men, women, children and even the animals. How the corrupt DNA passed beyond the flood is not explained, but the 4th verse of chapter 6 in Genesis, tells us that the Giants living in the Antediluvian world continue after that (after the flood). The giants became known as Nephilim, half mortal man and half immortal angels and because of that fact, even though the giant's flesh drowned in the flood, because of their mortal side, their immortal angelic side did not die and later became the evil spirits, talked about throughout the Bible*, also I believe, shadow men, that I have dealt with personally. You can also throw in those little green men that seem to be popping up all over the place. I doubt they are coming from galaxies billions and billions of light years away! They are coming from beneath our oceans and underground bases.

If given a chance, read about the military base and underground alien base in Dolce New Mexico. Those aliens we are continually hearing about today, I believe are demons created from messing with God's pure DNA he created for mankind and then corrupted by the intercourse of fallen angels with the daughters of men. That is why, the aliens are able to seemingly appear through solid walls, kidnapping people. Can I prove all this? No, not any more than all the evolutionists can prove we came from pond scum and then monkeys to became men! I received much of this information from the book of Enoch.

Another question I had answered, ever wonder how Cain went on to start civilization and build a city, since there were no other people on earth but Adam, Eve and his brother whom he had killed. The answer is in (Jubilees 4:9): "And Cain took Awan, his sister to be his wife." Verse 11: "Seth took Azura, his sister to be his wife." Yes, Adam and Eve gave birth to three daughters.

Here is a mystery for you. When Cain was driven from the face of the earth, Cain replied to the Lord, "And it shall come to pass, that everyone that findeth me shall slay me." (Genesis 4:14,15). Question: Who is everyone? Wasn't Adam and Eve and Cain and Able the only people on earth? Then where would the slayers come from? All this information was not mentioned in the Bible is explained by Jesus Himself: "Unto you it is given to know the mystery of the kingdom of God: but unto them that are without, all these things are done in parables." (Mark 4:11).

Cain's brother Seth lived to be 912 years old. Adam, his father also lived to be over 900 years. The Bible does not mention how long Cain lived, but it would be a good guess that he may have lived as long as Seth and Adam. He also was driven from the face of the earth to become a fugitive and a vagabond. This would make him separated from all his own relatives. If he did live quite a while there would be a heck of a lot of people roaming the earth given the length of the men's lives. The everyone Cain feared could possibly be a future relative.

*And now, the giants, who are produced from the spirits and flesh, shall be called evil spirits on the earth, and shall live on the earth. Evil spirits have come out of their bodies because they are born from men and from the holy Watchers, (Sons of God Genesis 6: 1,2); their beginnings is from primal origin; They shall be evil spirits on the earth, and evils spirits they shall be called spirits of the evil one (demons). [As for the spirits of heaven, in heaven shall be their dwelling, but as for the spirits of the earth which were born on the earth on the earth shall be their dwelling.] And the spirits of the giants afflict, oppress, destroy, attack, war, destroy, and cause trouble on the earth. They take no food, but do not hunger or thirst. They cause offences but are not observed (demons). And these spirits shall rise up against the children of men and against the women, because they have proceeded from them in the days of the slaughter and destruction, Enoch 15:8-12.

CHAPTER 28
"THE END OR JUST
THE BEGINNING"

The end of this book! The beginning, hopefully to some of the readers, the beginning! An awakening to the lies that have been propagated by the MSM for decades if not for over a hundred years

I will add a short glimpse of my life's story. My life should have ended before it ever began. It shows God's supernatural hand in keeping my father alive so I could be in the land of the living!

Besides having a Scottish heritage, I have an American Indian heritage on both sides of my family, Cherokee, Choctaw and Chickasaw, a very poor ancestry on both side of the Underwood and Wallace family. Because my Indian ancestors survived the Trail of Tears in the early 1800's, those many miles while suffering at the hands of the globalists, Yes, they have existed since time immemorial, just different in name and form, I am here today! I'll also mention for kicks and giggles, I had a great, great uncle, Edward Underwood, that was a Deputy Sheriff for Hanging Judge Parker in Ft. Smith Arkansas. My mother received a letter from an Underwood relative many years ago, stating that the Underwoods were also related to the Dalton gang. Since two of the Dalton brothers were also Deputy Sheriffs under Parker, I guess it is possible.

I will start with the birth of my father, Junior Paul Wallace who was born in 1921 in Panama, Oklahoma, Indian territory, who when moving to California in 1948, got to be called the prestigious name, Oakie! As I stated earlier, under very poor conditions. At birth, and I am only going by the source I received of my history from my great Aunt Maggie, my dad weighed only a pound and a half. He was given the comfort of incubation by being put under the heating lamps that was used for raising chickens.

My Dad was a bastard child, his mother being only 14 or 15 years old was, according to dear Aunt Maggie, her sister, was raped by a distant relative while spending the night at a family gathering. To this day my father now deceased, nor I, knows who his father or my grandfather was. That being said, he took on the name of his grandfather who raised him, William Wallace, giving my brother and sister and me a most famous name, thanks to the movie, "Braveheart" for which I am obviously very proud, not so with the Daltons.

The reason my great grandfather raised my father was on account of the abusive situation my Grandmother Mary and infant father were in. Mary ended up living with a man who in a fit of rage took out her eye with a fireplace poker and also abused my infant father. My Great Grandfather William, in a Braveheart moment, took a shotgun and descended on the property. He knocked on the door and told whoever he was to give him the child, thus causing my father to escape the future of one hellish life! My poor Grandmother Mary, because of the situations she was in, and an overzealous family, inflamed and indoctrinated in religion, was cast out of the family forever. Being so young she never made the effort to retrieve my father to raise him as her son, causing my father to never claim her as his mother, thus, wiping out any relationship I would have had with my paternal grandparents. I grew up not being told that one eyed Mary was my grandmother.

Grandma Mary Underwood with my infant father

So, as I had spoken before, because my Indian relatives having endured the death walk on the Trail of Tears, my dad being born weighing only 18 ounces in 1921 and then his life rescued by my great grandfather, I have to believe there's a reason and a purpose for my life, but I will tell of another incident greater than these, that pretty much sealed this belief.

It happened in the Hurtgen Forrest in Belgium in 1944. My father landed at Utah beach, D-Day the 6th of June. He was drafted into the Army July 1942. He was assigned to the 8th Medical Battalion Company C as a litter bearer and got to wear the easily targeted red cross on his helmet. His job was to pick up body parts and attend to the wounded and dying. He told me of times when he had saved the lives of those with blown off limbs by applying a tourniquet to keep them from bleeding to death. He was thanked by one soldier while my dad was at the army hospital, for saving his life. I always wondered why medics that risked their lives in open combat, saving the lives of countless men, never received a medal, or for that matter, very few thank you's if any from their superiors, for the extremely dangerous situations they were in. They couldn't hide behind a bush when the injured lay in an open field like their fellow soldiers. They were not even allowed to carry a weapon, which brings me to the time my father spoke of being captured by the Germans behind enemy lines for four days. He and two other medics aids were immediately searched for any weapons they might be hiding. Unfortunately for one of the soldiers, had carried a dagger in one of his boots which was against the Geneva Convention in WWII. My Dad went on to say that a German lieutenant took the man's dagger, had him pace off so many steps and proceeded to throw the dagger and stabbed him through the heart. The Germans pretty much obeyed the Geneva Convention and did not shoot at medics while the Japanese made medics open targets.

One day when my father's battalion was under heavy gun fire and launched missile attack. He was forced to run for cover when he heard the sound of a bomb, what I believe he called a Bouncy Betty, coming toward him. He was about to jump into his fox hole when he heard a voice behind him yell out, "Don't do it Red!" Red was my father's nick name. When he stopped running the bomb exploded in his fox hole killing soldiers who had made the jump before him. When he turned around to see who warned him, there was no one there! I never heard this story from my father but it was told to my brother by great Aunt Maggie. True, false, hyperbole I will never know. But if true, I am alive today to tell the story!

A similar incident happened on the U.S.S Liberty an American Navy vessel attacked on June 8th 1967 in the Mediterranean Sea by the Israeli military that confirms my dad's story. It is just another stain on this country's history. The ship was left to defend its self with no help or protection from the Navy's 6th fleet, why? The Liberty was to be a sacrificial lamb so President L.B. Johnson, who by the way had Jewish roots, could blame the Egyptians and give the reason to help the Israeli army in their war against the Palestinians. 35 servicemen were killed, 170 wounded. LBJ's intention was to sink the ship to the bottom of the sea to hide all evidence of Israel's, our so-called allies, involvement. Our Presidents wouldn't do such a thing, would they? Think 911, Ruby Ridge, the Waco massacre of over 80 men women and children, the Muir building in Oklahoma City killing a hundred innocent people, not to mention the assignations of John and Robert Kennedy, and Martin Luther Jr., all suspiciously having involvement from our government! The massacre of our servicemen on the Liberty to this day, has remained a cover up. As I was saying about the super-natural incident that happened to my father.

Such an incident happened to serviceman Ron Kukal on the Liberty, when hearing over the IMC," Prepare for torpedo attack." He was below deck. He hears a voice behind him say, "Hit the floor, now!" Whoever was behind him then pushed him to the floor. This was just before one of the five torpedoes had hit the Liberty, four had missed. He was just tens of feet away from impact. When he looked up from the floor to see who had warned and pushed him, no one was there! Randy and my father both had a supernatural experience. Now I know for sure, I, my brother and Sister are here because of my dad's supernatural experience!

Medical Clearing Station, Utah Beach Junior Paul Wallace

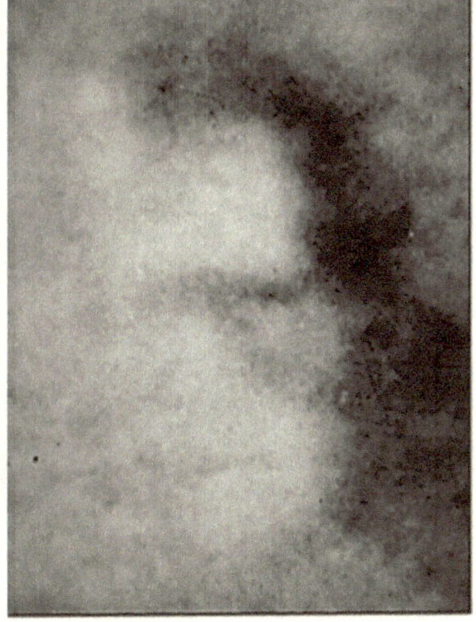

Great Grandfather William Wallace 1900, Ft Smith Arkansas. While looking at his picture I discovered what looked like a man's face in the backdrop. I enlarged the image and the picture at the right was the result. A mystry maybe someone can solve!

CHAPTER 29 MISCELLANEOUS

The emotional support dog after I get done telling it my problems.

UPS:
"Your package is in your city, on a truck driven by Mike. It will arrive at 6:27pm today."

FedEx:
"Your package is coming. You'll get it when we get there."

USPS:
"What package?"

Amazon:
"We are already inside your residence. Check the bathroom."

Facebook:
"We know you were thinking about getting a toaster oven yesterday.

GOD IS WATCHING YOU!

PRIDEMONTH
PRIDEMONTH
PRIDEMONTH
PRIDEMONTH
PRIDEMON

2021
2022
+ 2023
666

HEAVEN HAS STRICT
IMMIGRATION LAWS
HELL HAS OPEN BORDERS

If you think you are smarter than the previous generation...50 years ago the owners manual of a car showed you how to adjust the valves. Today it warns you not to drink the contents of the battery.

1940
2019

Hostess DING DONGS
10
Hostess Ho Hos
10

WELCOME TO THE NEW
ABNORMAL MASQUERADE
BROUGHT TO YOU BY YOUR
FAVORITE COMMUNIST PARTY

This is what we, who are aged 70 or 80 years plus, can look forward to.

This is something that happened at an assisted living center. The people who lived there had small apartments but they all ate at a central cafeteria. One morning one of the residents didn't show up for breakfast so my wife went upstairs and knocked on his door to see if everything was OK. She could hear him through the door and he said that he was running late and would be down shortly, so she went back to the dining area.

An hour later he still hadn't arrived, so she went back up towards his room but found him on the stairs. He was coming down the stairs but was having a hard time. He had a death grip on the hand rail and seemed to have trouble getting his legs to work right. She told him she was going to call an ambulance but he told her no, he wasn't in any pain and just wanted to have his breakfast. So, she helped him the rest of the way down the stairs and he had his breakfast. When he tried to return to his room, he was completely unable to get up even the first stair step, so they called an ambulance for him.

A couple of hours later she called the hospital to see how he was doing. The receptionist there said he was fine, he just had both of his legs in one side of his boxer shorts.

I'm sending this to my children so that they don't sell the house before they know all the facts.

An alignment like this won't happen until 2036. No sun glasses needed!

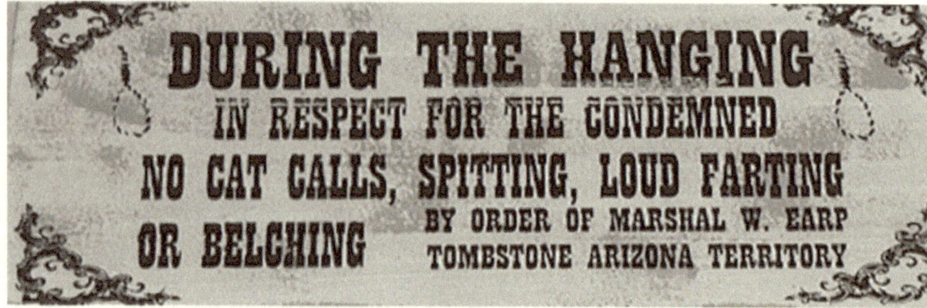

WHO INVITED YOU HERE?

Enough said. I feel I have at the very least presented information, whether you agree or disagree, that is not available in the unreliable news sources of the MSM. It is very easy to see that those who do not follow the party line will no longer be able to be in the party, Tucker Carlson just one of many kicked out because he started expressing personal opinions and individual thinking!

This is not new. In 1880, newspaper publisher, New York Times chief editor and orator <u>John Swinton</u> was the guest of honor at a banquet for the press. When a toast was raised to the independent press, Swinton reportedly had this rather surprising announcement:

THERE is no such thing in America as an independent press, unless it is in the country towns. You know it and I know it. There is not one of you who dares to write his honest opinions, and if you did you know beforehand that it would never appear in print.

I am paid $150.00 a week for keeping my honest opinions out of the paper I am connected with—others of you are paid similar salaries for similar things—and any of you who would be so foolish as to write his honest opinions would be out on the streets looking for another job.

The business of the New York journalist is to destroy the truth, to lie outright, to pervert, to vilify, to fawn at the feet of Mammon, and to sell his race and his country for his daily bread.

You know this and I know it, and what folly is this to be toasting an "Independent Press." **We are the tools and vassals of rich men behind the scenes. We are the jumping-jacks; they pull the strings**

and we dance. Our talents, our possibilities and our lives are all the property of other men.

We are intellectual prostitutes.

Now you understand. Our country has been high jacked for many years, and you thought you were living in a free society. The assignation of John F. Kennedy was the big red flag that should have awakened us all. He wanted an end to the Vietnam War, but most importantly he wanted to squash the Federal Reserve, to allow Congress to print our own money and put back our dollars into the pockets of the American citizens without paying exorbitant interests rates to the parasitic money changers! This was the nail that sealed his coffin! Who is the biggest stake holder of the Reserve, the Jewish Rothschild family, who have stated: "Give me control of a nation's money and I care not who makes it's laws" — <u>Mayer Amschel Bauer Rothschild</u>

Adolf Hitler was privy to their banking control schemes and refused the Rothschilds to place their central bank in Germany, the result, Germany's economy blossomed into the most prosperous country of its time, just like we would be today by ending the Federal Reserve. The cost of doing that, as Kennedy's future played out was death by assignation or suiciding, the more popular method! Hitler was accused of murdering 6 million jews, an exaggeration, sense the whole population of Jews in and around Germany in 1937 was 595,000, while the Zionist Jews murdered 66 to over 100 million white Christians during the Russian Bolshevik Revolution. The only thing they enjoyed more than murdering was torturing. Try to find that hidden information in the MSM!

Wake up Christian churches and leave the damnable evil prosperity Gospel so popular by these fake Christian TV Evangelists, and become the light shining from the hill tops you were supposed to be, or you will be joining your Christian brothers, sisters and children that were brutally tortured and murdered in Russia and happening around the world even today. You are the #1 target of the Talmudic Jewish Zionist Pharisee's. They hated and killed Jesus, which they try to deny, John 19:14-16, and cried out in Matthew 27:25, "his blood be upon us and on our children." And they hate you for being his spiritual descendants (the real Israel). I am not at all including Bible believing Jews who are against the Zionists that are committing genocide in Palestine today.

By the way, the true seed of Abraham is Jesus and those who have surrendered their lives to him are God's elect, Galatians 3:16, 3: 28,29.

We are seeing at this very hour a war against <u>white people</u>, code name for Christians, don't believe me, have you been listening to the MSM lately. Take a look at the Truth Bomb of ADL Jewish chairman Abe Fox,1987 to 2015 and read his quote:

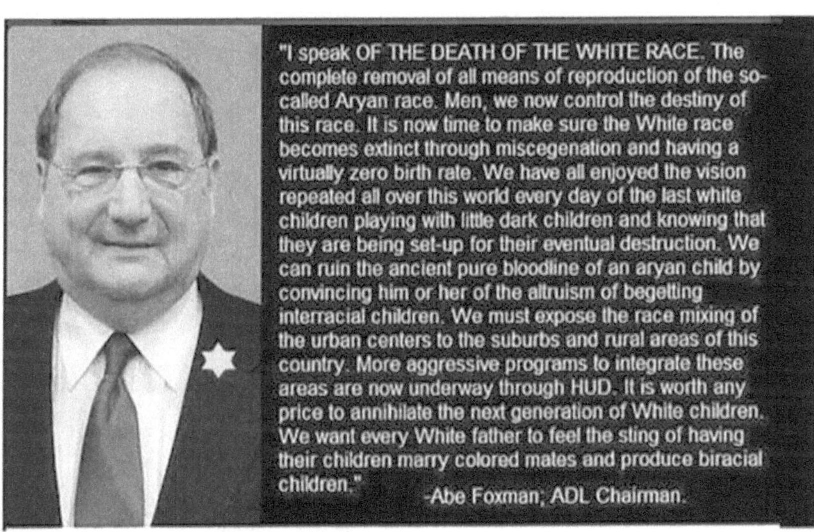

This also explains the black explosion in every area of the media today along with all the interracial marriages on so many TV commercials, all by the Jewish Zionist communist agenda to destroy the white race (Christians)!

But as I have included many scriptures on the previous pages, FEAR THOU NOT, Jesus the Christ, Yeshua Hamashiach is in control. As we are seeing the signs of his eminent return almost on a daily basis, is He in control of your life?

Braveheart Brothers

EVERY MAN DIES, VERY FEW MEN REALLY LIVE!

YOU CAN INCLUDE THIS FACT. I TIMOTHY 6:15,16 SAYS ONLY JESUS HAS IMMORTALITY AND THOSE THAT RECEIVE HIS GIFT OF SALAVATION, GIVEN BECAUSE OF HIS DEATH AT THE CROSS. YES EVERY MAN DIES, BUT YOU DON'T HAVE TOO. ASK JESUS CHRIST TO COME INTO YOUR HEART AND FORGIVE YOU OF YOUR SINS, ALL HAVE SINNED AND COME SHORT OF THE GLORY OF GOD, ROMANS 3:23. THERE IS NO IMMORTALITY EXCEPT THROUGH HIM.

YOUR ONLY ENTRANCE INTO THE KINGDOM OF HEAVEN IS THROUGH THE BLOOD OF CHRIST, JOHN 14:6 SAYS: "I AM THE WAY, THE TRUTH AND THE LIFE, NO MAN COMETH TO THE FATHER BUT BY ME." DON'T LOOK FOR ANOTHER. HE IS THE ONLY WAY!

ABOUT THE AUTHOR

Larry Wallace

Education:

Scholastic Art Awards, Junior and Senior year, Wilcox High School Santa Clara, CA. graduate.

AA Art degree at San City college, CA., study at San Jose

State college, BA degree Pacific Coast Bible College, Sacramento CA.

Associate Pastor: Calvary Chapel, San Jose CA.

Assistant Missions Director Calvary Chapel

County and State Delegate for Ron Paul 2008

Member of the Colorado Minute Men 2 years.

Big Fish Talent: Actor: Movies, TV Commercials, Internet Commercials.

Hosted TV program: "Victory in Jesus," Larry and Gary Wallace, Channel 2B San Jose California.

Author of: "The Xtra, Life and Times of a Nobody" Amazon

Created Book Cover for Ron DePriest Ministries: "From Hell to the Pulpit.

Fine Art America: My oil paintings for sale.